as a hand—though they hardly made up for what she suffered. What could?

Fan, closest to Louie as she was, didn't know what to think. For once she was stumped.

Over the years the sisters had amassed a large repertoire of names for Louie's girls. Floozy, bottle blonde, hussy. Chippie. Dime-store slut. Gold digger.

(But digger for fool's gold, surely? Louie never had a spare dime, was crafty enough to prefer "independent gals," as he called them. This meant girls who held down a job, weren't out for a free ride, could even chip in for the gas.)

On first sight Constance didn't fit any of the usual categories. She was no looker. Not sharp or slick or glossy. Lacking pep and any kind of flair. Charmless. No money to speak of.

What was the attraction?

Louie's girls always had a little special something that the sisters could secretly appreciate, even as they were bound to express official disapproval. This one could tell a joke. That one knew how to wear a skirt. "Vamp," Fan would sniff with satisfaction after Louie whirled his latest catch out for another snowy night on the town. "Cat in heat," Annie would sentence mercilessly, calmly. Any number of these vixens would come and go. It was to them, the sisters, Louie would always return.

Or so they once believed.

Following the ceremony, Constance sat stiffly in Fan's living room, feet planted squarely on the floor, and refused a second cup of coffee.

Her new sisters-in-law took stock:

Big feet.

No waist.

Flat as planed board.

Neck of an uncooked chicken.

Lipless mouth.

Bulging eyes.

(Thyroid? wondered Fan.)

Lil tried to call her Connie, but was corrected in such a way that no one used anything but Constance after that, Louie included. She held her purse tightly in her lap, as if one of the sisters might try to steal it. Not all brides glowed, it seemed. Constance took in furnishings and family with the same uninterested expression, and in a flat voice dealt out stingy helpings of information. Filing at the CPR. Thirteen years. It was a job. Could be worse. Her apartment downtown, she guessed. Big enough for two. Fourth floor. No elevator. A honeymoon not at the top of the list. Maybe later. Some people had to work tomorrow. Children? Messy. Loud. Don't mention pets. Movies worse. Eyestrain. Family still out east, far as she knew. Miss them? Why?

Before anyone could suggest a quick game of cards, Constance looked at her watch and told Louie it was time. These were her first words directed at him; until this moment she had not appeared conscious that she now possessed a husband and that he was also in the room. "Your wish is my command," vowed Louie with an uneasy attempt at the old swagger. Constance was already putting on her snow boots and car coat out in the hall. Long goodbyes were apparently not her style.

Clearing up while their husbands dozed in the rumpus room downstairs, the sisters remarked that Louie was looking old. Not so quick with the cracks, they observed. And going gray. (Though all his senior, the sisters still had their jet black hair and showed no sign of slowing down. The opposite, in fact.)

"Better gray than bald," sighed Lil.

Before the dishes were put away, the sisters had fallen silent. This never happened. "Just a minute," Lil would tell Stan when he came to pick her up at Annie's. An hour later Lil and Annie would still be steaming the kitchen window with laughter. The way life went, what could you do but laugh?

"If he lost his hair, Louie wouldn't be able to go on," agreed Annie at last, smiling weakly.

Now a 120-pound wrench had been thrown into the workings of their lives, throwing them off their gears, crossing their wires.

None of them was laughing now.

"Floozy, my foot," burst out Fan, throwing her tea towel to the floor.

None of the sisters had children. (Luckily, Michael and Carrie had more than their share; the family blood wasn't about to run dry.) They said it was because their little brother would always be child enough for three.

Naturally they had tried, they had all tried. But after her accident Lil's hope for a child was dashed again and again, and Fan and Annie had no better luck. The doctors could say what they liked, it wasn't meant to be. The sisters were never heard to regret their childless state, and hardly acknowledged its existence, but of course it made a difference. Especially later, when they were all getting on, it seemed something was lacking. Beneath the card table, ghosts of half-formed fetuses crawled among their legs and tickled their shins. Above the sisters' broad laughter soared a haunting harmony of clearer laughter.

"Did you hear that?" Annie would ask abruptly, turning her face sharply.

"Keep your mind on the game," Frank advised.

It was Fan, the oldest sister, who took Louie on when their parents died before anyone had even started to consider that a possibility. (Pneumonia got them both, one right after the other, in that hard winter of 1911.) Assuming legal guardianship, Fan and Stu raised Louie in the house on Broder Street. Never an easy boy, he didn't suddenly cease being an angel one day. From the beginning he tried to charm his way out of trouble. In spite of certain hopes Fan held for him, he insisted on leaving school early— not that there was much choice, with money so tight due to Stu's drinking on top of everything else.

First Louie delivered telegrams for Western Union, wheeling around Regina on that bike he kept polished bright as a nickel. It had a bell Louie liked to ring whether there was reason or not. A shiny sound that made you prick up your ears, turn your head. Sometimes you seemed to hear that bell and see that face, eager below the cap, everywhere you went. Louie learned to get around early. Right then, in his middle teens, he started to make the most of his possibilities and to milk any situation for what it was worth. The good news he delivered was really himself—and bad news wasn't so bad once he learned his ways. More than once Fan suddenly jerked the streetcar bell, descended to where that bike leaned against some front steps, marched without knocking into a stranger's house. A minute later she would emerge with one of Louie's ears pinched between her fingers. He would wince and stuff in shirttails and cast regretful glances back at the pretty housewife in the window.

Then Louie learned the value of a back door, a fire escape, an alley.

He got a reputation.

The mystery was that Louie wasn't a particularly good-looking boy—nor, later, man. He had the family's big nose, dark hair and strong facial bones. (His sisters were judged handsome, not pretty.) None of the family men were tall, or especially well built. Maybe it was enthusiasm more than anything that accounted for Louie's luck with the girls. He did play up his smile for all it was worth. His lips parted in continual anticipation, words smooth as silk slipped between his pearly gate of teeth. Darling. Sweetheart. Honey. Butter wouldn't melt in that mouth.

At first Fan said it was just too much energy. Louie should take up sports.

Really, the sisters didn't know what to think. Michael, the older brother, was always shy and clumsy where girls were concerned. He was grateful when Carrie came along to take charge and put an end to awkward dances at the Capri Ballroom and the Our Night Out Club. The sisters' own experience with the male sex was considerable; they had all been gay, high-spirited girls with a straightforward way that put the boys at ease. But it seemed Regina was not overpopulated with Romeos or matinee idols or Valentinos. Not at that time, at least.

Could it have been something to do with the climate? Or maybe it was the flatness of setting, the leaden rhythms of speech, the practical aspect of the architecture? What might appear romantic in Paris and sound seductive in Italian would, transplanted to Regina, have only been ridiculous.

There were enough polite, decent, steady men who knew how to buy a girl a box of chocolates and, perhaps once, a corsage. But these were not writers of love poems, walkers in moonlight, promenaders in the rain. You got married and settled down as quickly as possible—was there any good reason for waiting? Very shortly a couple resembled a duo of old friends, even siblings; comfortable with each other as a scuffed pair of shoes, they exchanged good-natured banter and a repertoire of jokes. They did not appear sufficiently involved with each other—not in any serious, essential way—to breed the kind of dangerous tension that often seems a necessary facet of romance. Passion, if it did exist, would not spark in public. Even when alone together the sisters did not discuss sex. Not as something that occurred in their own lives, anyway. There was enough of it in the movies—and that was something separate, wasn't it?

So Louie stuck out like a sore thumb. Of course he did.

For far too long Fan defended his flirtations. (What else could she do? She was almost his mother, after all.) She took pride in his popularity and called him a social success. Strange girls who came knocking on the door found Fan prepared to make friends. She was disposed to discuss Louie for as long as they liked, slicing up stories of his childhood—accidents, ailments, hijinks—along with coffee cake. Often these girls tried to get Fan to use her influence over Louie for their benefit. Fan remained neutral. She never favored one girl over another. "Good luck," she would wish one and all. "You'll need it."

Maybe Stu was resentful of the time she put in pressing Louie's striped shirts and keeping his suits so dapper. "You're aiding and abetting," said Stu. "You're an accessory to the crime."

Talk about honey to the bee. Louie was always rushing off to another assignation, his lips were permanently swollen from too many kisses. Lipstick flowered on his collar in and out of season. Just look at him: down on the corner he leans eagerly toward his girl and steams up the cold air with his compliments. Louie squirms and fidgets, he's so excited he can't keep still. She has the power to make him this anxious; all kinds of promises tumble from his lips. Of course she will meet him at midnight. She can't bear to see him suffer, she will give him what he needs. While she holds his attention, briefly, she's the only girl there is. The rest of the world dims and disappears. They stand together in a spotlight on a darkened stage.

A minute later, Louie's eyes would be darting in a dozen directions. Another pretty girl was always passing by. Maybe he could have them all. He was thinking where he had to be in an hour and where the hour after that. It was a miracle he could keep all their names straight and fit them into his agenda. His constant activities kept him rake thin: no matter how good a table Fan laid, he always had a hungry look to him. Lil once observed that there was something starved in Louie's eyes. She was right. Eventually none of his sisters could meet Louie's gaze.

It never was just tomcatting. Louie was always in love. He fell in and out of love a dozen times a day. A sickness, a fever: you wanted to take his temperature, feed him aspirin, believe there had to be a cure for this fervent kind of love you could die from.

"A cancer," diagnosed Annie, who always saw the worst side of everything. "It's eating him right up."

Sometimes Fan recalled that even as a little boy Louie's big problem had been concentration. A short attention span. Teachers had pointed it out in school. "He can't keep his mind on just one thing, or one girl, for any amount of time," analyzed Fan. "It's nothing more than that."

With Lil and Annie, Fan wondered if Louie's problem might have something to do with their parents dying when he was such a tender age. It was hard to know. Lil and Annie assured their sister that she had done a good job bringing up the boy. They wouldn't have done anything different. "You can't blame yourself," they said.

After one or two cheated husbands came hammering on Fan's door, the situation took a more serious turn. Then Louie was fired from Western Union as the result of an incident with the boss's daughter. His sisters began to fear he would catch a social disease. Louie became one more cross that needed to be borne.

Fan did her best. She asked him why he didn't settle down. Without going so far as to mention marriage, she pointed out the practical benefits of someone steady. Louie batted his eyelashes and claimed Fan was his only permanent girl. Next Fan made Stu have a private talk with him. She never did know what Stu said, but it was obvious nothing came from it. Once the whole clan took up the matter during a Sunday dinner. One after the other they outlined the error of Louie's ways, the wrong road he was headed down, where and how he would end up. Louie wriggled in his chair, dark hair falling into his eyes, lips pouting a promise of pleasure. Whatever the situation, however inappropriate it might be, Louie couldn't help looking like the cat that swallowed the canary.

He didn't change.

Over the Rummoli board his sisters began to make scathing remarks about Louie's girls. Soon they took the position that it was the girls who were to blame. "It's not his fault," they said. None of these chippies was strong or smart enough to take Louie in hand. Maybe they didn't deserve a steady man. They were snippy or flighty or loose. Badly dressed. No manners. "The one I saw him with downtown the other day," Lil would begin; then they were off to the races. The sisters howled with laughter until their faces turned as red as the Rummoli chips. They pounded the table with their fists until the game scattered and had to be started from scratch when they finally quieted down.

After he got the cab Louie was able to move out of Fan's and into a room on Coronation Street. This only made things more convenient for him and he got deeper into his various affairs. He began to run with a rougher crowd. Hearing he was selling bootleg on the side, the sisters didn't say a word. Louie was a grown man now. You couldn't always criticize. They only wished he wouldn't make it easier for their men to get hold of the stuff. Still, liquor was one danger they knew how to deal with— more than romance, for example. Teetotalers though they were ("We don't need help to have a good time," the sisters said), they knew what to do where booze was concerned, being married to a drinker each one of them. You could hide a bottle or pour it down the drain. You sober a man up, let him sleep it off, help him through his hangover.

But love?

He still came crawling back to Fan after a brawl over a girl. Louie was a less successful fighter than lover. The sight of his own blood scared him. Fan would clean up his face and put him on the chesterfield with a blanket. When he fell into a liquor sleep she went through his pockets and pulled crumpled notes from every one. She pursed her mouth and squinted. Some of these girls could hardly spell. *I'll wate at the usual place, same hour as beefor. Why haven't you bin bye? I can still taste yer kisses.* Fan folded the notes and put them at the bottom of her underwear drawer. Quite a collection gathered over the years. Sometimes in the midst of her cleaning she would go to the drawer, then sit on the edge of the bed with the notes heaped in her lap. She read them until she knew them by heart. "I can still taste your kisses," she said out loud. The clock on the night table ticked calmly. What was she doing? Fan got up and put the notes away. Louie never asked what happened to them. Maybe he didn't notice they were missing from his pockets. There was always another half dozen on him the next time he turned up in trouble.

Louie brought the odd girl around to show her off. On Fridays the whole gang gathered at Lil's for her famous *tochu*. Lil would have spent the morning grating potatoes, sifting flour, popping pans in and out of the oven. By the time she got bacon strips laid on the crispy cakes she was flushed red as a beet in her hot kitchen. When Fan and Annie showed up the three sisters invariably recalled that bedtime song they used to sing when they were little.

"Good night to little Tochu
He's saying his prayers
The window is open
His prayers have been said."

"Who's Tochu?" asked the girl on Louie's arm, looking uneasily around the room. They were such a big herd, the introductions weren't always that clear.

The men hammered fists upon raw onions Lil arranged by their plates. The girl jumped in her seat. With a thump the onions fell apart into their layers, then were eaten like bread with the *tochu*.

"We just got off the boat," explained Annie.

Maybe Louie's date wondered if the sisters always talked this loudly, all at once, or if it was something put on for show instead of company clothes. (They would be wearing their housedresses for these Friday meals, they weren't dining out in public.) No one, including Louie, bothered to fill in the background to the long, complex stories that accompanied the meal; they had been telling these tales for so long they couldn't imagine anyone not knowing them like the back of their hand. "And then the old man jumped off the roof," exclaimed Fan at the end of each story, to a fresh outburst of laughter.

What did that mean?

As soon as they finished eating, Lil herded everyone into the living room for coffee and cards. There was always time for a hand or two. It was the sisters on one team, their husbands on the other. Inlaws versus outlaws.

No one was able to explain the games. Did they even have names? Were there rules?

"The ace beats the two," said Annie.

"Except when the two is wild," corrected Stan.

"The two can't be wild," protested Lil. "When has the two ever been wild?"

"*Fan* was wild," recalled Stan.

"What do you mean *was?*" demanded Fan.

The girl slouched with a sulky smile beside Louie, who sometimes remembered to lean over and blow in her ear. Louie never missed a Friday at Lil's no matter how complicated his love life was. He kept score and spelled his brothers-in-law when they went to the bathroom.

"Lucky in cards, unlucky in love," chanted Lil, lifting her eyebrows when Louie made a nice play.

Eventually the men went out back with a bottle. (Lil wouldn't allow the stuff in her house.) The girl was left in the kitchen with the dirty dishes and the sisters. The latter weren't unfriendly or rude—no one could ever call them that—but they couldn't see rolling out the red carpet for some Miss they more than likely would never set eyes on again.

"Louie usually goes for blondes," Annie might remark.

"The last one was a redhead." This was Lil. "What was she called?"

"Ellen?" offered Fan.

"Ellen came before. There were at least five since that Ellen."

"What's your name again?" Annie asked the girl.

The same girl usually didn't turn up twice.

Louie looked puzzled when they asked whatever happened to that nice girl he brought by last time. His smile slowly turned mournful. He launched into some rigmarole involving a returned fiancé, an ailing parent, a sudden trip far away. The story was never clear. It was always hard to tell exactly who left whom, never mind the whys or wherefores of the situation.

Sometimes Fan didn't know whether to laugh or cry.

"I could write a book," she said.

No one was surprised when Lil was right. Constance didn't last. The ring and marriage certificate didn't mean a thing to Louie, if his behavior was any indication. He kept on with his gallivanting, even stepped it up. After seven months he was back in his old room on Coronation Street (had he ever left it completely?). None of them saw Constance again and they wondered if she left town. Come to think of it, who knew if there was even a divorce? Louie sure wasn't telling. "Who?" he would ask when anyone brought up her name.

The sisters wanted to understand why he married her in the first place. They could never imagine Louie and Constance alone together. It was too much work for their imagination. They say that opposites attract, but this was pushing it too far. "Why?" the sisters wished to question Louie; somehow they couldn't. This marked the beginning of a change. From now on they were not comfortable asking their brother too much. They bit their tongues. They really didn't want to know. "Ignorance is bliss," they said.

They had to be content to speculate among themselves—and there was certainly enough to puzzle upon, since during those seven months of Louie's marriage they didn't get to know Constance any better. At the beginning she came over with Louie on Fridays and Sundays, but the woman remained aloof. It wasn't from any sense of shyness or superiority, Fan finally decided. She just wasn't social. She would answer a question and throw in the odd remark. That was it. When the family got out the cards, Constance would bring out a piece of sewing and her glasses for close work. She stitched beneath the lamp in the corner, apart. Of course it was always hard to fit in with a new group of people; but the husbands had managed to integrate themselves, learning the sisters' card games and stories until you couldn't know they had not always been in the family. Constance didn't try. "We'll have to have you over," she said without enthusiasm each time she left Broder Street. One way or another an invitation never materialized; no one in the family ever saw the inside of her apartment—except Louie, of course. Not that they imagined Constance was hiding something. It would be a neat enough place, they supposed.

"*Too* neat," suggested Annie direly.

The first Friday Louie showed up at her door alone, Lil asked where Constance was.

"At home," he replied, and left it at that.

The writing was on the wall. Anyone could read it.

Later the sisters decided that Constance had caught Louie at a weak moment. In 1938, at thirty-seven, he would have been starting to fear growing old alone.

Well, none of them were getting any younger.

But maybe wiser.

Annie hinted darkly that Constance had something on Louie. He had to pay to keep her quiet. He was black-mailed into that ceremony. There was something shady about the whole business. Some people would do any-thing to get a man. Poor Louie.

At the time it appeared that Constance left no trace upon Louie or any of them. Soon the marriage came to seem of even briefer duration than it actually was. Hardly more than a Saturday-night date, a weekend fling. There were no photos of Constance lying around. She hadn't given any of them presents. Few of her words or actions stuck in their minds. What was there to remember?

Years later Fan would believe that Constance held more significance than was understood at the time. Up until she came along a certain number of possibilities remained open to Louie—his life could still take vari-ous directions. After Constance these possibilities became fewer. You didn't require Lil's powers to foresee that Louie would never marry again. He would never be a father. Never live in a real home or stay in one place. Never be happy.

(Did that last apply to just Louie? wondered Fan. Or to herself too?)

A mystery woman, Fan would think. What had they really known about Constance after all? She appeared out of nowhere and vanished the same way. A cat burglar. Carefully erasing her fingerprints from every surface she has touched. Leaving no clues of her secret, unseen visit behind, leaving everything exactly as it was. Except that something has been stolen, something precious is gone.

And no matter how expert the thief, a clue is always left behind.

Some invisible fingerprint. Some mark.

Fan stirred in the shadows of her Broder Street kitchen. (She stayed on there right until the end, alone. It was the Ukrainians she rented out half the house to in the last years who would find her.) Fan saw the image of a small, neat woman sitting quietly over some sewing in the corner of this very room. A needle flashed, glinted, flashed. The figure of fate? Fan shook herself in her chair. Your problem, she told herself, is you've got too much time to think.

It was just coincidental that major changes occurred in the family shortly after Constance made her quick entrance and exit. History happens how it wants to, nothing more than that.

Through all these years the family was poor, like most people—or at least everyone they knew. It wasn't until the end of the forties that any of them could stop worrying about money for one minute, though by then they had worried for so long it wasn't easy to stop. They were so used to no money that it was a familiar concern, like the weather. Yet it didn't stop them from enjoying life. It wasn't as if they had once been rich and didn't know how to be poor.

Still, by 1939 it seemed things were never going to improve in Regina—there was just nothing for them there. Stan got laid off from the gas company early in the Depression, then couldn't manage to stay off Relief for any length of time. Michael was in construction, but not much building was going on then. It was more or less the same for all of them. Lil did some cleaning for the Greeks. Carrie took in washing. They all just barely got by.

Then some cousins, the Keighleys, who had moved out west in '37, needed another man on their dairy. Michael and Carrie packed up and left Regina. Stan and Lil followed close behind—he got on at the smelter there in Brale. Next Annie and Frank thought they might as well try the Kootenays too. Fan was looking forward to the move herself, when Stu passed on suddenly. Heart.

Fan stayed on in Regina, though everyone urged her not to be a fool. To hurry up and get on that train before they came and dragged her away. What was left for her in Regina? It wasn't easy to explain. There were her sisters and one brother now all living in the same B.C. town, within walking distance of each other—and her two thousand miles away. She had always been so close to her sisters; there hadn't been much need for other friends. Now, alone at her age, it was hard to meet new people—not when she didn't go to church. Where? How? Oh, she *knew* more people than you could shake a stick at—everyone on the block and on the next block too, just for starters. But she didn't love them. One sure thing: she wouldn't marry again. Once was enough. She didn't have the energy to go through all that again, even if she did have the time. Somehow this meant she should stay on in Regina. She couldn't explain it even to herself. Least to herself.

"Fan is just stubborn," said her sisters. "She was always that way."

She made excuses and tried to pawn them off as reasons. Said she couldn't stand the thought of selling the house when they had finally just got it paid off. (And how they had managed that she would never know.) The idea of going through all the junk piled up over the years was more than she could face. This will give us a good reason to write some letters, she told Lil and Annie. Someone has to keep the home fires burning. Who would you stay with when you come back to visit? And someone has to take care of Louie.

He hadn't gone west, though he'd been out there any number of times. Louie hadn't *settled* anywhere, and showed no sign of ever doing so. After Constance he rambled more than ever, but always seemed to end up back in Regina. If you wanted to say he lived anywhere, that would be the place. Maybe it was because he had known the majority of his girls here. There were dozens he could call up still. Ask if they wanted to get together for old times' sake. Once more for the good times, he crooned into the phone with that bedroom voice.

No, he didn't slow down with age, not that you could notice. In the early forties he was still chasing skirts with as much dedication as always. But this hunt for love now seemed less pleasurable and more desperate. Louie had betrayed his bachelorhood with Constance; he could never really get it back however much he tried. Some purity was gone. And he was drinking more heavily now—he lost his taxi license over that. The booze may have been partly responsible for his losing what looks he had, too. All those coffee-shop and boardinghouse meals didn't help either. Fan had a feeling that the girls he was most interested in (young ones, to call a spade a spade) were not so easily within Louie's reach nowadays. Oh, he still had his charm—his attentive, enthralled manner that could make a woman float on cloud nine. He never completely lost that merry look of his, that frankness of face that made him seem all out in the open, all there for you to take. (An illusion, yes, but one that worked.) His compliments and appreciations never sounded stale, however often they tripped off his tongue. In his own way Louie was the most sincere lover in the world.

Maybe Louie didn't bring his girls around anymore because now it was just her. Or was it the girls who decided this? Either way, there were no more Fridays and Sundays with the whole crew together at Broder Street. Fan often felt a kind of ache on those days, a real pain in her bones. Was it arthritis coming on? She wondered if Louie felt this same thing and what he did about it. An extra drink or two?

She might see him downtown. Walking quickly along the sidewalk, in a hurry to reach wherever he was going, so deep in thought he would bump into people. Alone, believing himself unwitnessed, his expression was serious, nearly grim, completely unlike the face he usually showed the world. Which was his real face? When a woman was with him, Fan would notice that she was a good deal older than Louie's usual type, often older than Louie himself. Divorcées and widows, Fan imagined. Bank tellers and boardinghouse owners and the managers of coffee shops. Single women of a certain age who couldn't afford to let themselves go, who struggled against time and weight and gravity. They're braver than I am, thought Fan, who suddenly began to gain after Stu died and the rest of the clan went out to B.C.

Fan wouldn't quicken her step or cross the street toward Louie and his companion. It would be intruding. Somehow it was embarrassing to see Louie in this situation now, as awkward for him as for her. Like seeing a grown man playing cowboys and Indians. Or like opening a door to find him alone in a bare room, crying.

It was surprising how often he was alone. When she stopped by his place on Coronation Street he never had company, and there were no signs of a recently departed guest. Louie would be doing the crossword puzzle from the paper or entering figures into a little account book with a black plastic cover that he flipped shut as soon as Fan appeared. He would seem startled, as if he hadn't hoped for a visitor but expected to be alone.

A few times Fan had seen young girls look after Louie's thickened figure in the street. Turning to each other, they arched eyebrows and twisted mouths. "There goes the last Casanova of Regina," Fan heard one say once.

Of course when the war came along and Louie was exempted—Fan was never sure exactly why—plenty of these same girls were happy to have any kind of breathing man to squire them around. There was a shortage. During the duration Louie was in greater demand than ever. The pace of his romantic life increased and Fan hardly saw him. But she could imagine how it went with those girls young enough to be his daughter laughing on his arm. Daddy, they would call him. Pops. He would miss their jokes and not understand their slang. Bolder, brassier, harder: girls today were different. Inside as well as out—it wasn't just styles of clothes, of hair.

When the troops came home Louie was back in square one. This was when he really started to move around. He couldn't stay in one place longer than three or four months. It was more than he could bear. They all had a wide streak of Gypsy blood—hadn't they roamed halfway around the world to reach Regina? With Louie it was something more than that. There was no one to ask him to stay. No one to cry for him not to go. So go he did.

While she stayed.

He would stop by Fan's with some boxes for her basement. It always surprised her to see how little Louie had accumulated over the years. But things were looking up in Calgary and that's all that counted. A fellow there wanted to go partners in a wholesale concern. Then it was Edmonton he was headed to. Something to do with lightbulbs? Fan never could keep track. She often suspected these business proposals were no more than smoke screen; there was really a woman at the end of the road, she guessed. Each time Louie gave the impression he was going for good. He never said how long he was off for or when he was coming back. He was that confident of things working out this time around, he was eternally hopeful. An optimistic man if there ever was one.

Once every woman loved a dreamer. Maybe things were different now.

While away he didn't write or call. He vanished into thin air. Sometimes, during those long Regina winters, Fan forgot exactly when Louie had taken off and just where he had gone this time. Was it only in the fall he had said goodbye? What destination had he mentioned— Saskatoon? Sometimes Fan wasn't even sure he had left Regina at all. Maybe he was over on Coronation Street right this minute. Then she climbed down to the basement and bumped around in the dimness until she found Louie's boxes waiting for him.

The only news she received would be via her sisters. "What time is it there?" Annie or Lil would shout all the way from B.C., always unable to believe Fan was two hours ahead of them. ("You were always ahead of us," her sisters joked.) Then they might mention that Louie had been through. Maybe he had stayed for as long as a week, or headed straight on to Vancouver as soon as the road was rinsed from his throat with a beer. No, he was alone. Didn't mention any woman. His usual self. Nothing could get old Louie down. He looked as well as could be expected.

(Meaning: as well as any man who has lived alone too long, and suffered because of this single state, could be hoped to look.)

Old Louie's a character, they laughed to one another. That Louie would never change. There he is, coming through Annie's door on Columbia Avenue when no one had the slightest idea he was in the vicinity. Talking up a storm before anyone could invite him to sit down, wondering why no one was breaking out the cards, asking if that was coffee he smelled. Rubbing his head with one hand and looking like he could break your heart.

He was always a heartbreaker. He still broke Fan's heart. Every year her heart broke a little more just thinking about him.

He came back to Fan in the same unexpected way. It was usually the middle of the night when she heard him pull into the empty driveway, still in that ancient Ford of his. (Fan didn't own a car; she never had learned to drive.) Invariably she was awake. She found she needed less sleep as she grew older, and would go to bed to lie awake when she couldn't think of anything more to keep her up. He came in the front door without knocking. Fan tied the belt of her housecoat and switched on lights. "Been driving a thousand miles without a break," said Louie, rocking back and forth on his heels as Fan perked coffee. She took in his red eyes with the shadows below them, how his hands shook until she brought out the bottle she kept in the top cupboard for him. Now there didn't seem much point in being sticky over a thing like liquor in the house. Now many of the old rules appeared foolish, as though they no longer applied.

"I'll tell you," said Louie, adding whisky to his coffee. "It's good to be back."

He never said why he returned and Fan didn't ask. As he recounted things he had seen and places he had been, Fan hardly listened. They weren't what mattered. What counted was how he looked, the way his voice sounded. The angle of his back, the line of his shoulders. Those lines and angles were always changing—each time Louie returned they changed some more—but at the same time they remained the same. Old lines, new lines: they blurred, and there was more than one man before her. Fan saw a dozen Louies at once.

When he wound down they listened to the clock for a few minutes. Then Fan rose to get a blanket and sheets for the chesterfield.

"Like old times," said Louie.

"Don't remind me," said Fan.

The next morning he moved his boxes back to the place on Coronation Street. Fan never asked him to stay on with her, though she was alone with all that space.

Louie would stay in town for a spring or a fall. Every week Fan stopped by with some home cooking. (Louie had a hot plate in his room, but no kind of fridge. He ate out, Fan guessed. Or more and more existed on a liquid diet.) In turn he would come over and mow the lawn. Maybe for an hour at dusk they would sit out behind the house and slap mosquitoes. Then he was gone again. Finally he didn't bother to give a reason for his leaving, or even indicate the direction he was headed. Fan stood on the cracked sidewalk at dawn—Louie liked to get an early start—with a sweater pulled around her against the chill. Louie sat in the car and warmed it up. Fan nudged the sidewalk with her toe; it was crumbling, this whole neighborhood was falling apart before her eyes. When she looked up, the Ford was disappearing around the corner. Fan lifted her arm and Louie honked the horn. Fan put on another pot of coffee. From now on the only change in life would be growing older. However that sounded, it was true. For Louie, for her.

In her dream Fan sees a hobo. He is unshaven, his shirt is frayed at the cuffs, a belt of rope holds up filthy pants, there are holes in his shoes. How long has he been living on stolen apples and begged crusts of bread and the occasional piece of meat cooked over an open fire in some hobo jungle past the edge of town? He has been on the road forever and he will never stop because he has no destination. Sometimes he rides the rails, sometimes he walks. He travels through every season and he knows every province in the land. The road is long and dusty; each farmhouse is miles apart. The hobo knocks on another kitchen door and another pretty young woman opens it. Her husband is out in the fields; she hasn't seen a face all day. Though his belly growls and he is close to fainting from hunger, the tramp doesn't ask for a meal. "I lost something," he says instead. But he doesn't know what it is. Has he ever known or has he forgotten? The young woman is kind as well as pretty. This man looks broken and weary; she would help him if she could. A broom, a frying pan, a lock of her hair, a dollar bill. No, the hobo slowly shakes his head. No, he says to whatever she offers. It is never the thing he is looking for, the thing he needs. Both the tramp and the young woman are disappointed because she can't help him; in his own way each has failed. Only Fan, who is not in this picture but is somehow still there, knows what the hobo needs. She has what he requires; the power to save him with one word is hers. The word is right there on the tip of her tongue, but she can't get it out. What is it? It swells in her mouth. Does Fan really wish to speak? To help the hobo? She mutely watches him turn from the farmhouse and set out again upon his endless road.

This dream occurred over and over in exactly the same way, in the same flat, plain light. Yet each time it unfolded as something Fan had not experienced before, each time it took her several moments (or what felt like moments) to recognize this hobo as her younger brother. The awareness would spring upon her with the force of a shocking revelation.

Hadn't Louie always taken good care of himself? Even when drinking heavily toward the end (killing himself, as a secret voice inside her head told Fan), he was well groomed. A man who placed importance upon his visits to the barber and upon the rituals of manicure and shave. A shoeshine was an integral part of Louie's life. His clothes were painstakingly tended (a Lithuanian woman down the block did his laundry), though somewhat worse for wear in the last years. Vanity? Perhaps. Or a way of holding himself together. Of holding on.

It was always a pleasure to see Louie so nicely turned out, with a clean smell of soap and aftershave escaping from his skin—along with the inevitable trace of Evening In Paris perfume. (Lil used to say it was a first requirement of Louie's women that they wear this and no other scent. He ought to get a percentage from the company, Lil said.) Even when his face became blotched and bloated, with small red veins risen to its surface, Louie tried to carry on. On a Sunday evening Fan often found him sewing on a button or darning a sock in his room. This, too, was always neat and clean, but maintained the impersonal appearance of a hotel room only passed through and never really inhabited. Yet how long had Louie had this room? A decade or a day? (Mae Ruxtell, who owned the house, always managed for him to have his same third-floor room overlooking the street, even if it meant moving around other boarders each time he returned: Louie was such an old customer.) There were no photos of family about, and few souvenirs or gifts from former girlfriends—though Louie must have received a truck load in his day. Yet wasn't the past all Louie had left, more and more? Where was it, the past? Where was one sign of it? That's what Fan wanted to know.

Louie a hobo? No. Though there had been years when thousands of men were on the move all over the country, with nowhere to go and nothing to lose, Louie never was in that position. Those men didn't have family to fall back on, Fan always felt. That's what made the difference. Yes, Louie did travel, he did like to move around. But there was always some scheme cooking, one more iron in the fire—even if not quite on the level. (For example, he had that tire retreading contract during the war; there was something more than shady in the way it operated, the partner ended up in jail.) Careless as he was with money, Louie was lucky with it. Fan always said that if he put as much of his mind onto business as he did onto girls he would have been another Rockefeller. As it was, there were no savings at the end. Only debts.

Until the end of the forties Fan went out to B.C. every summer. She usually stayed a month at Annie's. (Though an outsider might not notice, Lil's old troubles became worse with age; it was hard for her to have company in the house, even if it was just family.) For those four weeks it was like old times. Food, talk, cards. Drives in Stan's new car. They never talked about the past. Why should they? It was being recreated every minute.

Then, despite her sisters' protests to the contrary, Fan would feel she was wearing out her welcome and take the train back home. Either Annie or Lil would make it to Regina once a year, and in 1947 Michael, Carrie and their kids came out. The oldest boy, Mitch, was quite taken with his Aunt Fan. They wrote back and forth all through his high school, and for some time beyond.

One summer Fan couldn't make the trip. She claimed the heat as the reason; she couldn't overcome it sufficiently to get herself packed and onto the train. "I'm just sitting here dripping," she exclaimed to Annie over the phone. "That weight I've been trying to get off all these years? Well, it's melting from me even as we speak." Annie agreed that the train was hard. Fan could fly out. Annie and Frank would buy the ticket. When Fan said she didn't think so, not this year, without giving further explanation, Annie was hurt. (Later, discovering what was really going on in Regina that summer, and how it had been kept from them, both Lil and Annie were more than hurt.) The sisters would still write and call each other, but future visits were never mentioned on either side again. They saw each other several times more, at funerals. But that wasn't the same.

Of course Fan couldn't wander off into the wild blue yonder that summer: this was when Louie became so sick. As stubborn as any man, he wouldn't see a doctor. Well, it didn't require a medical genius to see it was the drinking that had caught up with him. Blood pressure, liver, nerves—all kinds of damage had been done, and unfortunately Fan was well acquainted with the signs. (There had been her own Stu. And now John, on the dairy back in B.C.—though Etta denied it until the sun went down.) Louie had lost his ruddy complexion; his face became quite gray. He had trouble with his circulation, and balance became a problem. Suddenly, after being heavy for some years, he lost considerable weight. He wouldn't eat, hardly took in a thing.

And he drank more than ever.

Why did the sisters all marry drinkers and why did both their brothers also drink? Frank, Stan and Stu had all been fond of a bottle before they ever met, never mind married the sisters. At least no one could say these women had driven their men to the bottle. They liked some weakness in a man, so they could better show their strength in one of the few ways possible for women during those times? In the face of some fairly tough odds they would hold a home together. They would stick it out. (There was not one divorce or even separation in their generation.) You could take pride in that; it counted for something. And this battle against liquor, or its effects upon their homes, gave the sisters' lives a sharp focus that seemed lacking in the blurred shape of their husbands'. It gave them a clear, named enemy to pit themselves against.

None of the sisters had a problem with liquor themselves, though they lived in such intimacy with it for so long a kind of secondhand intoxication seemed the result. Even during their teetotaler years there was often a sweet, sherry-like giddiness in their manner. Later, when they relaxed their standards, they would grimly swallow a glass of straight liquor in one gulp, for all the world as if it were medicine, then turn unusually quiet and thoughtful for an hour. Not everyone was surprised to discover all those empty cough syrup bottles in Lil's basement when she passed on.

"No wonder," wrote Annie to Fan.

"With her life, why not?" wrote Fan to Annie.

"I would have done the same," Annie called Fan to say.

"Except I would have gotten rid of the empty bottles," Fan replied long distance.

Breathing hard and perspiring, Fan climbed Louie's three flights of stairs every morning. Louie would still be in bed whether it was nearly noon or not. He pretended to sleep while Fan opened windows to let in air; there was that smell of sickness she couldn't stand. Often vomit needed to be cleaned up.

Then she made Louie open his eyes, sit up, talk to her. She hadn't come clear across town in all this heat to be treated like a ghost. She tried to get something solid in his stomach. Maybe they would play a few hands of Honeymoon Whist. But Louie was tired and weak, without much to say for himself. What had he ever said besides his jokes and stories and love talk, anyway?

I don't know this man at all, thought Fan that last summer.

What did she mean by that? Of course she knew him. The way you know the blood that runs through your own veins; it doesn't have to speak beyond its pulsing. This was her brother. Not yet fifty. A young man still. Dying before her eyes. This is exactly how he wants it, Fan realized. This is what he has always wanted. To make me watch him die. Not lifting a finger, just watching.

She could do that much for him. She could do this one last thing.

Late in the afternoon she returned to Broder Street, almost too worn out to fix supper—not that it was ever easy to cook for one. (Often Fan found she made way too much, took the extra to the people who rented the other half of her house.) Those August afternoons were long; the light was nearly everlasting. Sometimes Fan went to bed before it was quite dark. She might have a nip of whisky from the last bottle she had bought for Louie's visits. It wasn't going to do her any harm at this late stage of the race. Didn't seem to do her much good either.

She thought of Louie in his room on the other side of town. Drinking, of course. She was sure he started as soon as she left in the afternoon. She could almost feel him waiting for her to go so he could get on with it. Where did he get the bottles? Fan didn't think he went out any-more. One or another of his women kept him supplied, she imagined. No doubt there was still a dozen dames falling over themselves to do Louie a favor, even if he was no longer any kind of lover. The kindness that kills. Twice

Fan passed the same one on Louie's stairs. An older, heavy-set woman with a sad, frightened face. Had Fan seen this woman years ago at one of Lil's Fridays? There was something familiar about her. The kind of familiarity that comes with bumping into your own reflection. Did that old flame of Louie's (if old flame she was) believe Fan one too? Meet me in the mirror, my lover, my self.

A dozen times Fan has gone to her window, lifted the curtain with one hand, looked out into the snowy night. Before her house stands a streetlamp. It illuminates the flakes falling thickly around it, but descending snow is also visible beyond this circle of light. The street is silent, and empty except for Louie waltzing with a woman near the streetlamp. They hold each other lightly (or is that only how it looks: is their grip really as tight as death?) and stare into each other's eyes. They are waltzing without music; they don't require violins. Louie's face is as clear as it has ever been, like the snow around him shining with all kinds of light; but his partner's face is blurred, just out of focus. Is this because Fan's vision is faulty? She rubs her eyes. Tears spring from them as she gazes at the girl's long dress. Fan knows what it is like to wear such a dress. She remembers how it feels, the way it moves. Louie is in uniform; perhaps all those buttons are why he looks so handsome. They slowly turn in three-four time, Louie and his girl, snow still falling around them, landing on their heads and arms and shoulders, powdering them like stardust. (In the Capri Ballroom there were small points of light that swept in circles around the walls and ceiling, swirling as you also turned and turned, making you dizzy, making you need to hold him tight.) Their shoes scuff the snow upon the ground and leave traces that show where they have danced. It must be cold out there, it must be twenty below. She must cling to him for warmth as they waltz away toward the dark end of the street.

Fan shivered. She dropped the curtain and realized several things at once. First, it had never snowed in August in Regina, not to her knowledge. It must be eighty at least. It was the heat that rose her from bed time and again. (Or was it the dream of Louie hunting and never finding?) Second, Louie never wore a uniform, he wasn't in the war. Right now he was burning up on Coronation Street, liquor flaming through his veins. He was in no shape at all to be waltzing in the street at midnight—which no doubt was against the law in any case. They had a bylaw against everything now. You couldn't keep a chicken behind your house, never mind a cow. This was 1949, after all. Cars, not horses. Indoor plumbing, not some stinking outhouse. Alone, not together.

Welcome to modern times, sister.

Careful, Fan told herself. Before you know it, they'll come and carry you away. Lock you up and throw away the key.

Or, at very least, throw it farther.

"I didn't see any need to put you through it," Fan would later say to Lil and Annie when they wanted to know just why she had chosen not to tell them how bad Louie was that summer.

"What would have been the point in ruining your summer?" Fan shrugged. "There's nothing you could have done."

Lil and Annie were buying none of this. They had a right to know. They had a right to be put through Louie's death and a right to have their summer spoiled. Louie was their brother, too. Fan wasn't his only sister, whatever she might think.

Fan had always been selfish. It came down to that.

It was true that Fan didn't wish to share Louie during his final months. She didn't want to fight with Lil and Annie over who could show the most concern for him. She wanted to be alone with him.

To watch him die.

If he needed her to do this, she needed it just as badly. They both required this experience: she must witness the rounding out of a life, must consider its whole, full shape and understand exactly what space that shape had filled.

Fan would believe finally that any clues she happened upon afterward were not left accidentally.

This time the woman who passed Fan on Louie's stairs was crying. Her face looked more frightened than before. Pull yourself together, girl, thought Fan. Once again she decided that Louie's women had never had any backbone. Constance included.

Floating to the surface of her mind for the first time in years, this name made Fan turn and peer sharply down the steps behind her. They descended into dimness. No figure was visible at their bottom, the only sound was the loud crashing of Fan's heart. She shook her head once, in emphatic denial.

These women were the reason Louie was in this present mess, Fan thought angrily—even as she knew that wasn't really true. They had made the bed Louie was lying in. They had lured him into it, then melted into thin air. Fan was inclined to give this woman on the stairs a piece of her mind next time. Then she remembered that her own blood pressure was something to take into account. Climbing these stairs was enough for her heart to handle.

Louie was dead. She knew it as soon as she opened the door. There was no need to hum and haw. By the look of it, he had already stiffened. Fan poked at him to make sure.

There was some cleaning to be done. She might as well get started right away. No use crying over spilled milk. Fan worked around Louie's room the way she did every morning, except this time he wasn't pretending to be asleep.

She looked around a little more closely than usual. This might be the best moment to see what he left behind— everyone leaves something behind, always, even if it's just unpaid bills. Fan poked through drawers and inspected the closet. She went through the pockets of the pants folded over a chair and pulled out a number of notes.

She knew what these were before she read them. *Darling, I'm still wating for you. I'll remember our nite together always.* Suddenly Fan moved her face closer. She wished she had brought her glasses. Reaching into her purse, she rummaged up a note Louie had once left on the kitchen table to say he'd stopped by. Fan compared handwriting, then closed her eyes.

She should have known. For one, Louie had never paid enough attention at school to learn to spell. For another, she just should have known. Louie had fooled them all. Good for him.

The question was: How much of it had been Louie's game? Had any of it been real? All that love and affection and adoration Louie had supposedly been object of. The thousand girls who were believed to have chased his elusive form through each and every Regina street. A whole lifetime dedicated to love—or to a chimera of love?

Once it had been real. Fan had certain proof of that. She had witnessed several indisputable scenes. At the beginning, yes. Up until Constance. But later? No. It had stopped years ago. She would put her money on it. His early reputation carried Louie along, sustained the myth of a lover when no lover remained. Only a man in a room rented by the week, alone, writing love notes to himself. A man who had reeked of solitude for as long as she could remember.

Hindsight, yes. But true.

And she would take the truth any way she found it.

Fan sat straight up, then walked back to the closet. Without fumbling she reached to its rear and drew out the bottle she knew would be there. Evening In Paris. It was one-third full. Fan sprayed a little on her wrist and sniffed. She saw Louie doing the same thing a million times, in this same room, before this same mirror. It wasn't quite her style—a little vanilla behind the ears was good enough for her—but she stowed the bottle of scent, along with the forged love notes, in her purse.

No one would have to know.

Fan got down on hands and knees beside the death bed. Instead of praying, she reached beneath it and pulled out the whisky bottle. Not for the first time she thought that Lil wasn't the only one in the family to possess special powers. She cast an eye upon the corpse and held the bottle to her mouth, placing her lips where Louie had placed his to take a final swallow. She had never drunk this way before, but there was a first time for everything.

In Regina they still told stories of Louie. Fan would overhear people talking on the streetcar, in a coffee shop. It surprised her to realize that her brother was a famous figure to this day. Imagine it. They said girls had killed themselves for his sake. Windows had been leaped from and rat poison swallowed because of Louie. Others withdrew from the world into religious orders or went to work as missionaries in China. Some remained in the city but could never look at another man again. There were those who had taken to drink or drugs. Louie had fathered more than five hundred illegitimate children. With just a glance he could make a girl lose her virginity—his eyes had a special power, something like x-ray.

This reputation hadn't been built in one day and it hadn't built itself either. Louie had gone to a good deal of trouble for a good many years to create his reputation. It had been his life's work. The least Fan could do was to play her part now. She could keep a secret with the best of them.

Casanova.

That was the name to put on Louie's headstone, so everyone would know who was really buried there. HERE LIES THE LAST CASANOVA OF REGINA. It had a nice ring to it. Lil and Annie would not be easy to convince, but they always saw things Fan's way in the end.

Speaking of her sisters, she had to get on the phone to them. And to the doctor. The funeral parlor. The newspaper. Fan set herself in motion. Nothing got done by itself.

Frozen Blood

"I could write a book," swore Fan more times than anyone could count.

Sometimes she said she *should* write one.

Depending on the circumstances, this could be a threat or a promise, spoken out of defiance or wonderment or despair.

No one took Fan seriously. She wasn't suggesting she was about to take out pen and paper, roll up sleeves, set to work. This was something all of them said when life twisted into a shape too fantastic to be contained within the Broder Street kitchen. One of the three sisters would shake her head wisely or with impatience throw hands through the air as she spoke about this book that ought to be written. Events slipped beyond human comprehension, and could not always be put to rest with spoken words or shrugged off with a laugh. Perhaps if bound between covers and printed in perfect, even type, they would seem less unreal, those outlandish occurrences. They would fit right in beside all the other marvelous made-up tales written down through the ages.

Take Lil's accident, for example.

Someone should write about that, they all agreed.

But no one was implying that one of *them* should do it.

Of course even if she found the time (and where would that be? in what corner of her days did unoccupied hours hide?), Fan was hardly literary. To begin with,

English was only her second language and she had forgotten her first. She hadn't yet started school before
they left the Old Country in 1897, traveling by boat and
then train to reach what seemed the end of the world
but was really Regina, Saskatchewan. Fan was still a little
bit of a girl then, only seven years old. What with one
thing and another she never did make it inside a
Canadian school as a student—there were too many
other, more important things to worry about in those
first years after their arrival.

(Later Fan would show an especially intense interest
in her younger brother Louie's education. After taking
Louie in—she had to, there was no choice—Fan was
always going down to the school to discuss his progress
or lack thereof. Not waiting to be called in, Fan dressed
up and walked over several times a week, timing herself
to arrive just when the kids were getting out, so she and
Louie's teacher could have a serious talk in peace. Really,
it was the sight of those neat rows of desks and the smell
of chalkdust that Fan absorbed more than the teacher's
words, though she would nod her head at appropriate
moments and wear a cowed expression unlike any to
grace her face at other times. Also, Fan was forever inviting these same teachers home for supper—she had an
idea that teachers ate poorly; they weren't ones to think
overly about their stomachs, she believed—until her
husband, Stu, finally told her to stop before the instruc-
tors began to think they were being bribed.)

For one, she had to work. They got her washing dishes
at a Ukrainian place on Victoria Avenue right away.
Standing on an apple box, she could reach the sink;

when the box was no longer needed, Fan was grown up. By this time, when she might have had the opportunity to get some education, she felt she was too old to sit in a room full of younger students. Fan wasn't fond of being behind anyone, ever.

Her younger brothers and sisters managed to get in a few years of schooling and considered themselves lucky. Louie, youngest of all, born right there in Regina, went to school like any Canadian. He could have finished, too, if things had turned out differently.

That was another story.

From the start they spoke only English at home. It was a rule. At first this meant long periods of silence before one or another of them could come up with any kind of phrase at all. But their father said they hadn't come all this way to stay the same. Even before they disembarked from the boat Michael altered the family name to make it easier for English-speaking tongues; he dropped a *vich* like it was a piece of extra baggage he didn't have the strength to tote to their destination. He never was in agreement with the way various groups clung together in their neighborhoods and churches and social halls, as if they had never left Germany or Poland or wherever. His idea was to fit right in—and he probably would have if he hadn't died before being given half a chance. The outlook for their mother, who passed away that same hard winter of 1911, was less hopeful in terms of complete Canadianization. Lena never caught on to the language at all, never progressed beyond a three-word sentence: *We eat now. Bring coat here.* She went around the house holding long, silent conversations with herself;

her constantly moving lips would remain a fixed image
in her children's minds: they remembered Lena as a
character in a silent movie without the titles. No one
ever knew on what kind of wondrous verbal flights this
woman privately soared, and later her daughters would
feel they had been deprived of all kinds of motherly
advice and wisdom. Except for a few words that seemed
without an English translation—these mostly described
foods and drinks nonexistent in Canada—the family
successfully erased an entire vocabulary and grammar
in a remarkably short time. It was a whole way of thinking they forgot, really. Especially with their parents'
deaths, it was as though something were wiped out. The
past was gone, just like that.

How could you miss what you couldn't remember?

How could you know if something valuable had
been lost?

Naturally the younger children—Lil and Annie,
Michael and Louie—picked up English as easily as a
common cold; they had the advantage over Fan, the oldest, in this regard. (Younger means easier, Fan realized
when she saw how things went in the family, and not
only in terms of language. In a hundred years life would
be so easy no one would ever have to get out of bed, no
one would have to fight for a thing.) But not for long:
eventually Fan could speak English with the best of
them. To the end of her life she refused to admit to any
kind of accent whatsoever. She would take offense if you
hinted that she pronounced a word incorrectly or gave
emphasis to the wrong syllable. She drew herself up to
her full five feet and one inch and turned indignant and

said she had been speaking English long before some people were thought of, never mind conceived. Later all the sisters spoke an especially slangy idiom learned from thirties movies. A jazzy, wise-guy style of speech, a Warner Brothers way of talking. It seemed almost another language than any heard in real life—no one talked that way in Regina, at least. "Get that Joe," Lil would mutter out of the corner of her mouth. "Nothing doing, mister," Annie informed her Frank. Even in the sixties the sisters were still molls addressing gangsters, though they knew perfectly well that this was not Chicago or New York and that the Depression had long ended. "Put a lid on it," Fan liked to advise.

Fan never regretted aloud her lack of schooling. She implied that education was fine for others because they were less quick. They needed that extra help. She could read and write, and she could do a lot of other things, too. She picked up knowledge like it was a dime on the street any fool would bend over and wipe on her skirt until it was something shiny you could use to buy what you needed. Fan looked at her sisters' schoolbooks, asked a question or two. "I already knew that," she would say once they gave an explanation.

Before she turned thirty Fan started to say she had already forgotten more than most people ever know. She had an opinion on everything under the sun—the best way to boil an egg, how the Americans controlled the banks, what Mary Pickford was really like—and she was always right. No one could tell her anything. They could save their breath or they could blow it out their ear.

Fan could write a letter and read the paper. For years she was fond of a book called *The Despair of Emily*, which she never seemed to finish. You would enter the living room to find her frowning into its dark, gloomy binding. Fan would stash the volume beneath the chesterfield cushions before you could blink an eye; cool as a cucumber, she studied her nails. Once, a dozen years later, out of nowhere Annie asked Fan the reason for Emily's despair and if this despair were ever overcome.

"What in the world are you talking about?" demanded Fan, denying she had ever known a despairing Emily or even a hopeful one.

People who needed to read books were people who had too much time on their hands or who were lazy or who didn't know that life itself is a book. You didn't need to buy it or borrow it from the library; it was there all around you, the book of life. Day in and day out its pages turned of their own accord, too swiftly for even a speed-reader to absorb, and you couldn't stop their turning if you tried. You couldn't pause at a favorite page you might like to read a second time. Even on the east side of Regina the world turned that quickly. Time flew like a scrap of paper in a windy street, and anyone who tried to run after it and catch it only lost their breath. You blinked an eye and you were ten years older.

What had happened to those ten years?

Where was it written?

It was Annie who was the great reader. She always had her nose in a novel. You couldn't get her to do a thing around the house because it interfered with her reading. She took on ten books at once, opened them during supper and in the bathroom and at work. She lost two good jobs because of her habit and turned down more dates than many girls are offered because she couldn't put down her book. This very reading was the reason why Annie looked on the dark side of things, felt Fan. It accounted for her brooding and her general gloominess. For several months, while Frank was courting, Annie also wrote poems at the kitchen table, after the dishes were cleared. Her cheeks flushed and perspiration gathered on her brow as she composed. These efforts she guarded in fierce secrecy—no one knew where she hid them; Fan once made a thorough search to no avail. Three weeks after her wedding Annie burned the poems in the kitchen stove. When she had to get glasses later on—she must have been forty by then, she was the first in the family to need them—Fan suspected that her sister had only gotten what she asked for, ruining her eyes for no good reason Fan could see. This was in spite of the fact that Annie had stopped reading years before. She just outgrew it, along with biting her nails and various other bad habits of youth.

Still, if there was going to be an author in the family, it would be Annie, not Lil or Michael or Louie. Certainly not Fan.

Like all the family stories, this one had a bottle at the bottom of it.

Picture a terribly cold February night in 1915.

Lil and Stan had been married for slightly less than a year, and the first baby was due in April. They were living on his family's farm near Davidson, eighty miles outside Regina. It wasn't much of a place. You could see that the spread (wheat: what else?) would never amount to a thing. The house was little more than a shack; a sieve offered greater protection against those cold prairie winds. It would have been cramped even if Stan's family had numbered fewer than the nine it did. Everyone was perpetually underfoot everyone else; Stan and Lil had no privacy whatsoever. And this was a grim, silent family. They didn't seem to know how to talk, much less laugh, and apparently cards were against their beliefs—they belonged to some kind of Russian Orthodox sect, Lil gathered. She wasn't sure what their religion was all about: there was no church-going or grace-saying or prayers that she ever witnessed. It seemed a negative faith based solely upon what it did not permit. Along with cards there was music, dancing, makeup, smoking: all disallowed.

But liquor was obviously not forbidden.

Quite the opposite, in fact.

Potato liquor. They all drank it, the whole family, from the youngest little girl, not yet six, to the old man who spoke some strange lingo—Estonian? Lil was never sure—when he spoke at all. They swilled the stuff from dawn to dusk. It might have been water, coffee, tea. There were gallons of it everywhere: a murky yellow-brown liquid that stank of something gone way off. The old lady was always brewing up another batch; she had to, the way they went through it. Her rotten potatoes and who knew what other ingredients took up the whole kitchen, so it was hard to fix a decent meal. The fumes that wafted through that house would have knocked over an elephant. Coming on top of her pregnancy, they were too much for Lil.

Sick, sick, sick.

Why, she sometimes wondered, couldn't they have concocted their liquor from a more pleasant ingredient, such as peaches, raspberries or plums? A nice, light cordial or brandy—that would have been an entirely different kettle of fish.

Lil had known Stan liked a drink before marrying him. This wasn't any surprise he sprang on her after the vows were said, not like his family. Lil knew she was lucky; you heard these horror stories of brides discovering the worst things imaginable about their men, however well they thought they knew them, the minute the I-dos were said. She didn't mind Stan's drinking, not really. No man was perfect—she knew that much after eighteen years upon the earth—and with Stan a few drinks only made him more himself somehow. His naturally good spirits lifted a degree or two higher. His cheeks flushed a handsome shade of red; he got an extra sparkle in his eye; he began with the jokes until your sides split open. Under the influence he never turned mean or sullen or violent, nothing like that.

The rest of his family was something else altogether.

The liquor seemed to have no effect on them at all. Had they become so used to it that it ceased working on them? It was strong enough, no doubt of that: although she didn't drink, Lil took a little sip of the stuff upon arriving at the house just to be polite, and she couldn't see straight for a good twenty-four hours. Yet you would have thought them each as sober as a judge even as they poured the stuff down their throats like it was going out of style. There was no slurring of speech, no stumbling or falling about. If anything, they turned even more silent and grim, Lil noticed. Certainly she witnessed little giddiness, merriness, fun. No, none of that.

Lil didn't even want to think about their livers.

It wasn't as if she were a complete novice where liquor was concerned. Though neither Lil nor her sisters would generally touch spirits (we just don't need it, they laughed), they had all gone with any number of boys who opened flasks outside Regina dancehalls, who couldn't get through a date without a mickey. The older brother, Michael, was partial to the stuff himself, and little Louie would more than follow in those weaving footsteps. If men drank, it was just one more difference between the sexes. One more weakness to be tolerated and understood. On a farm in winter Lil could almost see the point in wanting a little something to warm you up and take the edge off the boredom—there wasn't much to do aside from feeding stock and fixing harnesses during those months.

But there were limits to everything.

Lil didn't say a thing. How could she? It wasn't her house. She bit her tongue, however much it cost her— and especially where those children were concerned, it just wasn't right. She could hardly speak to Stan about the situation; everyone is touchy were family is concerned.

Of course there were no social workers in those days to keep an eye on such goings-on—not out in the country, anyway. No one knew what transpired on some of those isolated farms. You heard stories. Women kept as slaves, not just barefoot and pregnant. Insane uncles bound in chains down in the cellar. A little girl of twelve big with daddy's baby. Old people starved to death when they could no longer work. The simple, healthy country life.

You could keep it, as far as Lil was concerned.

She should have stayed in Regina that winter. Lil knew that now. Both Fan and Annie had urged her to remain in the city; neither had much space, not long married themselves, but they could squeeze her in somehow. She didn't want to have her first baby away from civilization, without the doctor, did she?

Lil decided to stay on at the farm. She felt it wasn't wise to spend that much time away from her husband, not during the first year of marriage. They had to get used to each other sometime, they might as well start right away. But of course she wasn't happy on the farm, regardless of the liquor. Lil hadn't grown up with the intention of living in the middle of nowhere. She wasn't familiar with farm life at all, and this first acquaintance did not encourage her to make friends. She missed her sisters and she missed streets and she missed stores. There was no chance of getting back to Regina after her Christmas visit; the roads were hardly roads at all, and with so much snow that winter you didn't want to risk the trip even if you had to.

As she got bigger and the stink of potatoes wormed its way into her clothes and hair and skin, Lil became despairing for the first time in her life. They were snowbound all of January. She had several dreams—nightmares, really—in which she gave birth to a potato-shaped baby with pale skinny roots for limbs, a few dirty indented eyes and not a speck of hair. Stan tried to keep up her spirits by promising that they would move back into Regina just as soon as he could get hold of something there. He might get on with the gas company in May. His family was different than hers, he knew, but they were good people in their own way and she would get used to them with time. When the baby was born she was bound to feel better.

Lil informed Stan that she was returning to Regina on the first day of spring if she had to walk all the way with the baby in her arms. She was leaving, and of course she wanted him to come with her, but he could stay behind if he so pleased.

These discussions would be held outside. There was no choice: two words could not be exchanged privately within the house. In the evening Stan and Lil bundled up the best they could against wind and cold, then went out beneath moon, stars. The world gleamed more silver than white; the landscape was turned lunar by snow. In other circumstances Lil might have found the scene beautiful; as it was, she could appreciate it only as a temporary escape. If the air was sub-zero and the chill factor more than you thought you could bear, at least the air was clear and clean, at least you could laugh out loud. Sometimes Lil screamed and shouted as soon as they were a distance from the house. Stan would encourage her to go ahead and get it out of her system.

There was a little sled (some might call it a toboggan), meant for a child to coast down snowy slopes, which Lil would ride. Stan draped the rope around his waist and pulled her along as far as she liked. They tried to stick to the county road, but sometimes cut across fields toward a break of trees. Stan floundered through drifts and stumbled down slopes to give Lil her ride. It didn't make up for everything, but he could do this much for her. Lil would sing on the sled to help Stan carry on and to interrupt the silence. "Flow gently, sweet Afton," she quavered in uncertain pitch while the baby bobbed inside her and Stan panted for breath. Maybe she and Stan would discuss names for it. A family name? If so, from which side? Would it be a boy or a girl? Would it take after him or her? They spoke too about the place they would get in Regina, how they would furnish it, what shape their lives would take within its walls.

When they returned to the farmhouse—they couldn't stay out long, it wasn't humanly possible—the stench of potato liquor would hit Lil with renewed force, almost make her regret the contrast of the clean air outside.

But she always felt better after these expeditions. More hopeful, somehow.

"They're all I've got," she said.

Stan knew what she meant. He didn't take offense and ask: Well, didn't she have him, and if he wasn't something, what was he?

Lil never blamed him for the accident. Yes, he was at fault, of course he was. But what good would it do to cast blame for something that had already happened and could not be changed? No one was completely innocent of anything, Lil knew.

This included her.

Picture a terribly cold February night in 1915, Fan was later to write in a dime-store notebook containing eighty-six pages ruled with pale blue lines and with margins drawn in pink. The cover was a cream-colored paper, stiffer, with a picture of a kangaroo in the lower left-hand corner. On this cover Fan printed, in neat capitals, *The Book of Life*.

Yes, it was a terribly cold night in February. For two weeks it had been too cold to snow and too cold for Lil and Stan to escape outside. Lil was going mad. She would be locked away, she would spend the rest of her life in a straitjacket, she would never see her baby. Various members of Stan's family were staring mutely into glasses of yellow liquor—this batch looked exactly like urine, Lil observed. Stan himself had taken more than his usual share of the stuff that day. Looking up from the baby dress she was trying to sew—she was now sure it was a girl— Lil threw Stan several significant glances. Then she put down her sewing—she was all thumbs, she wasn't getting anywhere—and began to wrap herself, layer after layer. Stan took the hint and bundled up too.

You could see a million stars, and the moon was nearly full. Lil sat on the sled, a scarf covering all her face except her eyes, and Stan began to pull her along. Cold had turned the snow's crust into a surface as hard and strong as cement, and Stan was able to drag Lil more quickly than usual, without sinking as far as his knees every other step. He trotted along quite swiftly.

After two weeks inside, the clear air went to Lil's head like one-hundred-proof liquor. She was drunk as a skunk, high as a kite. For a moment she understood exactly why people drink: she was a queen wrapped in diamonds and sables, riding a golden coach, waving to adoring subjects, heading for her palace. What exactly was happening? How fast was Stan pulling her? Was she whirling up or down? A white world wheeled by and Lil clung for dear life to the sides of the sled.

Later, when all she remembered was a blur of white, Lil would wonder if she hadn't urged Stan to run as fast as he could, then faster, and never stop until they were so far from the farmhouse that there was no going back—until they were outside Fan's place on Broder Street, right in the middle of the city. They would fall laughing through the door, into warmth and the smell of hot biscuits, and her sisters would look up from their cards and say: Well, look who's here.

With or without her encouragement, Stan began to zigzag as he ran, yanking the sled's rope sharply each time he veered so the sled tipped from side to side like a Kiwanis Fair ride. It was the liquor that got the devil into Stan, without question. And he was only nineteen, still a boy; sometimes he needed to play. Were they both laughing so that cold entered their lungs with sharp stabs? Was Lil screaming, shouting, swearing? Did she call for Stan to stop?

The sled tipped. Its hard edge hit Lil's stomach as she spilled onto the snow. Stan stood over her, gasping, then knelt beside her. The bleeding started at once; there was no time to do anything. What could have been done anyway, even if they were back at the farmhouse or in the city? Lil stared into the sky and saw the stars fall, the big moon shrink. Before morning a fresh snowfall—it began before Stan got Lil back to the house with the aid of the same sled that caused the tragedy—would cover the stain. Lil would never know exactly where her life turned upside down. Where it was buried.

The gas company took Stan on, and he and Lil moved back into Regina that spring. They got their own place within five blocks of both Fan and Annie, who were settled down with Stu and Frank respectively. Lil refused to return to the Davidson farm even for a visit; when Stan wished to see his people, he had to go alone. After what had happened, he could understand Lil's feelings.

It was the least he could do.

They never had children. Of course they tried. They were still so young; there seemed endless time and opportunity. Lil became pregnant six times more. On five occasions she miscarried in the seventh month, losing the baby at the same point she had lost the first one in the snow. The last time she carried full term, and she and Stan were filled with all kinds of hope. That one, a boy, was stillborn. He was completely formed, his parts were perfect. Joseph.

So they had the one funeral.

One small coffin.

That was something.

After this Lil no longer menstruated. She was still only twenty-five, but there was no longer the possibility of children. That particular door was firmly shut.

The doctors had a dozen theories. They poked around in Lil endlessly, did a whole battery of tests. But this was barely 1920; there was so much even the specialists didn't know. Would things have been different if Lil had needed help in, say, 1970? Later she sometimes wondered. Back then she listened with one ear to what the doctors had to say; her other ear was deaf to their jargon.

It was clear that words wouldn't help her.

Fan and Annie were also childless. They didn't manage a single pregnancy between them. Why was that? Strong, young women, healthy as horses, never sick a day. The doctors said there was something wrong with the family women. Something was lacking, they hinted—without stating exactly what this something could be.

They were incomplete? Freaks? Not really women at all? Nonsense.

And it was just the women. Their brother Michael had all those kids with Carrie. Louie, though never married, would be said to father a large number of—well, bastards, to call a spade a spade.

Without doubt their common childless state made the three sisters, always close, draw nearer together. More than ever they were like a small private club that operated under secret rules and admitted no further members. It wasn't that they were cliquish or exclusive—they took enormous pride in being the most sociable, ordinary women in the world. But shared experience, shared history, shared traits: these things, and now a shared lack of children, seemed a wall raised against the outside world. Even relationships with their husbands were plainly of less emotional intensity than those with each other. They didn't try to hide this fact, and the husbands would never have thought to try to change it; perhaps such capacity for acceptance was a chief reason why these particular men had been chosen in the first place.

If one of them had had children, the other two sisters would have felt their childless state more keenly. Bouncing a baby on her knees in front of those two empty laps, she would have felt bad. How could she do that to them?

This wasn't the end of the world. The sisters babied their husbands, spoiled each other, gave treats to themselves.

They discussed it alone together. Though the sisters would not speak directly about sex, ever, in the Broder Street kitchen they leaned toward each other and in vivid, specific detail discussed secretions and swellings, pains and tearing tissues, blood and eggs and the womb.

In mixed company they were more reticent. Lil's accident, they said. That night on the farm.

When Lil's blood froze.

She had the first fit shortly after the stillborn boy and the end of her periods. It happened one Sunday at Fan's while they were playing cards. When Lil fell on the floor and began to thrash like a fish out of water they thought at first it was a stunt she was pulling to protest a full evening of bad luck. It *looked* like a stunt. Just more of Lil's clowning.

Then Annie said, "Her tongue." She bent down and reached several fingers into Lil's mouth.

(Later Annie said she knew how to do this from reading a book.)

They looked on appalled. Lil's eyes rolled back in her head. She was slick with sweat; she didn't know where she was.

In a minute, but none too soon, it was over. Lil sighed heavily, then got up off the floor and took her chair. She looked at the cards scattered on the table and said she'd lost track of the hand. Whose play was it, sailor?

Epilepsy. They all thought it. Some of the doctors too, at first. Others disagreed. No, it was something else.

Definitely not epilepsy. But what? They were never certain.

Sometimes the spells took another form. Then Lil would rise from her chair and start cleaning. It wouldn't matter if it was a sister's or even a stranger's house. You couldn't speak to her, she couldn't hear you. With a distant expression Lil scrubbed the stove, wiped a wall, scoured the bathroom. By then she was a professional, having started to clean part time for the Greeks. Maybe she took her work too seriously, maybe she couldn't leave it at the office. There was something especially grave in Lil's manner when she wielded a mop during these moments; she might have been performing a religious ritual with her ammonia and her bleach.

It was hard on Stan. It was hard on them all. Lil had no memory of either the convulsive or the cleaning fits afterwards; she seemed less affected by them than anyone. No one could ever say they got used to these episodes —and they continued for thirty years, right up to Lil's death. Perhaps strangest of all was that in all other areas Lil's health remained top notch; the spells seemed isolated occurrences, unrelated to her general well-being. From now on there was a sense in which the whole family was always frightened for Lil and for themselves. Frightened of what could come out of nowhere for no clear reason.

It was doctors and more doctors. Diets and drugs until they were coming out of Lil's ears. None of them worked to speak of. Lil ran through all the Regina medical men, then she and Stan made trips to specialists. By train they traveled to Winnipeg and Toronto; once they crossed the border down to Rochester, Minnesota. These journeys were not something they could afford, and Stan would need to take off work. He had to ask Stu and Frank for help once or twice. When another specialist was suggested, this one in Boston, Lil put down her foot. Nothing doing, mister. No more quacks.

She would live with it if she had to. Whatever it was.

They all lived with it. The family still met twice a week, the sisters were at each other's any number of times a day. Together they ate and talked, laughed and played cards with as much pleasure as before. Never in real need of extra friends before, the sisters drew more tightly together after Lil's troubles began. Outsiders would be frightened of the fits. They wouldn't understand. They would talk.

As it was, Fan's Stu turned pale and had to leave the room whenever the convulsions came over Lil. He felt bad, he couldn't watch. It seemed men had weaker stomachs than women. The dark odors and liquids that were a part of life: why was it men seemed less able to cope with them? Why did they run away from them?

Stan began to drink more heavily at this time, all the men in the family did. Perhaps it was their age, rather than any particular occurrence, that set them off? Who would ever know? The women didn't comment, though those were the years they wouldn't allow a bottle in the house. The men did their drinking outside, behind the house, out of sight.

Fan and Annie had their theories regarding Lil's condition.

"It's because her blood froze," they agreed.

The blood Lil didn't release each month turned poisonous and backed up on her. It went to her head and caused these problems. That's what they thought.

Sometimes Lil wouldn't go out of the house. "I'm going to have a bad day," she might say when Fan or Annie suggested hitting the stores. She was always right. Without fail Lil would have a spell. "Think I'll get some cleaning done this afternoon," she'd grimace.

This was the first indication that perhaps Lil would be compensated for her difficulties. She started predicting the weather with far more accuracy than the newspaper. Once she suggested Carrie better not go out, and Carrie twisted her ankle getting down from the streetcar that afternoon. Stan made a small killing on the 1928 Stanley Cup thanks to Lil's advice. They learned to listen to her. It paid.

Lil took to reading hands. Without knowing a thing about the various lines and what they were supposed to portend, she could see a great deal. She looked at a palm and saw all kinds of things, and she didn't hesitate to share her vision however hard it might sound.

"Cancer," she sentenced.

"Stroke."

Lil was especially gifted in foreseeing illness, accident, financial ruin, heartache. Any bad luck. This went against her grain, it seemed—Lil always appeared such a sunny soul—and probably she wanted to describe happy fates. Probably she didn't want to think there was more trouble than joy ahead, and that was the reason for her predominantly gloomy predictions.

Later she branched out to feet. Then she started with the tea leaves and the coffee grounds. Eventually she could read a person's past, present and future by glancing into his eyes.

"Murderess," she stated in the street, passing an old woman with a harmless appearance.

"Adulterer," she mentioned to Annie in the market, indicating the butcher in blood-stained smock who was cutting their chops.

Annie spoke only half in jest when she suggested Lil set herself up as a professional. She could work right at home; her overhead would be nil; she and Stan could definitely use the dough. Just a simple sign in the window. *Madame Lillian.*

"I could open a cathouse too," Lil responded coolly.

Some gifts should not be used to turn a profit. This was Lil's intimation. If she could help someone, let them know what they needed to know, she was happy to do it. She just called the cards as she saw them.

There was no doubt, none at all, that Lil's powers were directly connected to her accident in the snow and to her ensuing difficulties. For one, there was the timing. For two, something is always given for everything taken away. You didn't have to go to the university to know that. Yet there was also a predisposition to this direction—the fortune-telling direction—a natural slant in which the family women were apt to lean. It was in all of them, Fan and Annie too. Lil's various troubles had only served to bring this tendency to the surface—to activate it, so to speak.

Fan recalled stories of female relations involved in all sorts of mysterious matters. A ring of salt around your enemy's house. Ashes in the mailbox. Three grains of sand in the newlyweds' sheets. This would have been in the Old Country, where seers and curers and spellmakers were more common and recognizable than in Canada. Had her mother or her father told her these stories? Or, as a small child, had she overheard a word here, a phrase there that she hadn't been able to understand or to piece together at the time? Perhaps she had glimpsed certain scenes, been witness to those aunts and cousins? They had frightened her?

Fan never felt the same about Lil after the spells began, not really. Although no one would ever notice, there was always a distance between those two sisters now. A space. Where did Lil go while in her spells? How did she see the world? For her was it a barren place stripped of secrets, robbed of shadows, without mystery? Or did clarity of vision make Lil's world a richer place teeming with spirits and ghosts others could not see, and thronging with every sort of being not yet born, still unimagined?

Lil's dark eyes gave no clue. Aside from her fits and her visions, Lil was the same old Lil, merriest of the three sisters, mad about the movies. She still took her coffee black and still adored the crusty heel of a loaf. Lil held herself neither apart nor above on account of the various peculiarities that visited her without invitation or welcome. She suffered them or made use of them, depending, with her usual good humor; of themselves they did not turn her more serious or thoughtful or self-important. In fact she would have been offended if accused of the latter, especially; there was nothing worse than someone who gave herself airs or thought herself special: these were sins against democracy. Maybe Lil even emphasized her carefree side after the onset of her troubles in order to nip such accusation in the bud.

These were hard years and happy years. When the sisters referred, later, to *when we were young*, they would be thinking of Regina in the twenties and thirties: the first clang of a streetcar bell in December; lemonade on Fan's deep front porch in July; veils of September smoke and sheets of April rain; and certain scents holding everything together, with the echo of voices that seemed to possess an unlimited power to echo. These were the years when the sisters settled into their marriages and their homes, and when they became comfortable with their bodies and began to put on weight. (Fan especially had to watch the scale; she just didn't have the height for extra pounds.) They no longer shifted the living-room furniture in search of a more satisfactory arrangement. Nothing was perfect, everything was all right.

The only change so far as Lil was concerned was that now she would begin to rock back and forth, as well as make a kind of humming sound, before one of the convulsive fits: you could tell Lil was working up to something, heading toward a destination, on her way. The humming was one monotonous note resembling more the sound of a machine throbbing with power than any musical expression. The benefits of these "warnings" (as they were soon called) were several: Lil could be led to the chesterfield or to bed; a pillow might be placed beneath her head; Fan and Annie could prepare to help Lil through her difficult time. There was no need to thrash around on a hard floor; Lil might as well be comfortable. With the element of surprise taken away, the spells were less upsetting to everyone: they became a phenomenon as familiar as lightning or thunder, known if still frightening. Thankfully, they never had to use ropes to prevent Lil from hurting others or herself. And she never foamed at the mouth.

As for the cleaning variety of spells, they had always been easier to witness and they remained the same. Of course it was an interruption when Lil suddenly rose and headed toward the Dutch Cleanser and the mop in the middle of supper or cards; but, to face facts, there didn't exist a house that couldn't stand a little more scrubbing. Often Fan and Annie would join Lil in splashing water and wringing sponges; though Lil would not know they were there, this was a way of feeling less distant from whatever strange world she was in and of keeping her company there. They did it for themselves, really. The boys (the husbands were still the boys, they would always be the boys) took advantage of the break in whatever was going on to head out back for a drink.

Lil's predictions maintained a high level of accuracy, though she was liable to become touchy if someone demanded special sight. She didn't enjoy being at beck and call in regard to fortune-telling or anything else, and might deliberately impart false or shocking information to teach someone a needed lesson. Maybe they would think before asking next time. If you got right down to it, did anyone really want to know what was to come? They already knew, everyone knew, it was no secret. Death.

In 1939, when they were all considering a move from Regina to B.C., it was Lil's last word, coming on top of a number of good reasons right in clear sight, that finally convinced them.

"Sure we should go," said Lil. "Things will work out better for us there. Take my word for it."

They took it.

One after another they left Regina. This would be the last time they would suffer such upheaval in their lives. (It almost felt like the first: their arrival to Regina, so long ago, was as distant and unreal as a historical event in a textbook. You don't doubt it happened, but it has little to do with you in the end.) First Michael and Carrie went west. Then Lil and Stan. Next Frank and Annie. When Stu passed on suddenly at this time, there was nothing to keep Fan in Regina except his grave. She would be alone there, not counting Louie—and by that time they knew not to depend on Louie for anything. Still Fan refused to budge from Broder Street.

"She'll come around," Lil predicted confidently.

"She's in shock over Stu," diagnosed Annie.

Fan shook her head. There was nothing she liked better than to prove her sisters wrong.

"There's still something I have to do here," she said.

Fan wrote letters to her sisters in the west. She didn't get the phone in until 1943; then it would be too expensive to call often—or should have been: for a while there Fan nearly supported the phone company. A stamp cost a nickel. A letter took five days to travel from Regina to Brale, B.C.

The letters were short. Fan found it hard to find enough news to fill a page. She had plenty to *say*, but words that might have flowed easily over coffee in the kitchen often didn't seem of sufficient importance to be written down and saved. Like her, both Lil and Annie were pack rats. Letters might be discovered in attic or basement trunks a dozen years in the future, dusty and faded and dried, to be read and found too fragile to support the weight of time. Possibly critical, analyzing strangers would view them as historical artifacts, curiosity pieces, rusty links to the past. Could they withstand such scrutiny?

Fan wasn't used to corresponding. Who had she ever written to before, when everyone she loved was right at hand? At the kitchen table Fan sat up with a cup of coffee. In between describing the weather, her health and what Louie was up to (no good, usually), her thoughts traveled a good distance in various directions. The space now existing between her sisters and herself, and how her mind had to travel so far to reach Brale, B.C., served to change Fan's way of thinking, to expand the boundaries of her thoughts. As well as stretching across the present, they went back in time to days she could scarcely remember, and circled warily around an image, sniffing it for possible danger. The first time she had seen the Qu'Appelle Lakes. Annie falling from the swing and chipping a front tooth. A boy who died one week after vowing love for the first time to Fan. That night Lil—was she sixteen? seventeen?—stayed out until dawn and refused to say where she'd been or what she'd done. A blue dress. Stu's hands. One autumn.

Fan wouldn't write about any of these things. Her letters were formal and stiff, entirely unlike the way she spoke in real life. *I trust you and Frank are enjoying good*

health. Let us hope that spring arrives early this year. Where
had Fan learned to write this way? Certainly not in school.
Perhaps her caution was stirred by knowledge of those
attic trunks waiting to be filled, those curious strangers
who would open them. Things lasted longer in those days;
evidence was less disposable.

Fan addressed and sealed her letter, then walked to
the mailbox on the corner. It was midnight. Broder
Street was sleeping. After dropping the envelope in the
slot, Fan would continue walking, and sometimes found
herself down at the far end of Victoria Avenue, an area
she normally had no reason to visit, without knowing
how she had reached there. Where was she going? It was
late. The beer parlors were emptying. Drunken men
stumbled and vomited and swore in the street. Only a
few women were about. Were they prostitutes? Fan was
uncertain, curious. Several men called after her—a
short, heavy, middle-aged woman. She knew not to listen; it was the liquor talking. She would feel almost too
tired to walk back home—but of course she had to
return to Broder Street, there was no other place to go.

She had chosen to stay on in Regina for a good reason.
Trouble was, sometimes she forgot what that reason was.
Lil and Annie wrote back equally stiff letters. These
might have come from strangers; Fan could hardly see
her sisters in them at all. The note Frank or Stan scribbled
at the bottom, usually a joke, would be the most recognizable, familiar part. Fan had no real idea what the
town her sisters lived in was like, or how their lives might
have changed there. Lil and Annie would have altered

beyond all recognition? They would be exactly the same? Fan discovered, surprisingly, that she wasn't especially interested in finding out.

Still, she did take the train out to B.C. in the summer of 1942, and nearly every other summer through the forties. The ride was long—and uncomfortable, since Fan couldn't afford a private compartment, had to sit up nights in day coach. She liked packing her bags and the sensation of moving and looking out the window at the scenery even if it was monotonous, at least between Regina and the Rockies. It wouldn't have surprised her if she'd been a traveler or explorer in another life. A Marco Polo, another Columbus.

In Brale her sisters' lives were astonishingly little altered. They might as well have stayed in Regina; only the background scenery—mountains, more trees—was different. It did turn out, however, that once again Lil had predicted correctly: things were indeed better for the family in the west—from a financial point of view, at any rate. (Really, this wasn't so difficult to have foreseen: it would have been highly unlikely that any place could be worse for them than Regina, where there was mostly just Relief.) Fan found that when she was with her sisters again she slipped right back into their old ways. Somehow she forgot to bring up matters she had thought about and questions she had formed in her Broder Street kitchen. There it had seemed urgent to know: Did this really happen? Had it happened like that?

Well, the old ways were good ways. Fan enjoyed her visits.

After four weeks in Brale she would be anxious to return home. She wasn't used to holidays. Neither Lil nor Annie would let her do much around their home: Fan's attempts to lift a finger were the source of an ongoing dispute. She could sit idle for only so long. There was something important she had to get back to.

What was it?

Lil and Annie worried about Fan, alone in Regina. They had no idea how she filled her days. Fan would not get out and mix sufficiently, they knew. Annie and Lil were concerned that solitude might bring out eccentricity in their sister; peculiarities that had lain dormant from birth might, under certain pressures, boil to the surface. The slightest misstep could set things off. Look at Lil's accident in the snow.

One or the other sister would try to make it back to Regina once a year, in spring or fall. Fan always seemed more or less the same. The Broder Street house remained entirely unchanged, like a museum. It was quite a battle to persuade Fan to get inside plumbing; that privy in the back was an unnecessary disgrace. If resistance to change was understandable, especially after a certain age, there were several other signs to cause dismay. One: When Fan got her electric stove she never used it for cooking, preferring still the wood stove in the basement. The new electric range she decorated with her doilies, one fitted nicely on each burner, and the back piled high with pillows, also handmade. Both doilies and pillows were rearranged or substituted with others nearly every day, but under no system that Lil or Annie could perceive. Fan had an almost unlimited quantity of handiwork; she was always clicking needles, she could never stand to sit with idle hands.

The stove resembled a kind of altar. What God did Fan pray to before it? Annie and Lil didn't like to ask. None of them were churchgoers. Religion didn't run in the family and they had gotten along just fine without it until now.

Annie and Lil secretly asked the neighbors to keep an eye on Fan. They left their telephone numbers with the people to the south just in case. Later, in the early fifties, when Fan suddenly decided to rent out half her house, it was a relief to everyone. A nice young couple moved in and stayed on right to the end.

"I need the loot," Fan said to explain her decision.

Presently Fan grew more silent. This was logical; she had fewer chances to talk, fell out of practice. Also she smiled and laughed less often. Annie would remark that it looked like Fan was busy making plans. Who knew what she would cook up next.

It was not until the middle forties that Lil and Annie really began to worry. That was when their sister started to call up in the middle of the night. A phone rings at that hour, you think something terrible has happened. An accident. A death.

It was nothing like that. Fan just wanted to know something. Could Lil help her out? She wondered if Stan's family still had the Davidson farm, or if they'd sold it and moved away. They weren't in the phone book. Also, she wanted to know if Lil could describe that fateful sled. What had it looked like exactly? How large? Painted a certain color?

Lil couldn't remember. Did Fan realize what time it was?

Immediately after hanging up on Lil, Fan called Annie.

"Lil knows more than she's telling," said Fan, then rattled on about blood in the snow as if the phone company no longer charged for long distance.

Meanwhile Lil would be trying to get Annie on the line but finding it busy. When she finally got through, Lil asked: "Was it her?"

"Three a.m. Who else?" Annie said.

Lil and Annie began to expect these late-night calls, this flurry of dialing when sane people were asleep. They would find themselves lying awake at four in the morning, waiting for the phone to ring. They tried not to sound irritated when out of the darkness Fan's voice would wonder whatever happened to that sled.

For a while they said Fan was just lonely.

"She's drinking," Annie finally told Lil, putting into words what both had been thinking all along.

Fan's voice did sound odd. Was it just the phone that made it sound that way—detached, without connection to a body, hovering in midair? Neither Lil nor Annie was quite sure exactly how a telephone worked. How could a voice travel so far with only the aid of a skinny wire, anyway?

This wasn't all they didn't understand.

"I'm smart enough to know I'm dumb" was something Annie was known to say.

When Fan's calls stopped, after about six months, Lil and Annie only worried more. They would feel frustrated to be lying awake until dawn for no good or even crazy reason. They would pick up the phone themselves. Fan sounded surprised to hear from them, as if this were the last thing she expected, as if she had never talked long distance in her life. Even in the middle of the day her voice was apt to sound sleepy, but she always denied napping. It might sound like they had interrupted her in the middle of something important, though Fan would say no, she wasn't doing anything at the moment. Sometimes she breathed heavily, as if trying to catch her breath after running to pick up.

In 1949, when bad feeling arose between Fan and her sisters over the circumstances of Louie's death, phone calls and letters between Regina and Brale became less frequent. Communication returned to normal in due course, if by that you mean that people who are separated lose each other to time and distance, misplace the habit of speaking to and hearing each other across space.

Anyway, Annie and Lil had less time to worry about Fan now. Trouble right at hand occupied them. Both Stan and Frank were drinking more heavily, and their health suffered for it. (Etta was facing the same problem with John. And it had been the bottle, of course, that had taken Louie.) Lil herself was turning queer. While her spells did not become worse during these years—if anything, they lessened in frequency, intensity and duration—her behavior in general grew alarming. She was getting quite a reputation in Brale; it was a small town, people were liable to talk. Lil now roamed the street in her housecoat and slippers to accost strangers with information that the most horrifying fates awaited them. She saw severed heads and gouged-out eyes and bodies burned alive. ("To a crisp," she elaborated, savoring the details.) Descending upon small children, she seized their chins in hand, stared fiercely into their eyes, told them they were the worst liars or thieves. Bands of children would dance after Lil down the block, chanting *Liar!* or *Thief!* to her back. Lil paid no attention. She entered houses without knocking and, ignoring inhabitants, rifled through cupboards and drawers, in search of something.

Between one thing and another Annie had her hands full. She felt burdened during these years. She wondered if Lil's prediction that the family would do better in the west had been one hundred percent accurate. Had their lives begun to go off track when they left Regina and Fan? Or had a wrong turn been taken long before then?

When Lil died in 1955 and they found all those empty cough syrup bottles in the basement, much of her erratic behavior was explained. Fan was unable to make it to Brale for the funeral because her own health was not up to scratch at the time. After the funeral lunch was over and the guests had gone away, Annie sat in her kitchen on Columbia Avenue and wrote to Fan. Dirty glasses and unscraped platters of food surrounded her. When had Fan last called or written? What was she up to in Regina these days? Phoning with news of Lil's sudden death, Annie hadn't been able to say much and wasn't sure what Fan said in return. It wasn't a time for chitchat. Now Annie carefully described Lil's last days, the funeral, the cough syrup bottles. She stated that Frank and Stan were failing. Michael held up well, but Carrie was mostly in bed since the late baby. Having Donald at her age was just too much for her. Of course still being stuck up on the dairy didn't help. They were all trying to carry on best they could. Who would have dreamed things would turn out like this?

This was the longest letter Annie had written in her life. By the end of it her left hand was sore and stiff. She could hardly manage the PS.

Did you ever find that sled? Annie added at the end, then swiftly sealed the letter.

"Picture a terribly cold February night in 1915," began Fan.

It was the summer of 1957. Fan sat on her front porch with her nephew Mitch, Michael and Carrie's oldest boy. He had just finished high school and was set to start university in Vancouver that fall. That would be a first for the family. He had been sent to Regina for several reasons: Carrie was doing worse and Michael didn't want the boy to see her that way; it would tarnish the memory of his mother, he felt. Also, through his Regina relations Stan found Mitch a summer job that paid more than anything he could make in Brale, certainly more than Etta would give him at the dairy. So he was at his Aunt Fan's for two months.

These two had met once before, when Michael and Carrie traveled with the children to Regina a number of years previously. They had hit it off well, this boy and his aunt, for reasons no one quite understood, and maintained a correspondence that surprised the whole family. What did they discuss in their letters? No one knew.

Mitch was at the mill six days a week. He left the house on Broder Street at seven in the morning and returned at five-thirty in the afternoon. Fan would have supper waiting. Dishes Mitch didn't know the names of, baked meats and potatoes, hot, heavy food. It was usually poorly prepared, either burnt or underdone. This surprised

Mitch; back in Brale they spoke in awe about Fan's cooking. On his Sundays off he hitchhiked out of town, going in any direction as far as he could without fear he wouldn't make it back to Regina that night.

Fan never asked where he went or what he saw.

"The Gypsy blood" was her only comment.

They spent the evening hours between supper and bed on the front porch, where they might catch a breath of cool air. Inside the house was too hot. The porch was deep, and sagged toward the street. The whole house tilted, tired of remaining erect. Paint peeled. One bathroom window, whose glass had broken, was covered with newspaper. There was a hole in the roof; Fan kept a pot strategically placed in the living room. All the rooms were cramped, dusty, dim; the basement was an impenetrable jungle of old furniture, boxes with mysterious contents, unnameable clutter. The yard was in particularly bad shape. It was hard to believe anyone had worked in it since Stu's death (and Mitch's birth) eighteen years ago.

Mitch felt he should do something around the place. Though accustomed to helping out on the dairy all through school, and to taking a bigger part in running it when John was on a binge, he was tired after a day at the mill. And he felt the job too large for one man. Where would he start? Fan never gave the least indication that her property was not in perfect condition. The few times Mitch began to trim the hedge or cut the grass, she told him to take it easy. She implied that the young couple who still rented the west side of the house would handle things upon returning from summer holidays. Somehow Mitch never fully believed in the existence of this couple, never mind in their ability to assist with maintenance and repairs.

Mitch didn't know anyone his age in Regina, and never ventured to a downtown movie or drugstore in the evenings. He was saving his money that summer. Anyway, it was assumed he would spend most of his free time with Fan; they had both understood this, without putting it into words, before he arrived.

They sipped lemonade on the porch. Fan's was spiked, Mitch knew. He wasn't a drinker's son for nothing. Periodically Fan took her glass into the kitchen and re-emerged with it a bit fuller, though the lemonade pitcher was right there on the porch. Mitch didn't know where she hid the bottle. He had the impression that the house was filled with concealed objects as well as incomprehensible artifacts—the crazy stove, for example—that stood right out in the open.

Once Fan went down into the yard to chase a child off her grass and came back to catch Mitch sniffing her glass.

"Better than potato liquor," she said.

She did most of the talking. When Mitch mentioned his day at the mill or his future plans, Fan smiled and said, "That's nice," then changed the subject.

She talked about the past, of course. There was so much of it. Her stories were difficult to follow, partly because her accent was so thick and partly because she seemed assured that Mitch was already familiar with them. Unexplained references and brief asides about people and events he didn't know at all gathered around Mitch on the darkening porch until he thought the warped boards would groan beneath the weight.

Also, much of what Fan said simply wasn't true.

"Regina," she replied when asked her birthplace, flatly denying the existence of some obscure country across the ocean. Where was Dobrudja, anyway? Who could find it on a map? Did it still exist?

"Canadian," she firmly stated, skipping over centuries of history as if they were nothing more than several squares in a hopscotch game.

Fan sprinkled her conversation with words in a foreign language (Polish? Greek?), which she left untranslated. He had no memory of Fan speaking this way on their previous acquaintance. Often he suspected these words were invented, nothing more than gibberish, only one more example of his aunt's slyness.

She would peer at Mitch after recounting with straight face another fantastic event that could simply not have occurred. Fan might have been daring him to protest the truthfulness of what she said, and seemed almost to hold herself from laughing when he didn't.

"I'm a tough old hen" was one of the favorite remarks she would make apropos of nothing.

"You're the handsomest man in the family so far" she also liked to assert out of nowhere—causing Mitch, who would remain a virgin until he married, to blush.

Even before darkness fell Broder Street was quiet. Two people, perhaps several more cars might pass before the house in the course of an evening. Sometimes there was the slamming of a screen door, a distant voice calling, a dog's bark. The muted street was lined with small, modest houses built at the turn of the century; many of them, like Fan's, were falling into disrepair, growing old and worn with their inhabitants. Children left, parents stayed.

Fan's eyes were bright black beads. "This street still swarms with kids," she said, glancing quickly at Mitch, then darting eyes beyond the porch. "More kids than you could count. In summer they hide in the trees, you can't see them for the leaves. They drop pebbles on you when you pass below. It's enough to scare even an old hen to death. It's enough to freeze your blood."

One fragmented story rose more frequently than any other through Fan's throat, Mitch noticed.

It seemed that on a terribly cold night in 1915 there had been an accident. Liquor was involved, Mitch gathered, but a sled bore chief responsibility. His Aunt Lil suffered this accident. What happened, exactly? After this things were never the same for Lil, or for the rest of the family either. The sled was the cause of all the suffering and misfortune to follow. It was painted blue sometimes, sometimes red. It could be large enough to hold five people, or so small that only one could ride it.

"There was blood in the snow," said Fan.

"An ocean of blood," she added, before they turned in.

Mitch woke in a pool of sweat. Another hot Regina night. He went downstairs to get a glass of milk from the ancient icebox. Fan wouldn't keep food in the refrigerator. Several times Mitch plugged in the appliance only to discover it disconnected later. Fan stored old letters and photographs inside it; apparently, these did not require cold for preservation.

Fan sat on the living-room chesterfield, beside a lamp.

She was writing on the desk of her lap. Hearing Mitch's step, she swiftly stowed her papers beneath the cushions.

"Hot enough for you?" she asked.

When she couldn't remember anything more, Fan switched off the lamp. The room descended into darkness. The other houses on Broder Street lay in similar darkness, and only light from a streetlamp across the road entered the window. The night was quiet.

Fan closed her eyes and saw three dark-skinned women with long, dark (and oily?) hair, and dark glittering eyes. They sat around a candle or an open fire; light flickered over them, burnishing their skin a copper color. These women, surrounded by greater darkness, were themselves composed of darkness, and only partly illuminated. Light caught strong white teeth, glinted off heavy rings encircling fingers and piercing ears. The three women spoke simultaneously, and more to themselves than to each other, it seemed. Rough voices; garbled sound. A harsh language that Fan could not quite remember. Did the small girl who watched outside the circle of light comprehend completely? Did she understand that spells were being incanted, cures worked, further darkness summoned?

Fan opened her eyes. She wished to go to the telephone and dial long distance. She knew the number by heart. But Lil was gone, and Annie would certainly not remember. Younger than Fan, only four when they left the Old Country, how could she? Fan wondered if she herself had really witnessed this scene or another like it. Or it had sprouted in her mind over the years from a seed she once overheard? She had read it in a book? It didn't have the slightest basis in reality? In history?

"They would have burned that sled," said Fan aloud.

Of course. Just as you shoot a mad dog or burn a false love letter or destroy a crippled horse. Get rid of what has caused pain and heartache and trouble. Yank out weeds at their roots.

"Her blood froze," repeated Fan another evening on the porch.

What did this mean? What was Fan suggesting about Lil's blood? Mitch recalled his Aunt Lil as a dusky-skinned woman brimming with vigor and health in spite of her peculiarities. He remembered a warm smile and a big laugh. The hot touch of her hand upon his cheek. No cold eyes, no icy skin. Lil seemed the furthest thing from a snow maiden.

Frozen blood. Liquid congealed into solid. Motionless in veins. Unmoved by heart.

Physically impossible.

Ridiculous.

"My blood froze too," said Fan, taking a gulp of lemonade.

On his last night in Regina Mitch couldn't sleep. He lay awake thinking of the train trip back to Brale, university classes to begin in a week, a whole new life. Although he didn't know it, he would not return to this house on Broder Street or see Fan again.

The downstairs was dark. Mitch pressed a glass of cold milk against his forehead and wandered the rooms. Behind a locked door waited the rooms of the absent tenants; they still had not returned and Mitch doubted they ever would. He bumped into an end table in the living room, rubbed his shin and swore.

Fan sat on the chesterfield. A bottle clinked on the floor by her feet. Her eyes were open; she was motionless in the dark. The image of an ancient pagan monument poised upon a black, empty plain stumbled confusedly through Mitch's sleepy mind.

He spoke Fan's name several times. She didn't turn her eyes his way or answer. Mitch paused. Did she sit up drinking like this every night? What should he do?

Suddenly he had a strong feeling that he should leave Fan alone. She didn't need him here. She didn't want to be disturbed.

The next morning Mitch was up early. Fan's bedroom was closed and the house was silent in the dawn light. Mitch carried his suitcase downstairs. On the kitchen table waited a brown paper bag containing one apple and two sandwiches wrapped in waxed paper. Beside the bag lay a small notebook, the kind a child uses for school, with the words *The Book of Life* printed on the cover.

Mitch opened the notebook.

It was a terribly cold February night in 1915, he read.

He skimmed the next pages. Quickly the writing turned into a language Mitch couldn't understand. The notebook was less than one-third full.

Mitch left the house with the notebook in his suitcase and the lunch in his other hand. He walked down the cracked sidewalk of Broder Street, heading for the station. Pebbles fell on his head from the leafy trees above. First he would try to forget, then to remember.

Buried
Secrets

Yes, I remember Riley, though that was just what we called him. We never did learn his real name, or anything else about him. So I'm afraid I can't tell you much more than Dorothy and Kay already have. But listen. If my sisters seem reluctant to go into the story, you have to understand that things aren't spoken of for a reason. What do you expect, anyway? You've been away for so long and now you turn up with all your questions. And it was so long ago. Still, it's funny what you don't forget.

You must already know some of the story from your father; the background, at least. How Michael and Carrie decided to come out west when it looked like things would never get better for us in Regina. That's right, 1949. It was just five children then, your uncle Donald hadn't been born yet. Lena and Annie and Lil, your great-aunts, had already made the move to Brale. And Etta, a cousin, married to a Keighley, had the dairy back up in the hills. We stayed with Etta and John at the beginning because my father couldn't get on at the smelter down here. His sisters didn't have the space to take us in at the time and of course there was no money for anything else. It wasn't charity, it was family. We all did our share around the place, Etta made sure of that all right. Considering John and her girls, how they were, not to mention the dairy itself, she was lucky to have us. And to have Riley. Maybe that was a connection between

Riley and ourselves right there: he wouldn't have ended up in such a situation either if there had been a better choice. What am I saying? A choice, period.

It was Etta who found him sleeping in the straw, there above the cows one bitter morning. This was our first winter on the dairy, and I can't say I've known a worse around here since. Well, that house was just a sieve, the walls were nothing. Imagine how it would have been for this man in the barn, just an old tarp over him, sick as he was. You could tell at once he was real bad. Burning up with fever, sweat streaming off him, shaking. All of that.

Right from the start there was an oddness to the situation in that Etta didn't turn him off the place. It would have been in character for her to do so without thinking twice, regardless of his health. She was such a woman then. One of the hardest lives, she had; you can't judge. Still, it made me stop to see her carrying a bowl of steaming soup across the yard to the barn, with a thermos of coffee tucked under one arm and a blanket in the other. Etta took it on herself to look after the stranger. She made a rough but capable nurse, I'd wager. Any kind of nurturing from her came as a surprise. I don't believe I heard her say one affectionate word to Uncle John during three entire years; he might have been just another hired hand rather than her husband. She'd lock the door if he came home drunk, wouldn't flinch to hear him scratch to be let in out of the cold. And she ignored those two girls of hers altogether, slapped them hard across the face if they so much as came near. I saw it. This was a woman with an arm as

strong as a man's, too. Really, there was no way of knowing June and April were hers unless you saw the birth
certificate.

So, yes, it was peculiar that Etta went out of her way
for this unknown man. He was a mute, you know, for all
intents and purposes. At first we thought he couldn't
talk because he was so sick. When he got a little better,
my father tried to ask him where he came from and
where he was going. Just who he was. Not a word then,
nor any time after. He could hear all right. His head
turned when you spoke to him, and I've seen his eyes lift
at the caw of a crow, a wind at the top of those trees. But
no speech at all. The most we heard—and this only con-
siderably later on, only in rare instances when he really
needed your attention—was a sort of moan. To my ears,
it seemed like a sound of distress. But don't we say a
sheep sounds anxious and a dog sounds angry when it's
just the noise they make and nothing more than that
noise? Nothing more than our need to make sense of
what we can't understand?

We wondered if it were physical. A condition from
birth or the result of some accident along the way.
Maybe he'd suffered a trauma that affected his memory
as well as his speech. Maybe his people were worried
sick looking for him. Or he just feigned the dumbness
to avoid our questions. We wondered about all of that.
You read such things. My mother wanted to have him
checked by the doctor in town, but that never happened.
I don't know why.

Michael and John did go down to the RCMP detach-
ment to talk with Bob Simonetta. They felt they ought

to, and of course they were right. The fellow could have escaped from the penitentiary at the Coast. We're so close to the border, he might easily have slipped over from the States. He might have been on the run from any crime at all. The things that went through my mind. You have to understand how isolated the dairy was, way up in those hills, far at the end of the gravel road, no one else around for miles. You've never been up there, have you? It was just the most unlikely place to end up, as I've said. Or the most likely, if you wanted to hide from the world.

Bob hadn't heard anything. He called the Coast and put the word over the wire, but nothing. He drove up to the dairy—that same day, I think—to ask some questions. Even with his uniform, he didn't get an answer. The man had no papers on him, no belongings whatsoever. I could take him in for vagrancy, Bob said—and I felt he wished to do that. The situation didn't sit right with him somehow. But Etta quickly said no, he could stay, she needed more help around the place.

Stay he did. Slept out in the barn above the cows, summer and winter, with just that blanket. I guess he used the old outhouse out back. He must have washed and shaved at the pump. Did he cut his own hair? You never saw him do those ordinary things, those human things; it was hard to think of him in such terms. I know Etta gave him old clothes, things of Michael and John that would otherwise have been thrown out. At mealtime she fixed a plate and set it on the step. You wouldn't hear him come for it; he was that quiet a man. The clean plate and the spoon would be there when we opened the door again. So far as I know, he never came inside the house. Wait: he must have, at least the once, because of what happened later. But I'm getting ahead of myself. I might mention now that after his arrival we locked the doors at night. That wasn't something we would have thought to do before.

There was worry for the girls—not for me; I was always older in more than just years. Of course we worried, though that particular fear wasn't in the air so much then. Not like now when it's all over the papers, the things that keep coming out. My sisters weren't to be alone with Riley on any account. Kay and Dorothy were frightened of him; we had no concern there. But you know Jeanette, always bold as brass. Even at seven or eight, as she would have been then. Though he paid her no attention you could notice, she liked to follow Riley around. That tall silent man and that merry little girl: it was curious. Nothing was said aloud, but I think we were all watchful, careful. It was Jeanette who gave him the name, wouldn't you know, that first spring he was there. Up to then, we hadn't called him anything. Well, my sister was always fanciful that way, always naming this or that. The cows. I remember a Daisy and a Daffodil. A Buttercup. Who knows how she came up with Riley, she wouldn't say where she got the name. It wasn't one any of us had heard before.

I have to say, though, I've wondered about June and April in connection with the man. They were always giggling together in a corner with some secret, those girls. Did you hear about the time they nearly burned down the house with one of their pranks? There was some sort of foolishness concerning Riley, I'm quite sure. One afternoon they kept looking toward the barn, then trying not to laugh. The next thing I knew, Etta marched straight into the house and without a word whipped them both. I never did find out why, though I had my suspicions. If I felt sorry for June and April, that doesn't mean I liked them.

Let's see. He was tall and thin, with dark hair. Not the kind of features you'd tend to remember. He must have been in his forties. It's hard to say. He didn't smoke or drink, though I guess John tried to get him to keep company with a bottle out in the barn a few times. Michael wasn't drinking so much in those days; it was like that with my father, off and on. With Riley, it was just the work; he was like Etta that way. And I do know he was a hard worker. Even she couldn't complain on that score. He was up before her with the cows, still moving around out there after supper was done. From what I understand, he knew something of livestock. So maybe that was a clue. And he was handy with machinery. Several times he got the old truck running when it seemed finished for good. I don't think he went to town once during our three years on the place. Imagine.

When I think of it, what strikes me most was that there seemed no indication of time working on him. From the beginning to the end, no sign of how he felt about things, no clues of likes or dislikes. Not a smile, not a frown. The weather, the chores, us: from what he let on, it was all the same to him. And I never had the sense that there were things he'd say if he could talk. You have to wonder how much you can know about anyone unless they tell you plain and simple. Unless they have people and belongings around that speak of them. Look at this old house: it says everything about who I am.

You really should ask Mitch about the man. Your father helped out with the cows after school; he had more contact with Riley. I was inside all the time. My mother and I ran that house, and let me tell you, there was plenty to keep us busy. We had no electricity or running water at first, just the stove for heat. Etta got the lights in during our second year and, say, that was something. Now it's hard to imagine, even for me. We had the cooking and washing for how many? Twelve? No, I was home already. I hadn't been to school since the polio, back in Regina. Carrie and I were used to working together as a team and we managed to keep on top of things, but just. I really don't know how.

So I saw little of Riley. When I went to hang a wash on the line, or to the pump for water, I might glimpse him across the yard, out in the back field. Often it seemed I spotted him just emerging from the brush or just disappearing into it. Suddenly there at the edge of my vision or suddenly gone. I'd be standing at the sink over my supper dishes and his shadow would cross the dark yard. It made me uneasy, I have to say. Something moved to the front of my mind, the shadow never left me for those three years. The time seemed an eternity, though now it's a snap of your fingers, just that, and a year's gone. But we'd come all that way out west, and things didn't seem any better than in Regina. As long as Michael couldn't get on at the smelter, we were stuck on the dairy. There didn't seem any real end ahead, and I got terribly down sometimes.

I remember once. It was after supper. Everyone had cleared from the kitchen, leaving the dirty plates on the table, pots that needed scrubbing on the stove. Did I tell you Etta wouldn't sit to eat? Standing by the stove in her boots and that big coat that must once have been John's, she'd clean off her plate in nothing. Then she spat into the sink, returned outside. She worked like a man out there. Well, on this particular evening I was resting a moment in my chair before starting the dishes. For some reason I couldn't stop staring at what Etta had trailed in with her boots. Mud and manure and bits of straw across the floor I'd washed that afternoon. Etta wouldn't take her boots off at the door and we really couldn't say anything. It was her house; we never forgot that. I started crying. It sounds silly now, but I was fourteen, everything mattered so much. My mother must have come up behind without my hearing her. I felt her hands on my shoulders, just resting there. A light, warm weight balanced evenly on either side. Then her hands lifted, and she turned to start the dishes. I suddenly felt so light. I felt myself rise and float in the air, all my burdens were left below. My mother had released me from them. She took them away.

I've always remembered that. A moment. You know, Carrie's health deteriorated quickly after Donald; the last baby was too much for her. She could do less and less. By the time we moved down to Brale, into Annie's, she was mostly in bed. I still feel badly about that time. We really left her alone. It became so hard to talk to her at the end; she'd always been quiet, I suppose. I know I felt relieved whenever Lena came around to sit and I could go out with Dorothy and Kay. Being in town was something new for us again, we were still only girls. Oh, but I was so close to my mother. After leaving school, I was with her day in and day out. She taught me everything around the house. It's funny. Carrie always seemed to move quite slowly, yet I'd turn around and she would have got the stove cleaned that quick. Dorothy and Kay tease, you've heard them call me a whirlwind because of how I dash about. I always feel, no matter how fast I move or how much I do, I'm still trying to catch up with Carrie. She's there, somewhere ahead of me, a glimpse through the trees.

What has my mother to do with Riley? What did he have to do with any of us? Not a thing. Except there was a connection. However hard to see, it existed. Yes. I know because of something that happened.

It must have been during our last spring at the dairy. By that time, I used to leave the house whenever I could, just a few minutes now and then. The place had become oppressive to me; none of the work I did would ever amount to anything, I knew. So one fine afternoon I went down to the little creek behind in search of pussy willows. I thought they might look pretty in a jar for the kitchen table. Some appeared beyond a patch of brush, that blur they make against the green. As soon as I moved toward them, my dress got caught in thorns. Maybe it was the wild roses we had around there. I couldn't move or I'd tear my dress, yet I had to get myself free. For a moment I stood still, as if the problem would somehow solve itself.

Through the brush I saw Riley. He was bent over a clear place on the ground. Then I could see he was digging. Burying something. A box, it looked like. I stood quiet. I felt certain he didn't see or hear me. The creek was loud with run-off that time of year. So when I heard Riley moan, I couldn't be sure at all. Why would he make such a sound to himself? I was so dumb, I didn't know what I saw. After he finished, he looked around, flattened the ground with his heel, then walked away.

I waited until he was really gone before approaching the spot. I didn't think of my dress or the thorns. I dug where Riley had dug. Yes, it was a box. Just ordinary cardboard, this big. Inside were photographs of us girls. My sisters and myself, not June or April. They were from the time a photographer came around and sweet-talked Carrie into having us sit. Oh, was that a big day. We got all dressed up in our best, with the hair washed and curled and tied with ribbon. Heaven knows where Carrie found the money. But she was real pleased with the result. And that upset when the photographs disappeared. You bet we turned the house upside down, but nothing. We blamed June and April, of course we did. It was something they would have done.

I stared at those four faces as if they belonged to strangers, or to people I'd known but forgotten. Who? I couldn't seem to recognize these girls, their serious smiles. I kept looking at one face and then another, as if that would help. The creek rushed so loud, the sound filled my head, I couldn't think. I replaced the photographs in the box, then buried it in Riley's hole. Stamped and smoothed down the dirt, leaving it the way he had. This must have been just a minute, though it seemed longer.

I walked back to the house without my pussy willows. I didn't realize my dress had torn on the thorns until Carrie pointed it out.

During the following days, I couldn't stop thinking of what was buried in that box. I pictured Riley digging up the photographs. Looking at them, touching them. Fingering our faces. Moaning. Despite my ignorance, it made me feel bad in all kinds of ways. Soiled, I suppose. Handled. And suffocated, as if we were buried alive without knowing it. All my unease of those three years on the dairy seemed to be in that box. I couldn't look at Riley at all, not even in the distance from the kitchen window.

Maybe I should have told someone, but I didn't. What I did instead was return to that clearing the next week. I didn't want to, I had to. Like that. I knew the exact spot to dig, but the box wasn't there. I don't know if Riley had seen me after all, if he'd moved the box to another hiding place. I don't know if I planned to take what it held away with me this time. I never would find out. I didn't see those photographs again.

It became a secret I kept without meaning to. I don't know that I ever told anyone, not even Ivan. The longer I was silent, the harder it became to speak. Maybe it was like that with Riley. Years later I did once ask Dorothy if she remembered some photographs going missing. What photographs? she wondered. So. You don't realize you have secrets, then you find them buried at the bottom of your mind, unfaded and unchanged, preserved like a pharaoh's treasure in the pyramids. But still alive. What is kept secret doesn't die; it thrives in the dark, assumes more importance and power, becomes immortal as the memory of God.

Listen to me go on like someone with a dozen university degrees.

After we moved down to Annie's, I would sometimes think of that box probably still buried somewhere on the hill. It made me feel, I don't know, as if part of us were trapped up there. As if we hadn't escaped scot-free after all. Something had been taken from us, something we never got back. The photographs—and more than that? Had Riley entered the house without our knowing it just the once to take what he needed? Or had he somehow or other slipped inside on a hundred nights? Leaned over our faces, shadowy and still in sleep, printed upon the white paper of a pillowcase. Stolen the sight, burgled the moment. Later, I came to feel the theft had been committed not so much by Riley but by that time and place. An empty hole yawned inside me for the longest while. Then I learned to fill it with my own secret.

I never went back to the dairy, not a once through all the years to follow. None of us did, except Mitch. Your father helped Etta out for a few summers in high school. She paid him, not much, but something for his university. And the dairy's just those few miles away. We could get in the car and be there in twenty minutes. Well. It was a time and place you were meant to forget. That's all it was for, that's all you could do with it.

But there's this. The spring after we left, the same spring that Carrie went, Jeanette took to speaking about Riley. When we were all gathered around Annie's big table, out of the blue she would pipe up in that clear, high way she had. Say that Riley used to talk to her. He had told her, in a voice like yours and mine, the names of flowers and birds. During the silent moment after Jeanette spoke, I felt the air in the kitchen change. It became more weighted, dense. Maybe this only seemed to happen more than several times. Maybe it was just another of Jeanette's passing fancies; she didn't bring up Riley, in any way, beyond that spring. I've always believed it had something to do with our mother's death, though I can't say why. And now it's too late to ask Jeanette. We'll visit all the graves on Sunday.

What more is there to tell? Etta tried to keep the dairy going for as long as she could. John died, then there was just Riley and herself. The girls had gone. June over to Ymir, where she was living with some older fellow. They had a trailer, I believe, and kids—but not the wedding. April ended up in Edmonton, working in a bar. We lost track. Maybe people talked about Etta and Riley up at the dairy alone. I'm sure they did, how they will. When I got a bit older, I started to invite Etta down for Sunday supper. It didn't seem right to me that Lena and Annie never had her over. I don't know what the story was there, but Etta was a cousin, wasn't she? She'd drive down in that old truck, still wearing her big coat and the boots. Dorothy and Kay used to joke she slept in them, I recall. Well, she took them off at my door, she ate at the table, there was no spitting in the sink. But she was a strange woman still.

One Sunday she said two men had shown up at the dairy wearing suits and ties. It wasn't the police. She didn't know who they were, they wouldn't say. No one from around here. They showed her a photograph of Riley, but she wouldn't say a word, not Etta. As they spoke, she saw Riley's face appear around the corner of the barn for just that second. Finally she had to order the men off her land. They'd become quite pushy, she said. There was something nasty in their tone.

That was the last she saw of Riley. For a few days, she thought he might be hiding back in the hills, biding his time until he felt it safe to return. But no one around here saw him again. Did he take the photographs with him? Did he leave something in their place behind?

No, I can't say I ever wondered where he went, what happened to him. For me he remained that tall, thin man in the distance, silently slipping into or out of my sight. An image pushed into a box at the dusty back of my mind. The photographs shoved farther back.

Not much longer afterwards, Etta sold the dairy. There never had been any real chance of making a go of the place; only her slaving kept it in operation as long as it was. That and the contract with the smelter for milk. There's a story for you. The smelter had been encouraging the men in the lead rooms to drink milk; they had a theory that it worked against the lead, coated the stomach, something. And then they found that the milk was leaded from the smelter. All along those poor men had been drinking in more of the same stuff they breathed. Now you read the obituaries in *The Daily Times*, all the cancer coming out, and you wonder.

I think they paid Etta off. In any case, she got enough for the place to buy her little house in Glenmerry. She took a business class at night. No one knew, but apparently she'd done some secretarial work before meeting John—back there in Winnipeg, I guess. Wouldn't you know but she flew through that course in no time, ended up with seventy words a minute plus the shorthand. Whatever else you say, she was a capable woman, a hard worker. She got on with the new high school, she got that one break. It was a good job for her. She ran that office for years, stayed on well past retirement age. Jeanette used to see her in the halls, dressed in a nice suit and blouse, her hair neat in a bun. The twists and turns that occur in a life. It's something, isn't it?

We never got close to her. She didn't seem able to relax, she stayed shut up so tight. All reined in. I don't think she was ever able to realize, not really, that things were no longer so hard for her. She made no friends down here that I know of, and of course her girls were long gone. I would say that at the end it was Riley who would have been the person to count in her life. Oh, your aunt Madeleine's just speculating, without a leg to stand on. But I believe he was the one she thought back on, the one she would dream about. Doesn't there have to exist, for all of us, that being to appear at four o'clock in the morning? You always wonder what was between them—no, not that. I'm speaking of what grows between people with time, in silence. What there's no name for, no speaking of. That's all.

PART TWO

Before I Was
Set Free

"We need, in love, to practice only this: letting each other go.
For holding on comes easily; we do not need to learn it."
—RILKE
"REQUIEM"

Ventriloquism

At the back of the furnace room the tin can lurks in mute darkness. Heavy and large, it is painted pale green, with silver at the dents. The tight lid eases off with a genie's sigh; an acrid scent of smoke rises from inside, mixes with those of oil and dust. I dig deep into my inheritance: pale cat's-eyes floating bubbles of trapped air; opaque agates; gaudy orbs. The globes of glass warm to my touch, then burn and moan and whisper. Beside me, the furnace switches on and the earth trembles beneath my feet.

My uncle swallowed smoke before my birth, leaving behind hockey sticks and baseball gloves and a universe of stunted spheres. In photos his face appears pinched and peaked, unlike those of squinting boys who in springtime lay stomachs against muddy grass, push hair from whitened winter foreheads, send marbles spinning toward a target. *I got you!* they crow at the click of glass on glass. My crystal eyes cloud beneath their breath, they make me twirl across the flat field until the world revolves dizzily, I can't see straight.

We never visit the cemetery on the hill where my uncle and grandfather practice patience. My father stares straight ahead as he drives us past; rows of white crosses blur by. The wiring of the Christmas tree lights was faulty, my grandfather forgot to unplug the cord that night. The old man and his youngest son were sleeping in the basement while empty rooms creaked and crackled overhead. (By then Carrie had already dug herself into the earth; my father and her other older children had already eschewed home.) The gaily wrapped presents beneath the tree turned brown, then black. Smoke stole down the stairs. They found the old man halfway between his bed and the window. The boy was posed in sleep, a lucky marble hidden in one hand.

They gave me his name. *Donald*, they say, and his voice emerges from my mouth. *Dummy*, they say when he will not move my lips. My bed is in the basement, beneath the surface of the earth. The world twirls slowly; now I am older than he ever was. I grip a favorite marble and sniff smoke. Without moving lips I chant a child's prayers; seven miles away they rise from beneath the graveyard's skin, muffled by snow as white and clean as the bones it blankets. I have passed through fire, I am as fearless as the phoenix.

There are years of cold winters and fiery summers in the small town split in two by a river that runs swiftly, icily, dangerously. From the bank I toss marbles into a watery mouth that opens then greedily gulps. The empty can floats from sight. Finally I am free to twirl and spin across the world, the scent of smoke clinging to me always. I chip and crack. I am easily lost and found. Indifferent hands warm me, roll me away to cool once more. *I never dreamed it would be like this*, the other Donald murmurs from my mouth as smoke from strangers' cigarettes curls knowingly into the corners of my cold hard eyes. At the bottom of a river marbles turn to stone. I drown with desire to be warmed by fire's hands, again and then again.

The Tattoo
Artist

It was not easy to find the tattoo artist, though his skill was renowned throughout the town and far beyond. Away from boulevards and cafés, away from lights and crowds, he lived among the narrow, twisting alleys behind the *quartier portugaise*. These were lit only by weak lamps attached infrequently to cold stone walls, and after dark rats roamed freely within the gutters and the waste. Few people passed over the rough cobblestones then; occupants were silent, if not sleeping, behind closed doors to either side; the doors were unnumbered as the alleys were not named. Except for a cat's sudden scream, or the squeak of a bat, there were no sounds except my footsteps and heartbeat echoing against stone. I knew it was possible to find the tattoo artist only on a night without stars, when he did not prick colored constellations upon the black skin of the sky.

Yet a sign did not hang helpfully upon the artist's door; nor did the door stand open in invitation. Within the labyrinth the tattoo artist's location itself remained as elusively unfixed as a fugitive's, though it was purported that his room was always the same bare, cement space illuminated by a candle, half-burned, whose light transformed the ancient dyes and needles into substances sheened with gold. If you could discover the secret way to the tattoo artist, the path of your life would be forever changed, it was averred in the tone of absolute certainty only ignorance can evoke: nothing and everything was known about this man whom the mute would describe in clear, precise detail if only they could speak. Perhaps he strolled through the *souk*, unrecognized but not disguised, to hear the stories told about him—all contradictory, all unproven—when we wearied of discussing the sixty lessons of the Koran or the reason for changing tides.

In the town we all grew up with mother's dire warnings that if we were not careful the tattoo artist would etch hideous, permanent pictures upon our sleeping skin. Later we learned that possibly his designs could attract the ideal lover who would not waver, who would not stray. Some said he substituted poison for ink when sought out by an evil man and some suggested that in certain worthy cases his handiwork could cure sickness and even extend life. There were those too who claimed that his instruments were the tools of Allah, and his images the Prophet's revelation. It was agreed that one needed to seek the tattoo artist at the correct time of life: overly tender skin would fester, blister and scar beneath his needles, while tough and weathered flesh would break them. The tattoo artist was a Jew from Essaouira, a *marabout* from Tarfaya, a Berber murderer or thief. Perhaps he was a distant cousin on your mother's side, the beggar disintegrating with leprosy before the Cinéma Le Paris, that pilgrim glimpsed yesterday on the road to Azammour. Stories shifted like Sahara sand blowing through the *derbs*, and changed shape and form from one day to the next, according to the wind. I did not puzzle at never seeing an example of the tattoo artist's work during my yearning youth: by the time I grew into a man and felt compelled one starless night to seek him for myself, I had come to believe his design remained invisible upon a subject until that being stretched his soul into a canvas tight and strong and broad enough to display the beauty that it held.

I had to ask infrequent strangers hurrying through the alleys for directions. Often they would not pause to answer, or only muttered brusquely that they didn't know; many spoke a dialect I hadn't heard before and couldn't understand, as if they came from the other side of the Atlas Mountains, or far beyond the Rif. If I knocked on a door to ask my way, those inside remained silent, or with a shout warned me away. Increasingly, I remembered how it was said that numerous people had vanished in search of the tattoo artist; whenever some restless, dissatisfied soul disappeared from our town the presumption was that he had passed through the gates of the *quartier portugaise* and had not emerged again. Some said these narrow alleys, dark even during day, teemed with lost spirits who on starless nights reached out with hungry bones of fingers for anyone foolish enough to seek the tattoo artist they had failed to find. This was home, it was rumored, to countless beings fallen into disappointment and despair, and that they sought consolation in narcotic and carnal pleasures was evidenced in sweet smoke and moans rising into the blue sky above our sensible town. "See what happens," mothers warned their discontented children, hoping one day these offspring would grow to feel happy with the prospect of a perfectly satisfactory, harmless tattoo of the kind offered every day and at reasonable price in the market; for example, a green cross of Islam, or a yellow star of hope.

I wandered until north and south became indistinct, and time and distance without proportion, before I found someone who would help. She looked at me with cold, suspicious eyes under the lamp where we met, and appeared undecided whether to speak or not. Slowly a knowing smile twisted her face, which was scarred and disfigured beneath heavy powder. "The next crossing," she finally said, placing ironic emphasis upon each word. "The third door to the left." Then she turned and walked swiftly away, drawing a scarf more closely around her head, leaving light, mocking laughter behind.

The tattoo artist did not answer my knock, but when I pushed the door it opened. In a room off the entrance he sat on a wooden bench between the small table that held his instruments and colors and the chair in which his clients sat when not required to lie upon the floor or to stand erect to receive his mark. He was looking in my direction as I entered but did not rise to greet me. The old man wore a dark robe, with a hood concealing whether his hair was black or white or disappeared, and partly obscuring his eyes. The garment made it difficult to know his size or shape; his fingers, unadorned with rings, were long and thin. No tattoos were visible upon the skin left uncovered by the hooded robe. Appearing absorbed in thought, and scarcely conscious of my presence, the tattoo artist did not speak.

I sat in the chair and explained that I wanted a tattoo unlike any other in the world. Commonplace tattoos—

a lover's name or initials; an eagle, snake or lion—did not interest me, less the heart, the arrow, the bolt of lightning; nor did I desire even a rare symbol of obscure significance. I wanted a unique tattoo, a singular tattoo: a shape that would clearly reveal to the world exactly who I was, and how the design of my being was in many minute ways indicated in his etching, different from all others. If I did not know how it looked or what it was named, this was because the mark I wished for did not yet exist except within the tattoo artist's imagination. There was only one thing I knew for certain: it should be imprinted upon my heart.

The tattoo artist listened, then left the room by a door at its rear. He returned to set a tray holding a small silver teapot and three glasses upon the floor. After a moment he poured pale tea into two of the glasses. Steam began to rise. Suddenly I wanted to tell the tattoo artist many things about myself: where I had come from, what I had seen and done, whom I had loved. I needed him to know how long I had been anticipating this moment, and how difficult it had been to find him, and how the doubts I had once felt about receiving his mark had vanished. He should hear me and see me, I believed, in order to know exactly what tattoo to place upon my skin; but the artist only watched the rising steam, seemingly uninterested in the material he had to work with, and I could not interrupt his silence. He turned to shift the candle slightly, then studied the shadow it cast upon the wall. He sighed once. Then he removed a small square of paper from the folds of his robe and untwisted it above one glass, spilling white powder. He handed me the glass. I drank its hot contents quickly, then loosened my shirt and lay on my back. The cement below me warmed as I fell asleep.

It was cold when I awoke. The candle still burned halfway down. The tray that held the teapot still lay upon the floor. One glass was empty, one glass was full, the third was gone. There was a burning sensation at my heart. I bent my neck and saw my tattoo. At once I knew I had never seen this shape before. It was unique. I did not know what the small shape symbolized; it called nothing definite to my mind, yet seemed at once to suit me and to describe me. Was there a suggestion of a wave, a hint of an eye, an allusion to an outstretched wing? Fastening the buttons of my shirt, I watched the tattoo artist use a wet cloth to wipe his needles of dye. When they were clean, he replaced them exactly in their former position on the table. He stared at his instruments with an expression that contained amazement or horror or pleasure, or a combination of these three emotions. He was unable to hear my thanks or to receive my offered payment, and I left his room.

For several years I was pleased with my unique tattoo, though long after the pricked skin healed it continued to burn in such a way that I could never forget its presence. When exposed it caused astonishment and envy, and those with apparently ordinary tattoos sought my companionship and approval. My mark became famous in the town and occupied a central place in conversation. On the corners old men argued endlessly over its meaning and at the shore small children tried to trace its outline with sticks upon the sand. Seers used the shape to predict the future. Holy men proclaimed it visible evidence of Allah's touch. In the dark, lovers pressed lips against those brilliant colors; tongues traveled its contours, and tried to lick it off my skin. There was a season too when many youths attempted to have my tattoo copied onto themselves by the everyday tattoo artists in the market; these imitations, however skilled, were always inexact, and appeared somehow grotesque. During this time I felt that even with my shirt buttoned to my neck it was possible for passersby to see through cloth to the colors stained upon my heart.

Later, though unchanged itself, my tattoo seemed to evoke a different response, such as distrust or pity or fear. My fellow townspeople fell silent when I approached down the street, and mothers placed hands over children's eyes to shield them from the sight. No longer did lovers line up to lie with me upon the sand; perhaps they realized their kisses would not erase my mark, less swallow it inside themselves. Now I was lonely, and separated from those around me by what I had once hoped would permit them to see me clearly and know me intimately. I tried to keep my tattoo hidden, as if it were ugly or obscene, wearing a heavy burnoose as armor even during the hottest season. "I hope you got what you wanted," my mother said, as another wedding procession wound past our door with its bright song of union. Ashamed of my mark, I wished it to fade or wash away, or to alter into an unremarkable design. At night, dreams concerning an undistinguished existence, with an unbranded aspect, afforded me brief release; awakening at morning brought more bitter disappointment. When I offered

tattoo artists in the market large sums to remove my
mark, their refusals were nervously adamant, and I was
driven to prowl the dark alleys behind the *quartier portugaise* once more. Hoping its creator could alter or elim-
inate the unwanted design, I searched for him on many
starless nights, yet in those narrow passages encoun-
tered only yearning youths with blank, unmarked skin.
"Go home," I told them.

One day my tattoo suddenly began to burn more
searingly, as if freshly pricked upon my skin. Now the
pain was so sharp that it would not permit me to sleep
or dream or pray. At this time I gradually began to wonder about the tattoo artist himself, seeking to recall
every detail of my experience with him and to find in
that memory some clue to the meaning of my mark or a
way of living with it. I mused upon the possible landscape of his past and the likely contours of his present.
What were his intentions when faced with the canvas of
my skin? What desires urged him to use dyes and needles
upon me in one way and not another? This was the period when I hoped to understand the implications of my
mark by knowing the being who had placed it there, as
we turn our eyes above the clouds to contemplate the
force that works upon us here below.

In this way my long journey began. First I roamed the
town itself and then the towns nearby in search of someone with the same tattoo as mine. I had faith that at least
one other being in the world wore that brilliant shape
that hovered over my heart; even accidentally, even a
single time, it must have been created before. It had to
have a twin. As years went by and my search did not end,

I journeyed farther from the town, crossing mountains and valleys, deserts and plains, rivers and oceans and streams. In distant lands I saw many things and met many people, but the single shape I hunted for did not appear before my eyes. I believed, still, that when it finally occurred our meeting would possess the symmetry and grace of a balanced equation: my mark would vanish beneath his gaze as his would dissolve under mine, and we would no longer each feel the same constant pain. "One glass was empty, one glass was full, the third was gone," I repeated as the road stretched far before me.

Though my end is growing near, I continue to roam from place to place in hope of discovering someone marked like me. The tattoo still burns above my heart; I have not grown used to its ache. While the colors of the world have faded, and stars dimmed with my faith, the tattoo still flames as brightly as in the beginning. Now it is many years since I have been to my town, and I do not know if my family and friends still live. I do not know if the tattoo artist still hides within the dark alleys behind the *quartier portugaise*. I do not know if he still pricks his stained needles into flesh, scarring it differently each time, leaving upon our hearts the unique designs from which we seek release.

The Beauty Secrets
of a Belly Dancer

"Don't ask me a thing about love," warns the belly dancer, though survivor of as many affairs as are grains of sand upon the Gobi, when I mourn the latest lover who has left. "I still don't know the first thing about the subject." At three a.m. she returns from the tapas bar on the corner, where a wealthy American has bought her drinks. "Older but interesting," she describes him without enthusiasm, sautéing diced garlic in a little olive oil. (Garlic is good for the scalp and relieves menstrual discomfort.) "He's taking me to the bullfights, he has season tickets for the shade, we'll see Curro Romero try to do his thing." I watch her kick off heels, wriggle out of the tight red skirt, sigh into a sheer Egyptian robe that floats and flutters around her thinness. (In dressing rooms for cattle-call auditions she can change beneath this garment, guard her secrets from other dancers' knowing eyes.) Reyna lights candles and incense, puts on a salsa cassette, settles down to eat garlic over bread in my living room—her bedroom during her yearly visits from New York. Then from my mattress in the curtained alcove I hear Luis Enrique sing the same song over and over. *San Juan sin ti*, he laments endlessly above the throbbing beat. I know my houseguest is rocking rapidly back and forth in her chair, like a camel's passenger who bobs for hours upon a humped back, dazed by hallucinogenic heat, surrounded always by the same parched expanse of sand, apparently not moving at all. *Cuerpo a cuerpo, sexo a sexo*, sings the boy too far from Puerto Rico, needing a body he can hold on to like it's home. Reyna expertly rolls high-grade grass she smuggled through Spanish customs, inhales deeply something more essential than oxygen. (She has long ceased trying to weigh the relief gained against the damage done: ice cubes beneath the eyes will be the only answer on yet another morning after.) Sweet smoke insinuates out into the Sevilla night, travels toward the south, the east.

Just before sleep, I hear the belly dancer change the tape; now Middle Eastern music jangles my neighbors' dreams. Reyna has switched into one of her working costumes, perhaps the silver halter with gold lamé harem pants beneath a bared midriff. While I dream her into a tent beside the mirage of an oasis, she kneels on hard tiles in the next room, hands resting on the floor before her for support. Her neck begins to pivot in frenzied circles, her long black hair whips the air, candle flames shudder and shake. The head dance, this one's called. ("Let's give them a little head," she jokes to her partner before they slink onto another Manhattan stage for the final set.) Somewhere in the desert, jarred by tambourines and drums, camels lift necks from water; it drips like gems through heat, sucking moisture from air and skin, falls back into the pool from which it came. The dancer's hair lashes more wildly at all the men who have failed to take her from this place: she would like to stripe their backs with blood. Now the beat slows, percussive blows jerk the dancer from side to side, sound she can't escape; but still

she smiles slyly beneath her veil, full of secret power.
Jasmine and myrrh smudge the shadows, coils of controlled muscle twist beneath skin still smooth and soft.
The men with money in her mind gaze intently, not missing a move. As flutes shrill toward a finale, the dancer's
face falls against the floor; she freezes into a posture of
submission at the feet of her invisible audience, waits for
bejeweled hands to clap her out of sight. (Always save
your best moves for the end, leave them wanting more
than you'd ever consider giving.)

Long after I'm far away in sleep, halfway to the home
that's never reached because of waking, Reyna cleanses
makeup from her face, washes away the black kohl
around her eyes. (In the end dancers are blinded by kohl,
saved from witnessing the disappearance of beauty, the
indifference of lovers, the melting of water into only
mirage.) Sallow skin emerges in the unkind bathroom
light; her head beats demandingly after the unseen
exhibition. When the show is over, dancers don't dare
attempt escape across the sand: sun would singe their
skin until it was without worth, or a moon would drive
them mad. Anyway, there's no easy end to the desert;
another dune always rises beyond every one that's
climbed. (There is no simple way back there, either; that
will be another lesson learned too late.) Sighing, Reyna
heats olive oil in a teaspoon over the stove's gas flame,
applies the thick warm liquid upon lines of fixed smiles
around her eyes, her mouth. There are always gorgeous
new girls elbowing youth onto Gotham stages; but can
they work a rowdy room, transfix an inattentive audience,

sidle smilingly through clubowners' tricks and traps? The belly dancer pins up the hair she will never blow dry, will wash only with a special shampoo found in a single East Village store. ("Imagine if I lost this," she sometimes laughs on those April afternoons when dark glasses conceal her eyes even though my living room is always dim. She fondly strokes her hair; it's slung over her shoulder, a favorite pet snake. "A bald belly dancer. How would I pay the rent?") In my dreams a harem waits restlessly for new summons of clapping hands, for warm wet lips pressed upon a veiled mouth. They glance mistrustfully at each other, wonder who will be chosen this time to be bobbed into oblivion upon the sea of love: the dance always leaves you needing arms that can hold you here if they can't take you there. Reyna abandons the mirror, leaves her image to peer shortsightedly from that window in the wall. Only opium permits us peace until the next performance—I am, in my fashion, a dancer too—some slumber in spiced shade. Beyond these canvas walls no skyscrapers rise to break flatness, interrupt empty vistas. Reyna, once we could see far through the burning air, deep into our common destiny. Did heat refract the reality before us into only illusion? Twist the truth that one day we must add to the dust of all dancers who believed beauty could lure the lover strong enough to carry them back where they belonged? Finally Reyna breathes drugged disturbed sleep, I call out my departed lover's name, garbage trucks groan through the dawn.

Why doesn't she save the ten-dollar tips tucked into her shiny costumes to vacation, for example, in Cairo or Beirut—rather than always here in Spain? I wonder but do not ask, respecting secrets fragile as my own, how they contain hidden explanations for apparent incongruity. ("How did you end up here?" they incessantly want to know. "Why don't you go there?") After five April holidays in Sevilla, Reyna has conquered the Spanish for many dishes, drinks and sexual positions. This is the extent of her vocabulary in the language; only mute does she pass as one of the city's striking señoritas. "They think I'm one of them until I open my mouth," she comments, originally just another California girl with Mexican blood on one side to explain her coloring. That grandfather was a professional gambler who robbed his bride from a Guadalajara convent and took her north; the old lady still mutters broken-English prayers in San Francisco, sends rosaries and crucifixes to a granddaughter also gone astray. "*Reina?*" they always ask her on these streets, ignorant of the name's spelling and confused by its phonics, disbelieving it wasn't assumed for the stage, one more showgirl aspiring to royalty. "Queen of what?"

"When I was little I wanted to be a nun," confesses the belly dancer over pulsing salsa, "but I quickly realized that wasn't my true calling." In the weak light of late afternoon, before candles can be lit, she appears tired and pale and almost old. Then her hips begin to sway; she entwines ten fingers into an intricate arrangement,

produces a snapping loud as a pistol's discharge. (This
secret took her seven years to master; others remain,
still undiscovered.) Arabs love the noise, but my upstairs
neighbors bang their floor in irritation. "Some people
wouldn't know a free show if they heard one," the belly
dancer states, rolling eyes heavenward, cracking the air
on the beat. Copper bracelets clink, scarfs swim through
space. "People have to pay a lot for this," she says, then
abruptly separates her hands to reach for the bottle of
rough red wine. (Never drink before five, always swallow a glass of water for each of less pure liquid.) We make
them pay and pay and pay: they can never give us enough,
they always leave us wanting more. ("Just once more," I
beg into the telephone, before he clicks a disconnection.)
For consolation we will hire a carriage with bright yellow
wheels to roll us through the park at dawn. While the
Gypsy driver slaps reins against the horse's shiny back, we
lap champagne and laugh along the leafy avenues, hear
harness bells and hooves announce our approach, how
we draw nearer to the end of what we've chosen to be:
entertainers who ignore that the tent has been emptied
and taken down, leaving no trace of spectacle behind,
leaving us here in western twilight to insist that once we
were not only ghosts in the Kalaharis of your mind.

"There's plenty where he came from," the belly dancer
consoles me for not the last time. She studies my skin
browned from radiant afternoons upon the rooftop; I'm
dark as an Arab boy. "Sun is the very worst thing for you,"
she chides, briskly whipping the white of an egg, spreading the stuff across my face. This hardens into a trans-

parent mask; if I smile, it will crack. (Don't show them how you feel, let them read their own emotion into your eyes.) The Queen of What rushes to get ready for another date, two hours late today. (Never show up on time unless cold cash is involved, anticipation will increase their eagerness and your beauty.) Married men and impotent cab drivers and unemployed waiters come and go, while surely somewhere sheiks in billowing white robes race Arabians across the sand, dark eyes unsmiling above dunes of cheekbones, every one of them an elusive Valentino in the moonlight. In ten days Reyna must squeeze back into her rooms in the least lucky letter of Alphabet City, negotiate anew that crackheads' neighborhood, again await the agency's orders to appear exotic at another fifty-dollar bachelor party or bar mitzvah. (A good man also expects her return; she carefully conceals fleeting infidelities from him: he has his uses, she may need to resign herself to his sober steadiness in the end.) "Go out and find another," my friend advises over her shoulder, falling out the door. "Get it while you can." But I stay at home with sentences, seduced by my punctuated rhythms, how they can sweep me breathlessly toward The End. Once upon a time Scheherazade told tales to divert the man, to forestall her doom: this was her way of dancing, this is also mine. A sudden sirocco stirs the palms along the boulevard, dies to make them droop once more. I touch my leathered skin; it will be tough enough by the time mocking laughter swells thickly around me, a sandstorm in which I'll stumble until enough grit is swallowed to end for good my hunger. Thinly sliced cucumber placed upon the face eases aridity. Beyond this secret lies another secret, just as above Saharan stars exist more stars, though we cannot see them. We must hang on to the hope that they are there. And we must keep searching for the lost oasis; this is our story, Scheherazade. *Once upon a time*, it always starts. You know the ending, but please don't reveal it yet. There is still time for several dances more.

"Semen's the only moisturizer that really works," the belly dancer remarks idly to her bullfight date, lifting his hand from her thigh, inspecting her face in a compact mirror. "It's the protein or something." In the ring Curro Romero is long past his prime; each year his costumes are flashier, his moves with the cape less elegant. Reyna remains in her shaded seat while the rest of the *corrida* audience rises to its feet, turns backs against Romero's bungling of another bull. The belly dancer blows the matador a kiss; he bows low before her, tosses her an unearned ear that causes the crowd to roar louder disapproval. Afterward, the wealthy American mistakenly believes he's purchased something beside seafood and wine for five thousand pesetas. "I'm going to make myself beautiful," the belly dancer evades, heading toward the restaurant's *Señoras*, slipping out a rear exit. "My kisses are not for sale," she proclaims back home, undulating anxiously before my eyes. "Feel this," she says, placing my hand upon her belly. Something inside her hits hard against my palm, a secret child bangs the wall of imprisoning flesh. Long ago Reyna brutally rid herself of who she used to be, left a fetus with her face in miniature floating by the foggy shores of Frisco, emerged a decade later as an exotic dancer, crowned herself Queen of Anything At All. (In illegal clinics of this country embryos are not wasted; they become the chief ingredient of expensive oils, lotions, creams.) I too have shed former selves as easily as snakes squirm from skin, freeing myself to coil around cacti, beneath flat stones. Reyna, we could spin from this city on the early-morning bus, cross the Strait of Gibraltar beneath birds and breeze, be back on the desert before shadow has stretched into darkness upon the sand. When was the last time we were there? In what lifetime long ago? It becomes more difficult to remember with each night we dance for sad fugitives of some Foreign Legion of the heart. This time when you leave me to return to your tenement across the sea, we will not reunite to share a sixth Sevilla spring. It is clear that one of us does not make the other stronger. Our journeys back to where we started will be separate or not at all. Perhaps it's too late to return, perhaps we have forgotten how to exist on dried entrails of armadillo.

"If I get another, we can make a Mickey Mouse hat," suggests the belly dancer, jaunty once more, holding her latest trophy up for me. Its blood has dried brown upon her skirt; she dabs at the stain while the unanswered telephone is forced to ring by another of the weak men who wish her or me to sway the hot still night. Already the severed ear has begun to fill the room with pungent scent; we will need no incense this evening. On the other side of the city Curro Romero practices imperfect pirouettes before an accusing mirror. He stumbles, shrugs, reaches for the bottle: accepts that the game is over. (His hotel room is otherwise empty, there is no one to remind him that alcohol as well as salt will bloat.) I paint the belly dancer's fingernails, one red, the next black. She is twenty-five or thirty-five or somewhere in between; anyway, the end of her career is also near, and the night will be shockingly cold even though earlier the day was too hot: you're never prepared for the desert's swift, extreme changes of temperature, no matter how many times you survive them. And belly dancers, like bullfighters, do not often have bank accounts, social security numbers or pension plans to soothe the future: it is difficult to save for a rainy day when you were raised to believe no precipitation would ever fall upon the sere landscape around you. I blow on Reyna's long thin hands until I'm breathless, unable to call out the name of the one who left no footprints in the shifting sand. *San Juan sin ti*, grieves Luis Enrique one more time, exiled always from his island. Outside, in Andalusia, Moorish music evokes camel caravans and somber Saharan sunsets and bands of thirsty bedouins through flutter, through wail. "Please don't ask me anything about love," repeats the belly dancer before each of us retires to his separate pillow. We lie awake in the narcotic night and hope for a breath of breeze to stir the air, caress our crumbling skin, touch our kohl-blinded eyes with one more kiss we cannot see.

The Murdered
Child

Once more something in the winter night, when the cold, dark lake leaks beyond the window, urges me to telephone my sister. Lily continues to live in the same square of stucco, one hundred miles from here, where we were once children. In those otherwise abandoned rooms, the only one left, she guards old secrets that refuse decent burial, meticulously tends souvenirs of skeleton, flicks dust from bone. Apparently, she can't or won't release information concerning what more than a decade of widening distance has failed to illuminate for me: nagging questions not hushed by the silencing Sahara; an image not choked from view by even Guatemala jungle.

That unseemly sprawl upon the surface of memory.

That obscenity in the snow.

Yet my reasons for being drawn to this cabin on this shore, almost counter to will, seemed less than specific upon arriving here from Lisbon at the end of summer. You must go back in order to move forward, I explained vaguely to myself, as if nothing more than that were wrong, as if survival were as simple as a mumbled mantra. If I were now within earshot of the past—near enough to squint at the source of its tug and pull, far enough to remain beyond reach of its dangers—no single question immediately clamored more loudly than others to be answered. And there were several questions: What finally happened to my parents and my brother? To Lily? And to myself? While summer people shut up cabins and retreated into town, leaving the lake to just a scattering of souls, allowing it to reassert its indifferent self, the aloof essence of a place not created primarily for pleasure, I delayed letting Lily know I was—am—this close. For the moment, my proximity seemed sufficient; it dissolved haste. I could thumb a ride or catch the bus to Brale any autumn afternoon. Instead, I scuffed fallen leaves in Lovers' Lane and rowed to the cliffs at Christmas Bay and learned a landscape almost familiar, nearly known, from before. I could imagine it was enough to understand that the evening train whistles along the opposite shore just after eight o'clock. I could believe that the wisdom whose lack I suffer was contained in comprehending that wind sweeps down the valley always from the west. I could convince myself, during darkening days, that I was here to learn the shape created by a group of Canada geese against the mountains, the sky.

Only after the arrival of cold that after my southern years seemed unusually harsh, only at a first sight of snow in all this time, did I begin to shiver from some sense of a child wandering in such weather. He is nine or ten or a stunted twelve. A second mouth has been slashed, beyond healing, into his throat. In bare feet and scarcely more than rags, accustomed to the elements after extended existence outside, long separated from home and school and other children, he steps lightly through snow to pause at the end of the beach, near the ferry landing, where he skips three stones across the water; before disappearing into the pines that cluster upon Greene's Point, face indistinct in dusk, made visible only by my memory, he turns to look through the uncurtained windows into these rooms where I am illuminated, as upon a stage, and where it is surely warmer, as in another climate of another country.

It became urgent that I see Lily. To feel out the possibility of a visit, whether or not my sister's condition would permit it, I telephoned our aunts in Brale. (I still knew that if you call one, you have to call all three; these women take offense easily, like to nurse slights like tall teetotal drinks.) Each sounded unsurprised to hear I was back in the area; anyone who goes away becomes unaccountable, expected of nothing less than the outlandish. "There's no work around here, you know," Dorothy informed me, briskly puncturing what could be the single sensible reason for turning up anywhere. "A cabin on the lake," echoed Madeleine flatly. "At this time of year." Just hippies and crackpots and people who don't curl would make such a choice, then pretend it was the superior option. "Sure she'd love to see you," Kay decided doubtfully, giving me Lily's number.

That was November. Now it's January. I've been to Brale and I've seen Lily and nothing has been uncovered by the experience. Or has it? There is this: at morning now a child's footprints, sometimes confused by tracks of deer and bear, lead to and from the cabin windows. There is a handful of pumpkin seeds, twisted within a scrap of silver paper, in my mailbox beside the road at noon. There is something in the bitter night, when the ferry becomes a glide of lights across black water, that every week or so insists, despite what did or did not recently occur between us, that I call my sister.

This is never a simple matter. Often Lily allows her telephone to ring unanswered, I suspect; or she disconnects the cord, forgets for days it is not plugged in. Maybe a recorded voice informs me that her number is not in service. For reasons I can't guess, Lily frequently changes or temporarily cancels or unlists her number. Worried, I will consider then decide against calling the Brale aunts; though the town they inhabit with my sister is small, they would not necessarily know if she is all right. By her choice, and to the aunts' injured puzzlement, they don't see Lily often. I am left to check periodically with directory assistance until a new number appears under—and this always startles me—our shared last name.

It has never been easy to reach my sister.

If she does happen to lift the receiver tonight, Lily won't speak first. Like a secret agent trained never to reveal herself to a possible enemy, she waits silently for the caller to identify himself. Learning this is only me doesn't ease her suspicion; nothing like a conversation follows. She is well, the house is fine, the weather is not unusual for this time of year. No, she hasn't been away. Yes, her number has changed. She won't ask how I am or what I am doing. She won't refer to November's meeting. She does not call me herself.

My sister has grown even more guarded than the child who concealed herself behind impassive features and covert movement and silence. I spent my first sixteen years living with Lily without fathoming how she felt or what she thought. I wasn't alone in ignorance; my older brother, MJ, and my parents, Ardis and Mitch, were also uncertain why Lily's bed yawned on summer dawns, who she met on the mountain in spring, where she went on winter nights as cold and dark as this night that conceals the answer to a question, the identity of a corpse.

Lily finds him on the mountain when the November world is frozen and stiff, still unsoftened by snow, five months before we will search for pussy willows and dam trickles of April thaw. "Come," she says, materializing in the doorway of the furnace room, wearing a gray felt coat, several sizes too large, that looks unfamiliar. Lily has stolen it from a house on the other side of Brale or from the change room at the skating rink. In my dim cave carved out of discarded furniture and abused boxes, and of hockey sticks that belonged to an uncle from whom I inherited my first name and sharp features and fear of smoke, I look up from the letter I am composing to Jesus. The furnace switches on; the pilot light hisses blue. The house suspends itself in uneasy Saturday quiet: Ardis engages in a series of naps in the big bedroom upstairs; Mitch shuts himself in his study across the basement; and MJ always spends the weekends with television and treats at Aunt Madeleine's, by the river. "Come," my sister repeats, in neither command nor invitation. Lily's speech is generally uninflected; little emphasis lies behind her words to lend them shade or nuance. Her communication is blunt and flat as that of cardboard Indians in the westerns Mitch drags us to see at the Royal Theatre, where from the front row he watches John Wayne, another simple man, with wide, admiring eyes.

"Hurry," says Lily, beckoning with one reddened hand. She always loses the mittens our concerned aunts bestow on her; it would surprise Lily to have this pointed out. She doesn't seem to feel the cold, and in winter roams unfettered by hats or scarfs. Lily has been outside all morning, I can tell: waves of dark chill pulse from her direction. She knows a way of leaving the house unnoticed; only halfway through a weekend afternoon, or long after the streetlamps blink on, does her absence cause remark. Where does she go? Mitch and Ardis don't ask; it's better not to. They accept that Lily lies as lightly as she breathes. "She's different," our aunts describe my sister, using the catch-all adjective applied in Brale to harmless eccentrics and nonpracticing homosexuals and tentative pedophiles, and to a thin girl of twelve who goes where she wishes, takes what she needs.

Unsettled by Lily's rare summons, I emerge from the back of the furnace room. I believed my hiding place, amid the asphyxia of oil and dust, to be a secret shared only with my buried uncle; but Lily always knows where to find me. Even after my sister stops looking for me, even during all the years when across the globe I cover myself beneath heavy blankets of time and distance, Lily knows where I am.

On a late-November afternoon I walk down Aster Drive, toward my first meeting with Lily in fifteen years. During my two brief visits to Brale in the early eighties, while she was enclosed in the hospital on the hill, Lily would not see me. The lingering power of those refusals, and the weight of all the years since then, made me nervous dialing her number from the cabin. When I stated my name, a long silence ensued. "Donald," I repeated. Fumbling with words that received little response, I tried to believe that the awkwardness of the call came from our not having spoken for so long. "If you want," Lily met my suggestion that I visit for several days.

My single small light suitcase brims with questions concerning what happened to my parents and brother while I was embracing distance. My knowledge of their fates has been gleaned from what lay behind and between the lines of several letters from the aunts: there is much I don't know, much that perhaps only Lily can tell me. Did she ever hear from Mitch and MJ, anything at all, after they disappeared from Brale? Was Ardis's death easier than her life? And how has Lily managed to hang on?

The house looks small, old, worn. A modest single-story structure, similar to others on the block, with a bare front yard and a vacant driveway. Though dusk has not fallen, the curtains are closed. I wonder if I'll learn anything inside it after all. I ring the doorbell, then touch it again when no one answers. Has Lily forgotten about my visit? As I am about to test the door, it opens.

She wears a gray skirt, white blouse and dark sweater. The clothes are cut simply, like a uniform, and look homemade. No jewelry adorns them. Though she is only thirty-three, two years older than myself, Lily's dark hair has turned mostly gray. The neat bun folds above a pale face that, once sharp, is puffy, perhaps from medication. The lines and angles of her body have also blurred, but with no concession to softness. She would feel stiff and cold in my arms, I suspect. Her gray eyes loom unusually pale behind thick glasses; they don't blink when I say hello. Glancing at my suitcase, she turns and retreats down the dim hall. It strikes me that each of her steps is measured to cover precisely the same distance.

Taken aback by her lack of greeting, then recalling her distaste for words, I follow my sister inside. She pauses, partly turns. "You can sleep in your old room," she says in a voice as toneless as ever, though pitched lower now. "There are sheets on the bed. Supper is at six."

Perhaps because she didn't initiate this visit, Lily continues with the housework it has interrupted, as though she doesn't have a guest. The living room she dusts appears painfully tidy and clean already. I notice that old furniture retains its old arrangement. The room that belonged to our parents is shut, like Lily's across the hall. Curtains from my childhood have faded in swaths, paths betray where the carpet has been paced. If the walls were ever repainted, it was with the same color as before. Turning on the back left burner of the stove, I place my hand above it. The element still doesn't work.

"Yes," says Lily, not looking up from her work when I mention that the house appears the same. "No," she says when I ask if I can help with supper. I linger nearby for a moment. I don't know how to give Lily the present in my suitcase. It's a book about what I imagined happened to us all.

I descend to the basement, place my luggage on one of the twin beds in the room I shared with MJ, then glance into the furnace room. It is still crowded with broken tools and rusted skates, and with empty jars that hold breath beneath a film of dust. The scent of oil

twines around my head, shuts my eyes. As if a finger of
bone traces my spine, I shudder. Across in Mitch's study,
outdated history texts weigh the shelves and the manual
Olivetti squats on the wide desk. Avoiding a sharp,
exposed spring in its corner, I curl up on the rumpus-
room couch that reigned upstairs until a new one
replaced it. At card-table islands, MJ, Lily and I bent over
homework in this sunken space, while Ardis lurched
through hours above and in his study Mitch toiled at his
memoirs. Although their title was *A Simple Man,* my father
was not blessed with a sense of irony.

"It's time to eat," Lily calls down the stairs.

The kitchen table is set with two plates, two forks
and two glasses of water. Lily serves a casserole made
with macaroni and tuna; soft and bland, a child would
enjoy it. Her eyes focused on the wall behind me, Lily
eats steadily. She pauses only to sip water and to respond
briefly to my tentative remarks. The neighbors to the
left have moved; she doesn't know who lives there now.
Yes, downtown Brale has changed. No, thank you, she
prefers to clear the kitchen herself; she knows where
everything belongs. Her movements before the counter
appear carefully considered and executed; each hints of
an obscure ritual, an invisible significance. I realize how
difficult it will be to ask the questions that have brought
me here. Her back still turned to me, her hands plunged
into scalding water, Lily lets her shoulders loosen, then
sag. Steam appears to rise from her body, drift from her
skin; it lingers around her head. Lily stands before the
sink as if she has forgotten what she is doing or where
she is. The tap drips a persistent reminder. Abruptly, her

back stiffens again. She pulls the plug, shakes her hands, dries them on a tea towel. "I expect you're tired from your trip," she says, her back still facing me. "Good night."

She turns the corner of the hall toward her bedroom. Or does she sleep in our parents' room now? Water runs in the adjacent bathroom. A door opens, then closes. It is seven o'clock.

What have I expected? What do I deserve? To be eagerly welcomed as the long-lost brother? To be greeted with open arms? Yes, Lily, I am tired from my trip. My trip has been longer than a hundred miles from a cabin on a lake, I hadn't realized how long my trip has been until circling back to where it began, it's been too god-damned long and it isn't over yet, not by a long shot, not by half. I grimace at my reflection floating on the kitchen window. Though I can't see through my image, I know a maple tree, bare at this time of year, rises halfway across the backyard. Beyond the fence runs another row of single-story houses; past that, the high-way. Then the mountain looms jagged and forbidding, scantily clad even during summer, splintering the chemical sky. Sometimes we tried to reach the top to discover what lay on the farther side. But we never could conquer the peak; the slope was too treacherous, too steep. "I'll reach it without you," Lily said after the last time she allowed me to attempt the ascent with her; before she began, at twelve, to scramble alone upon the mountain, along the cold, swift river.

No. Not quite the last time. There was at least one more time. Yes.

A November Saturday.

Something like a scrap of paper stirs in a dark room in my mind.

The house stands silent. Has Lily already gone to sleep or does her light still burn? She lies on her narrow mattress and looks upward through the dark? Or tosses in the wide bed where Ardis sweated pills, where Mitch planned escape? I am tempted to steal down the hall and look for a stripe of light beneath a door, then remember that several floorboards creak.

All I know is that, after the age of nineteen, Lily passed in and out of the psychiatric unit of the Brale Regional Hospital earlier haunted by our mother. I know only that, five years ago, she was permanently released. From what I understand, Lily doesn't have a job or own a car or visit our nearby aunts. Though everyone in Brale knows everyone, she is without friends. There has never been a lover. Solitude and the quiet of this house may be essential for her stability. She may be unable, rather than unwilling, to answer questions. It may be wrong to remind her of the past. It may be necessary for her to forget.

Downstairs, I sift Mitch's study for his memoirs, without hope. Failing to discover the manuscript during my pair of Brale visits a dozen years ago, I was convinced that Mitch had destroyed or taken with him his story upon vanishing in 1978. I inspect the basement bedroom for evidence of MJ's childhood: baseball mitts, model planes, unblinking eyes of marbles. Though his transformation into thin air was apparently less carefully planned than my father's, nothing telling remains behind of MJ, either. Yet I recall that on my previous returns at least some souvenirs of my brother had survived.

The house is the same, yes, but with a difference. Every significant artifact, all mementos of the presences that abandoned it, have been scrupulously removed. Hidden away or destroyed. I envision Lily methodically clearing out closets and drawers, carefully wiping fingerprints from surfaces, stripping space of evidence until only the intangible secrets remain. In the backyard, she stands before a bonfire, unflinching when flames leap at her face, inhaling smoke while wisps of ash snow upon her head. With a stick she stirs the coals, prods their hiss, makes the red eyes blink sparks.

I lift my opened eyes to the narrow window set high in the wall, above MJ's bed, at the level of the ground.

It lies out there, in the cold, dark night, the question I need answered.

It's not a question concerning Ardis, Mitch or MJ, after all.

Hours later, finally sliding into sleep, I'm disturbed by a known sound from above. The click of the front door. My watch glows three o'clock. I push away sleep and wait for Lily to return. Didn't she always come home eventually, when we were children, when we saw the truth?

The child stands above my bed of frozen earth and jabs a stick. "He can't feel anything," she informs the presence that hovers behind her. The point of the stick presses against my bared belly, seeks to pierce the skin, gain entry to entrails. The child pokes harder with her tool, she wants to see inside. The gray felt coat flaps from her effort; the sharp face frowns. She is angry that I don't cry, moan, plead for her to stop. My eyes refuse to close against the intent face above. My gashed throat grimaces. A bubble bursts from my blue lips, escapes into the sky. "His name is Billy," she says, dropping the stick and turning away. The pulsing shadow leaves her, nears me, bends low. Its warm hand, the same size and shape as mine, strokes my stone cheek. Scented breath urges me to speak.

At the kitchen table, Lily bows her head before a cup of coffee.

"Good morning," I say, foggily filling a mug. My hands wrap around its heat. I'm cold, despite the groaning furnace. Though it is early, I feel I've slept too long, too deeply. I can't remember hearing Lily return last night. She wears the same neat skirt, blouse and sweater as yesterday. Has she been to bed at all?

"Did you sleep well?" I stare at the scars. The one on her right wrist is thicker than the other. She did it in the back of the furnace room, Aunt Dorothy wrote me at the time. Ardis found her; the rest of us had left Brale by then. Come, my uncle summoned Lily in the blue basement light. Dig deeper, he urged. See what's inside.

"Yes," replies Lily, rising from the table and leaving the kitchen. After a moment, the front door opens then closes. I move to the living room and part the curtains. Without a coat, Lily passes slowly beneath a slate sky, between the frosted yards.

The house has to tell me something that Lily can't or won't. I open the door to our parents' room. Obviously, Lily hasn't made it her own; the wide mattress below the spread lacks linen. Nothing litters the dressing table; the closets and bureau prove bare. The adjacent bathroom contains toothbrush and paste, soap and towel. The medicine chest holds several full vials of pills, with a prescription made out to Lily several years ago. Chlorpromazine. Across the hall, Lily's old room is uncluttered as a nun's; even during her childhood, it lacked girlish touches. The narrow bed is neatly made. A Bible rests on the night table. One drawer contains underwear; like the closets, the rest are empty. Not even a small white valise, locked tight, lurks anywhere.

Wandering back to the living room, I realize with fresh force that it has no television or music system, no framed photographs or magazines or books. A small radio perches on the mantel. I discover that it is tuned to static; the buzzing seems to rise in volume inside me. It says that these curtains upon the street are never opened. The telephone and doorbell rarely ring. My sister wears the same clothes and eats the same bland food each day, and late at night walks to the same dark place.

She lives simply, that's all. Not everyone hoards old photographs and love letters, torn ticket stubs and tattered maps. Lily exists on a monthly government cheque that is probably not enough. She can't afford sleek machines and the latest gadgets and an extra pair of shoes. Apparently, she no longer takes what she needs. Or no longer needs.

I move toward the old-fashioned rotary telephone. Aunt Madeleine expects me to visit today. In her house by the river, we will sip tea and nibble cake and skim lightly over the past and present. Lily will be mentioned cautiously, if at all. We will visit Ardis's grave in the cemetery where my uncle also shivers. We will drop in on Dorothy and Kay, end up playing dice and cards for change. (When I went out into the world at sixteen, the single piece of advice offered me, by Dorothy, was to bring a deck of cards along: everyone likes to play; it's the best way to meet people; you'll never be lonely.) I'll catch my aunts peering at me sideways for clues to how their younger brother would have looked as an adult. I won't ask them if they remember the murder of a child more than twenty years ago. I know their resentful answer already. Children have never been murdered in Brale, B.C.

"This way," she says over her shoulder, walking quickly. Where are we going, Lily? She won't wait for me, I know. I hurry to follow her across the highway and through brush on the mountain's base. Lily threads her way surely up the lower slope. Her breath puffs signals that vanish before I can read them.

My sister stops in a narrow gully and bows her head toward the ground.

What is it?

I don't want to see, don't want to know.

"Look," says Lily.

A boy. There's something wrong with him. He's wearing only running shoes and socks. The left shoe is torn at the toe; green peeks out. It's cold, he should be dressed, why didn't we bring him a shirt and pants? My drawers are filled with clothes that would fit him, he's the same size and shape as me, nine or ten or a stunted twelve.

Something else is wrong. His throat shouldn't look like that.

A second, messy mouth. Torn lips caked with rust.

"Who is he?" I ask Lily. I don't recognize him. I haven't seen him among the boys who yelp like wild dogs across the schoolyard. Maybe he goes to the Catholic school with the Italians, lives up in the Gulch or down in one of the shacks on the river flats.

"His name is Billy," says my sister, poking his stomach with a stick.

His hands curl around something that isn't there. His legs twist at odd angles and dirt sticks to his white chest. He stares at Lily as she jabs the stick. He won't close his eyes, he won't cry. His lips are blue. He must have been eating berries, no, that's not right, berries don't grow on the mountain in November, we slather their juice in July.

"He doesn't feel anything." Lily drops the stick. She turns and faces me.

"He's mine," she says.

I bend over the boy and touch his face. Cold skin tingles my hand.

"It's going to snow," Lily says behind me. "It's going to get dark."

"Billy," I breathe. "It's time to go home."

After my walk from Aunt Madeleine's, the house seems very warm. It feels empty, though something is baking in the oven.

A muffled thud sounds from below. Steps ascend the stairs. Lily walks past me and opens the oven. "Greetings from the aunts," I say, attempting lightness. Silent, Lily peers into the dark cave barred with glowing light.

Downstairs, I throw my coat onto MJ's bed, where the few contents of my suitcase are strewn. I start to leave the room, turn back. Is something different about the things on the bed? In their appearance? Arrangement? The book I brought Lily is gone. I search the space, even kneel to look beneath the bed, without success.

"It's time to eat," Lily calls down the stairs.

We have the same supper as the night before. I suggest we see the movie at the Royal Theatre. "We'll sit in the front row," I propose. "It wouldn't surprise me if John Wayne still exterminates Indians on that screen. My treat."

Lily declines. "It's going to snow," she says. As she clears the kitchen, again refusing help, I feel as if I have sat in this room every evening of my life, as if I have never gone away. There has been only a single supper and a single evening. Long ago, time stopped, stiffened, froze.

Before Lily can finish at the sink, I move to the living room and turn the radio on. I fiddle with the dial until I find the CBC. Voices cant about Quebec. Perhaps Lily will settle on the opposite couch; even if we don't talk, that would be something, a start. Water runs in the bathroom down the hall. Lily enters the living room, walks to the radio, turns it off. Before I can speak, she has left the room. Her bedroom door closes.

I can't remain in this silent house. I slip on my coat and step outside. Cold jabs me awake. Lily's window is dark and the empty street is quiet. I move past curtained squares that glow with yellow light, leak cancer from television screens. Lily, is it going to snow?

"Yes," she says in 1972, parting the curtains and looking into the dark street. Snow is late this year. Though Brale stores preen with Christmas decorations, the ground remains naked. "He's still there."

I haven't been back to the gully since Lily showed me what it holds. "Stay away," she has warned, sidling up beside me. In the schoolyard I study the shouting boys, puzzle whether one is missing after all. Maybe Billy was here all along, maybe I didn't notice him before. His parents must be looking for him, they must know he is lost. His toys must wait for his hands to fold around them. He must shiver where he lies. I still want to bring him clothes, but I'm afraid. There was something the matter with him, something more than blue berries and a second throat, I can't remember.

"Don't tell," says Lily, dropping the curtain.

When she slips from the house, I know where she is going now. She sits on a flat rock near Billy and tells him things she won't tell me, describes what is locked in the white valise at the back of her closet. He will never betray her secrets; my uncle won't reveal mine.

Down in the furnace room, at the warmest part of the house, I coil in my hiding place. My uncle swallowed too much smoke when he was twelve. The Christmas tree caught fire, there was something wrong with the wires of its lights. The boy tried to crawl through the smoke, it was thick and white, he couldn't get out. His can of marbles sighs from the corner; his hockey sticks stir the shadows. My pencil presses against the pad of paper I have taken from Mitch's study. "Dear Jesus," I print. Dig deeper, my uncle whispers. There is something different about his voice. My uncle sounds like Billy now. Dig harder, he pleads. I press the pencil until there is only a hole where Jesus was.

I can't find the gully in the dark. Dear Jesus, it's cold. Stumbling across loose rock, I wonder if the features of this slope have changed since my childhood, altered as though a million years of weather have done their work. Or has sly memory played another of its tricks? "It was just a game," Lily told me in January that year. "He was just pretending. Billy lives up on Shaver's Bench. He goes to the park there all the time. He's probably there right now. We just wanted to see how your face would look." His face looked pale and thin; a smudge of dirt clung to his risen ribs. I saw the shoe with the hole in the toe and a clue of green sock so I wouldn't see something else. As winter passed, my memory of Billy froze into a picture of my uncle in my mind. The same face. Speaking shadows in the furnace room turned muffled, then mute. Only the deepfreeze hummed. He was silenced so he would never tell.

Lily walks quickly toward the mountain through the snow that finally falls. I don't think she knows I am behind her, at a quiet distance, until she stops and turns. "Don't follow," she calls, standing still, becoming white. The snow will bury Billy until spring. It's too heavy and thick, he can't dig himself out from the hole where Jesus was. I retrace a dozen steps; my trail has already been covered. I stop to look where Lily stood a moment ago. A shape of darkness moves through falling flakes. The white curtain closes, the white valise snaps shut. Billy's heart beats against my chest, hammers the cage of bone. Let me out, let me out.

Falling, no longer a nimble child, I grunt. A small, sharp stone presses into my spine. I can feel it, Lily. My hands curl as the sky begins to shred white scraps of a letter from Jesus. Something like glass glints over the earth; a shape of darkness breathes nearby. I try and fail to close my eyes against the intent face above me. The puffy features. A white blanket covers me with warm weight. I'll never tell, Lily. My blue lips will never ask why.

Snow won't stop falling through the past. It fills the hole as quickly as I can dig, forbids me to find the face. I can't reach Billy. Dig harder, he calls up to me. Dig faster. Dig.

The house on Aster Drive hovers in darkness amid descending snow, though I left the living room lit. My iced feet feel their way quietly down the hall and stairs. This way, Billy. In the black hole, I fumble for the edge of a bed. Objects fall to the floor as I pull back covers. We've climbed into MJ's abandoned bed instead of mine. It feels the same. Billy's skin feels as cold as mine. We shiver in synchronization, chatter teeth in tune until dawn.

At morning, silver light gleans the kitchen. The snow has stopped. Six white inches conceal the features of the landscape. The blanched bones of the maple rise from the backyard, foreground to black and white mountain.

A cup of coffee rests on the table. My dipped finger discovers cold, dark liquid.

"Lily?" I call. My unanswered voice sounds thin and frightened as a child's.

Let's go, he says. Hurry, he urges.

My suitcase is packed. Should I leave a note? Dear Jesus ... Fresh footprints lead from the front door, bend in the direction of the mountain. Shivering, I stall. My feet start to follow my sister's trail, then turn the other way. Toward downtown Brale and the bus that will carry me back to the cabin on the lake.

The fire in my stove has gone out and the cabin is cold. Beyond my wall of windows, the small ferry still floats across a black hole yawning between white shores. Still pursues the endless back and forth. On the farther side, lights from scattered cabins peer down into liquid darkness, seek the contents of its depths. Steam rises through the falling snow, from the lake, as someone down there sighs.

The receiver in my hand is warm. How many days have passed since my telephone has rung? Since my voice has spoken? My lips kissed? I glance around the cabin. After four months, it still looks unknown. There is no television or music system. No framed photographs or sleek machines or glossy magazines. Only a few pieces of shabby furniture left behind by previous tenants. I don't hold a job or own a car. My clothes are washed in the sink, hung to dry on a string above the stove. Taking what I need for warmth, I steal wood from distant neighbors. There is no money to buy a cord of larch for the stove, curtains for the windows. I am exposed in this cabin hugged from behind by brush and cottonwoods and ponderosa pine but in front perched boldly upon the shore. Anyone driving on or off the ferry can see inside. "He's different," people have begun to mutter.

How and why have I ended up in this flimsy structure, this unlikely location? I sense I am experiencing someone else's life. My own existence has ended; this is afterlife, though the empty shell of self still sings. In some indeterminate season, the source of my ghost wanders the clearing above Lovers' Lane, hand in hand with my uncle among berries and thistles and weeds, up where the cold wind blows.

I dial Lily's number. A measured sound fills my ear. He was raped and killed and left upon a mountain. Once, searching the slope for pussy willows during the following spring, I found myself by accident in that narrow gully. Not even a pair of running shoes remained there after the April thaw. "You lied. He doesn't play on Shaver's Bench. Where did he go?" I asked Lily, who had turned more silent that season. Inside a locked white valise, she was already storing razor blades and pills, with other secret things. My sister didn't answer me, or even turn her face toward my question, as if its sound had failed to reach her.

Is it possible? In a small town, children are apt to hear disturbing news that adults might try to keep secret. The sexual murder of a boy would have filled *The Brale Daily Times*. The town would have bristled with panic, shivered with fear. Doors would have been locked at night. The park and other places where children play would have been deserted after dark. Uniformed men would have combed the mountain and dragged the river until they found a body. They would have knocked on every door on Aster Drive, seen the white valise at the back of Lily's closet, discovered the green sock inside.

A sound like nails of fingers scrapes against the window at the back of the cabin. Or it's just a branch. I've been here too long already. It's time to leave. I can no longer share the cold with you. Donald. Billy. Whoever you are. My shell of self must seek warm climate again.

Snow shakes steadily through the dark; the cabin roof groans beneath its weight. The buzzing in my ear persists, swells in volume. I glance at my watch. Is it too late, Lily? Ringing violates the house on Aster Drive. It won't stop until I put the receiver to rest or until my sister disconnects the cord. I never told, Lily. I never asked who, I never asked why.

Phantasmagoria

They say that you were just a dream, but now the night is over. At chill dawn I waken once more in the cabin on the lake, with pines pressed behind and the meadow farther back. There is the shape of your head indented upon the pillow, the scent of your last cigarette stale in the air. Night turned traitor, inhaled, and held its breath while you stole away, while I slept unaware.

If I believed them, we never scattered yellow leaves on the road to Redfish Creek or rowed the boat to Sunshine Bay to drink wine upon the midnight cliff. I search drawers and corners and beneath the bed for proof of your presence. Where are your shirts that furled within the closet, the razor rusting beside the sink? All evidence has been immaculately removed (by you?), and now with insistent voices empty space demands to be filled. You were here, I know—even as they repeat that imagination plays pranks and desire conjures phantoms that hover like mist above cold water before they fade. I remember that you never said you'd stay.

The long grass stiffens with frost and the kettle steams upon the stove and a boomerang of birds slides above the slate lake. Sometimes the damp morning earth betrays spoor of prowling through the dark. Claws, hooves, paws.

So at night I turn the pages of my books and hear the ferry cross back and forth nearby, connecting this side to the other. Tomorrow I will see you standing on the farther shore, shrunken by distance into anyone at all, dissolved into blue and green and gray, reflected upon the still water. And I will glimpse you walking through the woods above the old man's farm. You turn once to glance behind, then continue toward the clearing where we lay in tall weeds through summer afternoons languid with bees. Even now I know the shape and size and texture of the muscles that strode your legs from me. From a distance well-intentioned neighbors arrive at noon to say that I will soon forget, or will dream a new lover in the night.

Each week darkness arrives earlier and the snow-line lowers. A descending lake exposes small stones that were concealed by water before. Already it is winter, and summer people have retreated into town. Cabins are locked tight; they twitch with ghosts. We listen for the last train to whistle above the water, we split enough wood to warm us from November until March. There is coffee in the morning, a candle for the night. The refrigerator buzzes. Mice rattle between the walls.

Perhaps your voice draws me out this afternoon, and I find myself on the point beyond the wooden bridge.

I realize that I've been here before. I know this landscape that you are coming back to breathe with me. In the meantime, another Kokanee wind sweeps down the valley and my warm breath puffs above Lovers' Lane. Bears curl in safe, dark caves and deer descend the mountains in search of food beneath the snow.

PART THREE

After the Glitter and the Rouge

*"After the glitter and the rouge
There's nothing left to lose
And everything to win
The world, you feel it spin
The music starts again
It's time to let it in
Another dance begins
After the glitter and the rouge"*
—PATRICK ROSCOE
"AFTER THE GLITTER AND THE ROUGE"

Honey

They took me away from Honey, they said she was unfit. That was the end of the two of us on the Jupiter Circuit, orbiting together between Tacoma and Portland, Seattle and Spokane. All the rooms above the bars where Honey danced her golden self before men hungry for something sweet beyond their reach. "We're troupers," she'd say each time we unpacked old things and spread them around to make every place like home. *Live Girls!* stuttered bright letters I learned to read outside those hotel rooms at six. For eight years I listened to some dangerous heart beat below, *boom boom*, while in the musty bed I waited for Honey to finish her last show. Then she floated upstairs with Diamond Lil, an aging star, huffing at her heels. There was ice down the hall for sticky drinks, there was Lil becoming blurred and calling me her Little Ladykiller as I fought to stay awake. No life for a boy, they said; it was all the life I knew. Or sometimes late a man would trail Honey's sweetness into the room; she was always a little breathless then, fixing me a bathtub bed until the man quit making noise and the door clicked goodbye, so long. "He's gone," Honey breathed above me in fresh perfume, in her silver robe. That was when we would curl before the window and watch drunks fall to prayerful knees in the street below, see colored lights shake scared when it rained. "This isn't so bad," Honey might say between a sigh and a yawn, a blue pill and a red. Tomorrow we could sleep all day, tomorrow we could sip thick milkshakes in cafés. Lil stitching a million sequins onto costumes, Honey swaying before the speckled mirror, being sad on Sunday: all these things I would first try to remember, then try to forget. How at the Greyhound station Honey wrapped her smooth scent around me one last time. "I could never change enough to please them," she said, flicking yellow hair from the messed makeup around her eyes, taking one step back to look at me once more. She held my arms so tight, she left red marks that would fade too soon. "You'll run away from Ruth like I did," she promised quickly; then her heels tapped away, my bus started north. *Miss you like crazy*, read the first postcard I received at the trailer on the outskirts of Brale where I came to stay with Ruth. "Out of sight, out of mind," muttered the old woman when I asked why there was no second or third card from her daughter, my mother. Ruth scrubbed the trailer some more, it was always too small, she could never get it clean, boys were dirty. So she gave up again, fixed herself another drink during the commercials, told me to go play out. Behind the trailer was a partly cleared field dotted with stumps, weeds, rusted machinery. On blond afternoons bees buzzed there, nothing better to do; later Jupiter would rise from darkness, float beyond my reach. One stump was hollow, bees flew in and out of its secret space. Honey was inside. I reached to take some for myself, the stinging started, welts rose like a red constellation upon my skin. It hurt until the world turned once. In September school would start; then other things would happen.

The Real Truth

For a long time there was nothing to reach out and touch to know the real truth when Ruth swore she'd never heard of anyone called Honey, in a high mocking tone spit out the syllables like something tasting bad, what kind of whore's name was that? There was only how I remembered Honey's voice sounded telling me about Eureka, California, while we curled close on the fire escape overlooking Spokane or above the bar in Bellingham. The way it turned scratchy and rough in the Greyhound station when she wouldn't say goodbye, this was only adieu until we reunited in Eureka, OK? Beside us Diamond Lil, always the wise sidekick, shook her experienced head, swayed some more upon her heels. "It isn't right, it isn't right," she kept repeating like a prayer, kissing another cigarette pink then squashing its end like a burning beetle beneath her toe. A cardboard suitcase decorated with six shiny stars rode with me on the bus north, across the border to Canada, when they took me away from Honey and Diamond Lil and my only life till eight. Inside were some clothes and a photo Honey made me promise not to lose. You could touch our paper features, feel us together in the arcade booth. Making funny faces and wearing our favorite hats as quarters fed the hungry slot, during the pop hiss flash. Plus Diamond Lil gave me one of her eight-by-tens from way back when, the good old days when stripping meant show business and dancers were entertainers, smiling coy with her boas and feathers, the stilettos and the big bouffant. Also a plastic whistle from a Jupiter dancer named Jewel. "Just blow when you want me," she liked to pucker and wink beneath her Bacall bangs. A Cracker Jack ring from the sad one named Star who Harry was always advising to sell it sweetheart with a smile. Just things you could touch to make you think of other things that weren't there. "Cheap goods," muttered Ruth, pursing her mouth and unpacking the suitcase when I arrived at the trailer on the outskirts of Brale. "Cheap as cheap." The next morning everything but the clothes was gone. I found the empty suitcase out in the field later on, blistered and warped by the sun and the rain, hidden among those tall weeds that scratched. The six green stars were no longer shiny but now each faded and sad like Star. I never learned what happened to the photos, the whistle, the ring. "What're you talking about?" demanded Ruth when I wondered. "Wake up, kid. You've been dreaming again." Everything I remembered was apparently a lie; those endless identical gyrations of the Jupiter Circuit across Washington and Oregon had never been. See, you couldn't prove that once-upon-a time before Brale, B.C. Not rub it between your fingers, not relearn its texture. Something gritty and smooth at once like sand in the sheets at Salem. When Ruth took her bottle to bed, I would wander from the trailer, lose its lone light to distance, allow the dark to touch me everywhere. Wind shoved down the mountain, pushed a smell of rust across the river. Slowly the glitter and the rouge of before receded, Diamond Lil's sequined shape shimmied out of sight. Now was separated by a border from then; bygone Eugene and Olympia belonged to the map of another country and not to me. All those cities where Honey still danced moved far away as stars in the big black sky above the stumps, the brush, the thorns. A boat drifted up there, too. My daddy floated between Jupiter and Venus, traced circles among the constellations, orbited a sickle moon. His sailor cry sounded clearer than the crickets, closer than the owl up in the twisted oak. He was still a child, Honey said, just turned eighteen. Another tall boy on a three-day pass/Too far from home, he stumbled in to see her dance./He never said he'd stay. So how could he know I breathed, folded inside such dreams, while Ruth's TV snowed static through another winter and time scuffed by. Drop a curl of bark into the Columbia, cold current pulls it south toward Spokane where Honey always liked the cowboys, over from Idaho on a dare, their faces frank or sort of shy. See, the Circuit was that unwavering, its rotation so fixed I could still be sure where Honey headlined this week, when it was on to Walla Walla again. You didn't need an itinerary tucked in your pocket or beneath the pillow to know. And not a postcard to learn the news about miss you, love you, wish you were here. The lipstick kiss for a signature, sure. How one night I realized something had happened to Honey: her lilt no longer lifted to meet Daddy's high ahoy inside my head. Abruptly the air around me lacked the one sweet arrangement of ions—insinuating as any aroma, subtle as some pherome—that from the very beginning, even despite miles and months, had always fed my blood.

Now my lungs inhaled a thinner, flatter element instead; my tongue tasted the zinc puffing from the smelter stacks like Lil's cigarettes in the downriver distance. Maybe Honey and me would never meet up in Eureka, California, some day after all. Maybe she did her bump and grind in Heaven now, burlesqued with stagestruck ghosts above. Down here, everything was holding breath; more than ever it was only longing. In Portland or Tacoma, Diamond Lil had to laugh with just Jack Daniel's, or else her sad pal Jimmy Beam, about the weirdos and the creeps who filled the blackness before the stage, shifted tensely beyond the spotlight's glare, unseen. For years Honey had sensed a bad number out there, the unluckiest one of all, anxious to stop her dance for good. She could almost glimpse his face if the blue pill didn't work at five a.m.; that was when she would lullaby to me about Eureka or discuss the sailor until light. After I was ten, it got darker. Ruth stuffed cardboard over the trailer windows for insulation; the next spring she wouldn't take it down, said perverts liked to gawk at her, the curtains weren't enough. At the end of the dirt road, across the frozen mud beyond the ditch, the school bus jounced by again. River kids flattened features against the windows; their glassy eyes slid out of sight. They liked to caw *Yank go home* across the playground if I was there, if Ruth didn't keep me home because Sodom and Gomorrah ruled the classroom and I didn't need to learn more lies. "Filth begets filth," Ruth fretted in her gumboots before I learned not to mention Honey anymore. Her stick poked into the burning barrel, turned the trash, stirred sparks. "Flesh and fornication." She brooded aloud about dirty boys more often as I got older; the ragged wind flapped her complaints like flags. It was always the stink, the stink of sin, enough to make you sick. No wonder her throat retched vomit, the poison needed to get out. A rank pool of everything gone wrong beside the couch at dawn. A sharp, angry language, almost English, in the dark. In the end we couldn't have the trailer lights on much; it would only attract attention. That social worker and her fellow spies snooped plenty as it was, there was an abundance of Satan's interfering agents around. Beelzebub buzzed secret code through telephone wires strung above the road to town, belched smoke signals from the smelter stacks. Something dirty over there in the sky. Ruth gurgled another prayer to her own sweet Savior until *damn it to hell* the bottle knocked over again. Scotch stained more thin pages of the Bible, soiled the skimpy trailer air. The wrong way things were, it made you picture an abandoned car rusting in some February field. I wasn't old enough to find my fantasy, to discover the magic door leading to how it ought to be: the way to all Eurekas. If I waited, one day when I was thirteen, my daddy's call would reach out and pull me to the cities by the sea. Where late at night I'd prowl the harbor, in a tavern full of tars hope to find a hungry touch was finally his. I would lick away the anchor Honey said was tattooed on his shoulder, the left or was it the right. (Who can recall/that long ago, it was back so far/when Diamond Lil was still a reigning star.) I would love and not forget his salty lips, I would slide inside his gap-toothed grin. Waken to receive his squint, sometimes blue and sometimes green, just like the sea we'd sail across, so far from Ruth slurring to the sandman, from cramped space trying to squeeze my dreams. "Hold on," counseled Honey in my heart. "Sustain." To pass the time until my turn came to abandon Brale like she had before, I strung shiny sounds into a necklace in the night; names of strippers we'd trooped with sparkled the dark like sequins. Brandy, Crystal, Ruby. Champagne, Jewel, Star. Maybe people would say those weren't their real names. Maybe Diamond Lil was just Louise and Honey only Hannah. But I came to believe that what is really true and more than true is always what you wish, how you hope, the way it all must be. Beyond the facts, besides what's black and white, deeper than anything carved in stone: there the real truth shines the color of your stars. Six green planets glittered above the trailer and the wind and the dark. Emerald islands, Honey. Pacific ports of prayer to sail toward during sleep. One day we will waken where we need to be.

Sometimes
a Sailor

Sometimes Honey said he was a sailor
Though still a child, just turned eighteen
Another tall boy on a three-day pass
Too far from home, he stumbled in to see her dance
He never said he'd stay
Love drifts away ...

Sometimes Honey said his eyes were blue
Or else they're green
Just like the sea he sails across
So far from you, too far from me
He doesn't know their shine
Has been reborn in mine ...

Sometimes Honey said who can recall
That long ago, it was back so far
When Diamond Lil was still an aging star
We bumped and ground the world to its knees
Gave a sweet taste of what they need
Life's long striptease ...

One day, Honey do you know, his voice called me
My daddy's arms reached out to me
And drew me to the cities by the sea

Sometimes a Sailor

Where late at night I haunt the harborfront
And hope I'll find their hungry arms are finally his
That salty kiss ...

Tonight, Honey, a sickle moon
Floats in the sky, do you see it too
Way up so high
Just like the one he sails beneath
So far from you, too far from me
He never said he'd stay
Love drifts away ...

Eureka,
California

Until the end I believed that Eureka, California, was part of every prayer you send to Heaven to tell of what means the most on Earth. Maybe that's because Honey had such a way of speaking about where she delivered me to the surprising world. It was more than a backdrop to the famous year she and Diamond Lil temporarily retired from the Jupiter Circuit on my account, and with mixed results reacquainted themselves with civilian life. Afterward, the place served as a setting for each of Honey's poems and psalms. Always on her lips its name sounded less an exclamation ringing out upon an original discovery than the muted murmur that what had once been known and then forgotten was found again.

Less: I see; I understand.

More: I am reminded.

Eureka, I remember.

Sure, I'm coming, said Diamond Lil upon learning about the baby and California. She could take a break from show business, get that shine back in her star. Plus she'd always wished to play the fairy godmother. Maybe for a moment Diamond Lil felt miffed that the father stayed a secret whose face, unlike mine, would not be revealed after nine months; but Honey wasn't going off alone in her condition, not a chance. Right from the start—since finding Honey strung out on speed and spreading in the rough Red Room, since teaching her costumes and music and lights, since paving the way for her to join the Jupiter—Lil had known it would be hell or high water, no questions asked. Though Harry didn't like losing his two headline dancers for so long, with his cigar sulked some over who would fill their star billing, they left Seattle that October on the southbound bus. There were different stories later. Diamond Lil claimed they ended up where they did by accident; their ticket money took them just that far, ten more dollars would have meant another town. According to Honey, she had always wished to experience Eureka, the name had long floated inside her head, and chance was not involved at all.

They found a small wooden house once painted green but now faded almost gray, with a deep front porch that slanted toward the south because everything about the place was old. There was a living room and a kitchen and a bathroom, and two bedrooms with gable windows like curious eyes upstairs beneath the eaves. A real house, Honey repeated on the fire escapes of the hotels that were the only kind of home we'd know afterwards. A backyard with a crooked plum tree and a front yard surrounded by a low wooden fence, also faded green, that tilted this way or that like it couldn't make up its mind. On one side lived a blind old woman who wore her white hair in a long braid down her back and with her fingers read cracked photographs from when she could still see. On the other side was a family with two children, one boy and one girl, who would have become my friends if we'd stayed forever in Eureka, California. They would have lent me their tricycles and invited me to spend Saturdays in a treehouse high among the apple blossoms and the birds.

Honey would tell me about Eureka, California, when I became sad or frightened on the Jupiter Circuit where, six months after I arrived, she and Diamond Lil orbited on stage again. Other girls on the bill helped look after me. Star and Jewel and Crystal changed diapers in G-strings and pasties, shook rattles in stilettos and silver robes. Harry groused he wasn't running a day-care center, then bought me a miniature banjo for my first birthday. Still, sometimes in the hotels funny things would happen that made my heart *boom, boom* like the music in the bar below. That's when Honey's voice placed a soft hand upon my head, reminded me that on the street where we lived in Eureka, California, no one locked their door at night. The children played hopscotch all after-noon on the chipped sidewalk and old people slowly walked arm in arm around the block at evening, and through the cool dark husbands and wives would dance on their front lawn to music from the radio even when it rained. They waltzed over the wet grass, *one* two three, or did the twist beneath the dripping trees.

Honey didn't dance a single step during the whole year she spent in Eureka, California, but slept instead. It was so quiet there she could sleep all night and half the day. Maybe that's why it would feel like a lullaby when Honey told me about the place where you don't need cigarettes and pills even on mean Monday. More things my mother didn't do there: paint her face into a picture for the funny men; strap her feet into tall shoes like stilts that made her sway; pile her blonde hair so high upon her head. She wore a ponytail with a rubber band and learned to click the knitting needles while two blocks away on Main Street in the Rise and Shine Café Diamond Lil worked as a waitress to keep the wolf from the door. This part of the picture she painted with words always made Honey smile: Diamond Lil getting up with grumbles at the crack of dawn for the breakfast shift when she was used to stumbling to bed at that hour; complaining that her arches were falling faster than the rain that sloped past the mountains all winter; moaning that in this two-bit town her sex life was now extinct as any dinosaur. Lil left the Diamond behind on the Jupiter Circuit, along with her sequined costumes and her sex life; for one year she was just Lil who poured coffee and served eggs over easy and asked if you wanted pie with that. She had a uniform of cheerful yellow and low white shoes like a nurse and a name tag with a crooked star dotting the *i*. In the evening she would soak her feet in a basin of warm water that made her sigh how to this gal's eyes the sleaziest stage was starting to look pretty good, never mind the weirdos and the creeps, while instead of scotch Honey sipped a big glass of milk so I'd be strong. If you listened, from the plum tree in the yard an owl would hoot once, twice, three times.

Oh, it was just a tiny town in those days, Honey would recall, as if Eureka, California, had happened so long ago, as if she'd been back there since to see how it had grown big like me. Often I had the plainest feeling that my own eyes witnessed the whole year. I didn't so much hide inside Honey for half the time as sort of hover near her on the slanting porch where she rocked away the hours while radio jingles floated from windows yellow as Lil's uniform, from cars slowed by teenaged boys wanting a look at Honey even when she was heaviest with me. Their horns honked like passing geese. Light from streetlamps had to reach and find its way through leaves of trees that lined the sidewalk, and from the mountain sank the smell of bears bumbling through berries while Honey muttered knit, pearl, knit beneath her breath, worked wool that would keep me warm. Eureka was cool, though it belonged to California; you shivered when fog strayed in from the sea. It reminded Honey of a tall boy's breath made visible by condensation, shapes of unheard words fluttering like salty flags along the shore. We must have paced the sand with the wind in our faces; we surely held a shielding hand above our eyes and at the gray Pacific squinted for sight of his boat. Sometimes late, when all the town was sleeping, Honey slipped from bed and through the quiet streets wandered beneath the same stars he steered by. He was just eighteen, still a child, another frank boy on a three-day pass. In Tacoma, too far from home, he stumbled in to see her dance. He never said he'd stay. Then I was an island floating in Honey's saline sea, turning with her tides. And still the sunshine and the movie stars remained in the distant south, as far away as any sailor. I could see Eureka, California, so clearly when Honey told me about it, I'd think what you remember is any place that has made you happy, even if you were blind.

But once in a while Diamond Lil would say things to make me suspect I was mistaken in my memories of

Eureka, California. Honey was sick as a dog the whole time, Lil would mention. For months after your birth she worried every minute, sat up night after night to watch you sleep. The tips at that greasy spoon were so lousy Yours Truly had to steal from the grocery more than once. There wasn't a decent bar in town where a girl could go for a little drink or two. The neighbors wouldn't talk to us. The roof leaked and it never stopped raining. Don't even ask what I had to do with the land-lord to get us that shack in the first place. Talk about your weirdos and your creeps.

Then I might wonder, while Honey spoke about Eureka, California, if she were really remembering another town instead. I knew how the red pills could make her mix things up. Maybe she was talking in fact about where she had once lived as a little girl in a wooden house painted green but now faded almost gray. While she described the children playing hopscotch and the dancers in the rain, Honey might stare straight before her, as if she were blind as an old woman next door and couldn't see me there beside her on the fire escape above Tacoma or Portland, Seattle or Spokane. Or as if she spoke about long before there was a sailor, long before I found my secret way inside her. "It was just any place," she answered if I asked where she was born. "Any place," echoed the flat voice she used with the funny men who sometimes trailed her sweetness into our room late at night. "It wasn't Eureka, California." She would hardly talk about before the Jupiter Circuit; neither would Diamond Lil, even when the sixth sticky drink made her slur other secrets. After she swallowed a blue pill instead of a red, or when I asked at the wrong time about the sailor, Honey would tell me to shut the fuck up, leave her alone for once, could I please just do that? Then she would disappear from the hotel until the next night's dancing and I would rap my knuckles five times against the wall to invite Diamond Lil to visit from her room next door where as usual she was practicing bumps and grinds before the speckled mirror, fighting off the competition again, young girls were always coming up. "She had to go," the aging star would say about Honey leaving the Carousel Hotel now. Or about her leaving wherever she had lived before becoming something sweet that swayed on the stage beneath the colored lights. Honey didn't have a mother and she didn't have a father. I knew that from the way she held me tight, whispered into my neck, licked my eyes to make me shiver. No one had ever told her about Eureka, California, when she was frightened or sad, I guessed.

Lil shook her head. Upon her face, slathered thickly with cold cream, white as a Kabuki clown, played a pensive expression. Honey wasn't like this before Eureka, she said. So restless, so nervous. Missing cues every night on stage, her mind a million miles away. Sometimes it happens like that. A girl takes a step away from the gig, she can't come back to it with the same feeling. Maybe she recalls what should have stayed forgotten. When Honey came back to the hotel from feeling bad, she would slowly explain that she went to California to have me because she always thought it would be really something to be born there. She couldn't give me a tricycle or a treehouse, but she could give me Eureka, California. Always remember, she would say, painting the picture on her face for the funny men once more, preparing for the next inevitable shimmy and strut. Always remember that no one can ever take Eureka, California, away from you. Could I please just do that?

I tried. After they took me away from Honey, I tried to remember the place where she promised one day we would meet again beneath a crooked plum tree or upon some slanting porch. Once more it would be three of us in Eureka, California. A new kind of three. Not Diamond Lil to make us one more than two but a sailor whose eyes like mine were sometimes blue and sometimes green, and sometimes faded like everything forgotten though, Honey, I promise I tried.

Lucky

You could call her Lucky or you could call her Luke, but never Lucille. That name belonged to a sap who cried and tattled and was frightened of the dark, not to someone who could spend day and night outside in winter without feeling cold, plus run swiftly, climb high, jump far. When I was ten, two years after I was taken from Honey to live with Ruth, Lucky appeared in the brush at the far side of the clearing behind the trailer. The world can be such a sudden place; a door closed for so long opens in a pulse. As soon as they saw her, my eyes understood they had been waiting without knowing it to be filled by just this figure made of sharp angles and brusque lines. How sometimes you realize you're hungry only after taking the first bite. Like that. She was building something from old boards—a fort, it looked like—but stilled when my shoes crunched the frozen grass and weeds. Through narrowed eyes gray as any November sky, she judged whether I were an enemy— or, as she would say, one of Them. At first I thought Them referred to a gang of older country kids; later I realized it meant almost everyone. Maybe I wasn't one of Them because like Lucky I didn't have a winter coat or mittens or such. Maybe because when on Saturday Ruth went into town for a minute that lasted until closing time, locking the door so my dirty hands wouldn't touch her things, Lucky knew I had to crouch against whatever side of the trailer was protected from the wind, shove my hands deep into the heated pits of my arms; or I ranged the fields and thought about warm subjects such as California and Honey's eyes and the way Diamond Lil would laugh like hot chocolate in those rooms above the bars where she and Honey danced. Maybe it was just because that, now camouflaging her fort with brush so They wouldn't detect and destroy it, Lucky asked: "Are you going to help or not?

"Incidentally," she mentioned, "my name was never Lucille."

From the start I called her Lucky instead of Luke. She liked that best, how it fit. Like Billy described the boy I was. ("No," agreed Lucky. "You're not a William and you're definitely not a Bill.") The way all the dancers on the Jupiter Circuit had names that told what they really were; for instance, Ruby and Crystal and Star.

I wondered if she could be someone I had known in another place before. South across the border in Washington or Oregon, any of the Jupiter Circuit cities over there. It was as familiar to witness her smoking her Marlboros or aiming a stream of spit at a difficult target as it had been to watch Honey paint her face before the next show. That happened sometimes. A face across the schoolyard turns and in that movement is a face glimpsed just once through a café window in Tacoma or Eugene. Quick as a camera flash, and the photo stays, unfaded by light, in the album of your heart.

"Over there," she answered when I asked where she lived. One long, thin hand waved vaguely behind her. There were no houses or even trailers in that direction, only partly cleared fields dotted with weeds and stumps and rusted machinery, more clumps of brush and a tumbledown barn, then the bald mountain. I puzzled why I'd never seen Lucky in school or, if she did live nearby, in these fields I roamed whenever Ruth started again about Satan who had turned her precious baby into a whore named Honey, given her a dirty boy like me in return, filth begets filth, sin always stinks, she smelled it on me, get out of here. Soon I had an idea that Lucky had been nearby since my arrival to the outskirts of Brale, B.C. I'd been unable to see her not only because she had this way of blending in with the landscape but because my eyes needed to learn to find her: they weren't wise enough when I was eight and nine, I guessed; my heart hadn't yet taught them how to read many words of the world. Lucky suggested it was because I was busy daydreaming. Herself, she'd seen me lots of times. Following the train tracks by Waneta Junction, climbing the creek up the mountain, hiding in tall summer grass while planets shimmied in the sky. It made me funny to think someone had been watching me when I believed I was alone. I remembered how, during the first year apart from Honey, I thought her eyes could always see me however far away she danced. But that feeling had faded, taking Honey with it.

"I have to go," Lucky announced abruptly, though the fort wasn't finished and light still tried to wash the muddy sky. She didn't say goodbye, so long, meet you tomorrow by the bridge. That wasn't her way, I'd learn. Each time she left you didn't know if you'd see her again in the skirt with the drooping hem—part of a Girl

Guide uniform, though Lucky didn't belong to anything
—that bounced against her bony knees, flapped legs
thin and white and constantly scratched. On her feet
were gumboots with a hole in the left toe; now and then
she would stop and take off the boot to empty water,
later melted snow, that leaked inside. The boots were
too big and she wore no socks. Lucky also had a sweater
that didn't fit, the kind someone's grandmother such as
Ruth might like, brown with yellow buttons, shiny
where sharp elbows poked the wool thin. I watched
Lucky move quickly toward a voice I couldn't hear, slip
past the elderberries at the edge of the next clearing,
disappear. I found out her ears were so much sharper
than mine; they could hear a snake coiling through
grass, a deer at the far side of the field. And she could see
in the dark as though her feet had developed eyes that
allowed her to step quickly and surely even when there
was no path to follow, only unlit stones and roots.
Sometimes she would freeze—in one motion, without
slowing—and push her face toward the wind. Her gray
eyes closed. She was learning what the air carried.
Proofs of unseen presences, scents from far away.
Something in the south, sweet as apples in Oregon.

Maybe it was already getting dark by the time the bus
dropped me at the end of the road after school. In the
trailer Ruth would be changing channels and working
on another bottle while waiting for Dear Jesus to save
her from the filth and trash. It wasn't hard to pass that
lone light, head back where Lucky might be. Like wad-
ing into black water. Even after I learned some of her

places, I could never find Lucky. She always found me. Her way was so quiet, I wouldn't know anyone was near until she stood right there, breathing light and quick from running. Or she'd be a bit farther away, at the edge of what I could see in the dusk, bent near the ground to study tracks left by some brown bear. Without a hello, before I reached her, she was talking. It made me think we had never been apart except in my imagination. "Incidentally," she continued.

I never did learn exactly where Lucky lived, whether she had a mother and a father, some brothers and sisters. There were certain subjects she didn't care to discuss; if I brought one up, she would say I sounded like one of Them. "Twelve," she replied warily, after a minute, when I asked her age. Many things that mattered to Them, like school, were of so little importance to Lucky they didn't exist even incidentally. It could be that was why I wasn't able to picture her in the classroom, with rows of desks and everyone alphabetical, or anywhere in town. She didn't fit with Ruth in my mind at all. They refused to inhabit the same snapshot, shoved each other out of the frame. I knew never to mention Lucky in the trailer because of Ruth's habit of speaking about what counted most, how Honey became that whore. And though she knew where I lived, Lucky wouldn't knock on the trailer door for me. Ruth was only one of Them, not worth our while to talk about even when her hand lifted and made the colored lights dance inside my head. What mattered was smoke rising from a fire we guessed a hobo had left smoldering beside the tumbledown barn. Strange steam that one afternoon rose from the creek as if an invisible housekeeper ironed the water. A raccoon hat Lucky pulled from beneath the broken seat of one of the cars, abandoned and rusted, that littered our landscape. We took turns wearing it like Davy Crockett despite the smell of something gone bad. Lucky had such things hidden far and wide, liked to spread herself around, claimed as her own this area They didn't much want. Suddenly she bent down, pushed some rocks aside, from a shallow hole lifted two wrinkled apples wrapped in dry grass. "Those damn squirrels," she swore when nuts saved for supper were missing from another hiding place. Anyway, thick milk could always be coaxed from Old Man Johnson's bad-tempered cow if you were careful. Slowly I began to understand that all these fields, this entire open space, was where Lucky lived. Picture a big room without walls and only sky for ceiling. Stereo birds, lightbulb stars. Lucky curled beneath the cottonwoods when it rained hardest. She spent the night in a boxcar or in a wrecked Ford or in a tumbledown barn. She slept here or there. It reminded me of following the Jupiter Circuit with Diamond Lil and Honey, those different towns, a new one every week.

Lucky liked shiny things especially, say steelies and a tin whistle and brand-new coins. Whatever caught and gave back light was valuable. "Possession is nine-tenths of the law" went one of her favorite sayings. So you didn't ask where she'd gotten the army knife with seven separate blades that could pry open the door of a boxcar forgotten on the Waneta Junction siding. A blanket and a half-burned candle took up one corner of its splintery floor, plus three comic books starring superheroes who could rescue any being no matter what the danger, save any situation no matter how desperate. "Sort of," she replied when I asked if she'd settled here for the winter. Lucky would answer questions more often now, though every one still made her stiffen as at an alarm.

I found out Lucky didn't go to school because, as she pointed out, the Fathers of Confederation wouldn't do her much good when she became a rodeo girl. She knew how to ride with a saddle, sure, but most often went bareback, the bridle fashioned from binding twine, on one of Old Man Johnson's mangy horses. Lucky had given them names of her own; they sounded like dancers. There was Jewel and Satin and, her favorite, Champagne. In secret they went down to the dam at midnight, galloped along the bank of flat, hard-packed gravel. Her specialty was racing barrels; yet Lucky also had a length of rope, worn as a belt around her waist when not in use, and she could spend hours twirling it above her head. Snaking shapes in the air, capturing stumps in its noose. "Watch this," she bragged, showing me a trick mastered while I'd been learning fractions and capital cities and *je suis, tu es, il est*. The rope floated a circle through the dusk like one of Lucky's smoke rings, snared a fence post gleaming white as Lucky's legs with the first snow of winter. Beneath the bridge, while Lucky discussed Spokane three hundred miles south where there were big rodeos with cash prizes every summer, I tried not to shiver like a sap. If air at once too sour and too sweet from bottles licked my skin inside the trailer, at least it was warmer there. I wondered whether it were getting too cold even for Lucky to live in a room without walls and beneath such frigid sky. I wondered why she didn't find some long pants and a heavy jacket to possess nine-tenths of. Then I understood. That was what a Lucille would have done, not a Lucky or even a Luke.

One Sunday in December Lucky's legs were marked with more than just scratches. The red stripes looked like they'd been drawn evenly on her skin; a few days later, they might have been outlined, just as carefully, with a black crayon. My eyes had missed seeing the real truth before them. Those scratches on Lucky's legs had been something else all along.

"That Lucille is such a sap," said Lucky when she caught me looking. "She doesn't know how to fight back and she doesn't know how to run away. Serves her right, what They do to her."

Lucky began to speak often about Lucille, as if that girl mattered more than incidentally now. The subject made her fretful. She sneered about the sap the same way she did about any of Them; but something else was in her voice, sound behind sound, a river in back of a wind. I learned that Lucille loved sweet things, every kind of candy. If she became a rodeo girl, Lucille would curl her hair, put on makeup, and wear fancy costumes with rhinestones and fringes to barrel race. Of course Lucille was excited that Christmas was almost here; it was just the kind of holiday a sap like her enjoyed most. She adored the colored lights and the carols and the shiny paper that wraps the presents beneath the tree. Lucille was crazy about all that jazz.

"Dance naked?" demanded Lucky in disbelief when I told her about the Jupiter Circuit, how it had brought us to Spokane lots of times but never to a rodeo. "People pay to see that?" As I described Diamond Lil's feathers and boas and fans, then Honey's long blonde hair and high silver heels, Lucky's gray eyes narrowed as if refusing to allow such visions into their sight.

"Well, maybe in the States," she admitted finally as the only possible explanation for naked dancing. In a grudging way, apparently against her will, she asked over and over about the music they swayed to on the stage, about staying upstairs from the bars, about the funny men who sometimes trailed Honey's sweetness into our room late at night. How I'd have to sleep in a bathtub bed until they stopped creaking the big one and the door clicked goodbye, so long, at last he's gone. Lucky needed to ask about such subjects over and again just to express her astonishment and disdain; yet each time I could hear the river behind the wind, its yearning flow.

Lucky's sharp eyes peered south toward the border, Washington that close beyond Waneta Junction. They could see a host of dancers spinning in a spotlight on the other side. A shiver passed across her face, fast as a minnow's dart and flash through water, the same shiver as whenever she noticed the smelter stacks rising above distant Brale. Maybe Lucille almost flickered in her features. I wasn't sure. Before I could decide, Lucky's face had become extra alert, more intent than ever.

Something dropped from her skirt pocket as we skidded through snow to scare bats in the tumbledown barn. I picked up the rag. There was just enough time to unwrap an old lipstick and a little compact before Lucky grabbed. "See? This is exactly what I mean," she spat. "This is Lucille to a T." Her strong arm pitched the things across the fence, that far. They flew like birds then suddenly plummeted to make you think a hunter had taken good aim.

"Unless you wanted them," taunted Lucky, running on toward the barn.

I stole a package of cigarettes from Ruth and a bag of Hersheys from the Kresge's in town. Christmas presents for Lucille as well as for Lucky. I had to leave them where Lucky would just find them, could just claim them. She wasn't a sap who hoped for presents; she could steal whatever she needed, incidentally. On my way to the boxcar at Waneta Junction, I wished for once that Lucky wouldn't find me. I hid the cigarettes and candy beneath her blanket, then sat to read again about the hero who in the best comic book always saves the day. On the inside cover, blank last time I'd looked, someone had been practicing printing. It was like when you're six or using the wrong hand, unsteady as Ruth after a bottle. *Lucky*, it said a hundred times.

I thought how, when we discussed the comic books, Lucky sometimes got the story wrong. That happens, reading just the pictures.

"If there's anything worse than a sap, it's a sneak."

For the first time I heard the voice Lucky used to speak to Them. But I'd seen those marks on her face before, dark against the white. Lucky had explained about learning a new rodeo trick: standing tall on Champagne's back while he trotted, twirling a lasso instead of holding on. It was hard, you fell a hundred times, it didn't hurt.

The face was gone from the open boxcar door. I didn't see Lucky during the next days. Maybe there was the flash of a Girl Guide skirt through those trees. The crunch of gumboots on snow. Two alert eyes across the air's invisible wall.

On Christmas morning Ruth gurgled with the empty bottle cradled like a precious baby in her sleeping arms. I searched the trailer in case some presents were hidden anywhere, then stepped outside. Cigarettes and candies were sprinkled over the snow, as if they'd fallen out of the sky, dropped from a sleigh speeding through the air. I dumped them into the barrel where Ruth liked to stir the smoking contents with a stick, mutter about filth and trash, trash and filth.

Lucky still found me after that, but less often. I could wait beneath the bridge, by the boxcar or inside the tumbledown barn for hours without anyone showing up. Then one day she appeared again. But now Lucky spoke as if I were incidental, looked intently toward the trees like her words were really meant for them. What was different besides was how Lucky's shiver at the sight of the distant smelter looked more like a shudder and how Lucille never came up at all, as if she'd died before she was born. But without asking about the dancing there, Lucky mentioned Spokane more often. You could ride to the rodeos in the back of a truck, she mused. Anyone could cross the border beyond Waneta Junction in the summer; then only college kids worked at the little building with the gate across the road. You just walked around when the dopes weren't looking. Once she showed me an American quarter she'd saved though it didn't shine brand new. "It's worth more," Lucky said, suggesting you could buy anything you wanted with it, quantities of cowgirl costumes with rhinestones and fancy fringes everywhere. I didn't like to hear so much about Spokane, even about the rodeos anymore. It picked the scab on my heart to remember. The Paradise Hotel where we'd ended up for one week every second month. That desk clerk with the left eye of glass and his wooden leg. Lonesome miners over from Idaho for a good time on the weekend. How Honey appeared as through a window of thick, foggy glass these days. You could wave and call but she didn't see you, didn't hear.

Lucky's blanket, candle and comic books were gone from the boxcar. I couldn't find them in the tumble-down barn or in one of the wrecked Fords. It was hard to say where she slept while January turned colder. Her eyes wouldn't let me ask. "This damn smoker's cough," she complained as it got worse and worse. It was brown where she spit on the snow. Her hardest rodeo trick, standing on Champagne's back without holding on, didn't get better either. She fell more often than before, it looked like from her face. Now when she said she had to go and moved out of sight, I tried to follow her tracks in the snow. Always at a certain point they would suddenly trace tight circles that crossed each other in confusion without one clear path leading from the maze. I bent over the puzzle, words I should have known how to read, then lifted my head at a snort of laughter.

"Hurry up," said Ruth when I came home from school one day in February.

We were moving into town right now. It was a house. I'd heard about the place on Columbia Avenue, how the City had stolen it from Ruth the way everything was stolen from her. Somehow it was hers again. She wore a tight, satisfied smile, like she'd pulled a good trick.

Old Man Johnson's truck was already loaded up with Ruth's things, all her treasures my dirty hands were never allowed to touch. There wasn't time to run to Lucky's places to say goodbye if she were there. I couldn't even dart beneath the bridge where I'd buried three things Honey had made me promise never to lose, three things Ruth missed when she burned the contents of the cardboard suitcase that came with me from the south.

Town was just five miles away, but everything was different beneath the smelter hill. Smoke from the tall stacks made my throat burn, my eyes itch. I couldn't see as good as before; it was harder to make out the real truth of things. How Honey had once been a girl in this old house with the slanting porch and peeling paint and the missing front step. Her room above the porch was locked; the door wouldn't pry open with the army knife I'd taken nine-tenths possession of from the Kresge's on Cedar Avenue. I slept on a cot in Ruth's room, she liked to keep an eye on me these days. That was different, too. Before, she never minded if I were out all hours in the fields with Lucky trying to trap rabbits with a snare of string. "Why'd you bother coming back?" she'd ask when I came through the trailer door at last. "Since you're going to leave like that slut in the end." Now I had ten minutes to make it home from school or else.

For the first few weeks at Columbia Avenue Ruth didn't buy bottles. We cleaned the filth and trash, scoured the stink of a slut from the floors and walls. Then it started again. Jack Daniel's always hanging around to make Ruth sick and sad, to lock me in the closet with the coats. Ruth praying to Dear Jesus on the other side of the door, the colored lights dancing in my head when it finally opened and her hand lifted. I tried to remember that all this was incidental. That the world was one big place without walls. Sky for ceiling, lightbulb stars.

I had to go to another school, it was closer. The rest of the kids were still always on the far side of the playground yelling *Yank go home*. One recess I thought I saw Lucky over there by the swings. I rubbed my itchy eyes, tried to see better. Same sharp face, same thin white legs, those flat gray eyes. Though March was still cold, she didn't wear a coat or mittens or scarf.

"Lily," called a boy about my age and size. As they turned to him, the girl's eyes saw me. They narrowed, she frowned. Then she ran away.

Three times, after the snow began to melt, I caught the schoolbus out to Waneta Junction as if I still lived in the trailer at the end of the dirt road. An old man and woman had moved into the place. I saw her wandering across the field with a rope tied to her wrist, the other end dragging on the ground. "Marie," the old man called after her, over the thistles. "Marie," he called again when she didn't turn. She wasn't wearing any shoes, not even ones with a hole in the left toe.

I waited for Lucky in the same places as before. A wrecked Ford, a boxcar, a tumbledown barn. There were no signs anyone visited them anymore. Lucky refused to emerge out of the air. Now she really believed I was one of Them, I guessed.

"Lucky," I called loud as I could.

It sounded like a question, something doubtful, unsure of summoning what was good and hoped for in the world.

"Luke," I tried.

"Lucille."

She wouldn't come at a call, I knew that. "Are you insane?" she'd asked the only time I tried, before knowing her well. "Do you want Them to hear?"

It was dark and late by the time I walked back to Brale. There was hell to pay. William was too weak, he couldn't fight back or run away, he deserved what he got. The second time was worse than the first, like falling from a horse in the sky. I had to stay home from school for a week so it wouldn't show. That was when I began to think about the sailor Honey had said was my father sometimes. He came to me on account of the tall man who lived down the street. His eyes were blue or green from squinting at the sea. His back was strong from pulling up the heavy anchor. Another man, also young and tall, lived in the same house. They were worse than filth and trash, said Ruth. In the closet, I pictured them and thought I heard my daddy's voice calling from the cities by the sea, waves behind a wind.

I knew I could go out to the fields to look for Lucky just once more before Ruth made sure I never went there again. Before I left Brale for good the way Honey had, how she promised one day I would. The last time had to count. I had to plan carefully while Ruth's marks faded from my skin like memories of a mother.

All the snow had melted. The creek was loud and fast with run-off from the mountain. The air felt almost warm at four o'clock. Soon it would be summer, time for rodeos in Spokane. I waited in Lucky's places just in case, though I didn't hope she would really appear. I thought maybe it would be Lucille or, who knows why, a girl named Lily.

What had been buried beneath the bridge was gone. They weren't even shiny, they were just three things.

When it started to get dark, I walked to Lucky's favorite spot for practicing rope tricks. A clear patch of ground behind the tumbledown barn where once, we guessed, a corral had contained dancing horses. The world twirled around like a lasso in the air as I bent to scratch big letters with a stick into the ground.

"Incidentally," I printed as neatly as I could. "I'll never be one of Them," I wrote, though knowing Lucky couldn't read my promise.

After the Glitter
and the Rouge

"At least it's only the one side," said Diamond Lil, the last of the old-time strippers, appearing out of the pale Portland sunlight to take Honey from the hospital. The doctors had only been able to do so much, the grafts hadn't taken exactly as hoped; there were certain complications, the men in white explained. Lil's gaze refused to flinch. Blue bodies on the bathroom floor: she'd witnessed worse. Nothing to do but unsnap an elastic from a roll of twenties and settle the bill and hand Honey dark glasses. Then the marquee outside the Golden Arms made a promise that got bigger as the cab drew nearer: *Live Girls!* Honey watched the driver try to keep his eyes from the rearview mirror; before people had stared for another reason. "Everything heals," Lil glossed over later in their room, expertly packing feathers and boas and fans, preparing to follow the Jupiter Circuit on to Eugene one more time. They drank a last champagne toast, to the tune of shattered glass vowed they'd work together again, hell or high water. "Maybe a mask, a bit of classy kink," Lil mused, snapping her makeup case shut and sealing the possibility tight inside, once more hardening herself to the fact that she was pushing forty like it was a boulder you had to heave uphill or else be crushed. The Circuit was unaffected by accidents; its orbit would bring Lil back this way again. They'd bump into one another here or there or in Eureka, California.

Sure they would. Lil laughed thinly at the lies you have to live by, grimaced at sentiment too expensive to buy even on installment. Honey stayed on at the Golden Arms with her costumes and Camels, lotions and pills. Lou let her keep the room for old times' sake. Till the end of the month, kid, you understand. Food ordered in, curtains kept closed, a new face floating in the speckled mirror. One night she tried to see what makeup would do; it only made the left side flame more brightly. Red neon stuttered *Dancing Nightly!* through the curtain, buzzed inside her dreams. Out in the hall complaining batches of new dancers trooped down to the Showroom in stilettos and robes; she knew their dissatisfactions by heart. Rain dropped in straight lines along Centre Avenue and traffic lights changed like the colors of a lost boy's eyes according to what arcade photograph hovers inside your heart. Then quarters were falling into a phone booth slot during the northbound Greyhound's ten-minute stopover in Tacoma. "I'm coming home," she said, after Ruth's thin voice needled through a bad connection. "Frances," she said, knowing then she'd have to forget being Honey. Or Blaze or Star or Crystal.

"Well, it's not pretty" was Ruth's greeting at the screen door Frances had last slammed sixteen years before. "He went," she commented on the subject of the boy they'd taken from Honey and sent to Ruth when he turned eight, heading off questions no one had the right to ask. She'd done nothing wrong, only the best anyone could do. You can't change trash, she'd learned that the first time around. Look where her charity had got her, a whore under her clean roof. Then and now again. She glanced at the single cardboard suitcase, pushed at her wig, went back into the kitchen and made reheated coffee spread bitter fumes. Frances recognized furniture in her old room above the porch, pictured girlhood things she'd left behind cremated in a backyard fire. Heard *slut slut* hissed at sparks and smoke. She unpacked, then balanced on the edge of the bed until that flat accent called up some supper was ready. Soon you knew Ruth went out only to the Safeway and the liquor store, to cash her monthly check. "The house is mine" was her sole volunteered information that summer. The bank had tried to pull a fast one and take it back, she'd been in a trailer out by Waneta Junction for a while there with the boy.

"The same ones as always, I guess," Ruth replied impatiently when Frances couldn't ask how tall Billy had grown by the time he left, where could a boy of fourteen go but across the seas like a sailor whose arms you know a single night before he must be back on board; could ask only who lived next door these days. The smelter had been laying off the last few years, plenty moved away, good riddance to bad rubbish. Still too many dirty dagos in the neighborhood, crowding down from the Gulch with their spaghetti and their pervert Pope.

Frances walked past the old high school, over the bridge, downtown. Not many people around to gawk, none she could recognize; Brale itself appeared unchanged. Same metallic taste to the air, same banks of black slag. Smoke still coughing from the stacks up on the smelter hill. She didn't take more walks after that one time. The doctors had told her to stay out of the sun from now on; she spent the days inside with the TV while Ruth cleaned and carried on a long monologue of complaint. "Greasy Italians," the old woman muttered in the midst of frying meat, boiling up potatoes. "Filthy Wops." They ate early, the afternoon still hot, food steaming the kitchen damp, curling the corners of what you saw. Afterward Ruth went up and closed her bedroom door. There was the clink of the bottle against the glass, the whine of prayers to Jim Beam and Jesus. Frances sat out on the deep front porch; the boards were warped, the gray paint peeling. *I'm your private dancer*, moaned radios of cars cruising Columbia Avenue those summer evenings. Drivers were boys with grandmothers who'd never learned English, with last names like Lorenzo or Catalano. Maybe they were heading down to Gyro Park with gallon jars of papa's homemade wine. After, they'd get brave enough for the cold fast river, try to make it to the flat rocks midstream. That last summer, when she was sixteen, the boys didn't call her Little Orphan Frannie anymore; but Brale girls still didn't trust her. The wine was red and rough, cast-off clothes assumed subtle shapes on the bank, a moon touched the current white. The first time she reached the rocks, Frances knew she'd be gone by fall. "It was an accident," she finally said in September, when Ruth still hadn't asked. She reached for her mother's hand, drew it to where her face was shiny and tight as the scales of a fish. Puckered, pink.

First the doctors then police had explained that he must have planned well in advance. The acid was quite rare, difficult to obtain, used only in specific laboratory experiments. He'd been someone unseen beyond the pink and purple boring into her eyes, one of the hot angry men sending up smoke to cloud the lights, waiting for her next blonde move. She'd felt him out there for years, ever since Lil found her strung out on Seattle speed, spreading in the rough Red Room whenever she could get herself together. "There's more to this business than young pussy, those little girls burn up in a week," said Lil, teaching her costumes and music and lights. Soon they were trading off the headline spot on the Jupiter, doubling up in hotel rooms, living steady and sober and straight. They had their winter in Eureka for the birth of the boy; they had eight years of revolving on the Circuit as three instead of two. After Billy went north, there was something more you couldn't afford to remember, something else to never mention. That hot coal out in the audience glowered greater rage, made her nervous as sixteen again. "I come every time I'm on that stage," joked Lil, herself always staying in after work these days, eyes hungry insects crawling over pages of books, going through one after another like a chain-smoker. Honey would try to force herself, all those nights in Salem or Olympia or Eugene, to sit by the window and sew a million sequins. Wondering which of her moves would make something click in his head, tell him she was the one who had to wake up in a motel room with fire feeding from her face. He'd stop her dancing, he'd make it so the hot lights never dimmed. They'd still sear into her head as on all those staged nights, burning pieces of before into ash and cinder, current like something white wiping away what made her restless. "I don't remember," she said when they asked who he was, how he looked, what took place that night she'd become tired of waiting for it to happen. Afterward she was immediately calm, always peaceful.

She went up to the room above the porch as soon as night cooled. The pear tree used as her midnight ladder before becoming a trap for his paper planes was gnarled and bent outside the window now. Waking with steady heat on her face, she was still on stage, her shadow kept moving on the wall. By the end she could pick clues up blind, close her eyes and feel the difference between red and blue. *When a man loves a woman* and *Misty blue* and the one about the rain against the window: she'd made them all into movement. Downstairs in the dark her fingers found the old piano hadn't been tuned since the last time she'd practiced for her Friday lesson with the teacher with the cats. She'd forgotten how the pieces went, or they'd flattened into something else. Behind her a black shape loomed in the doorway. "I always knew you'd be back," said Ruth, satisfied at last. From now on everything would be quiet and slow.

PART FOUR

The Truth about Love

"I learned the truth at seventeen"
—Janis Ian

"Hay quien muere de amor y no lo sabe"
—Antonio Gala

The Truth
about Love

There is a time bomb concealed somewhere in the minefield of our lives—in your heart, to be precise. I press my ear against your strong, broad chest and listen helplessly to its click. To diffuse this danger would be to dismantle your love, I know: the same mechanism caresses and kills. Steadily the ticking grows louder; sounds swell as that decisive, explosive moment nears when we will be blown into bits, scattered like fireworks through the sky. Sometimes I try to calculate how many weeks or months we have left together, you and me, before you are taken away. (Or are there only days?) Yes, it is you they will handcuff and lock up; but, clearly, we will both pay for your crimes.

How we met, how we fell in love: seas of memory wash inside me, bubble in my blood. They are the same memories cherished by every lover, banal if spoken aloud, gold turned into dross when exposed to objective elements. We do not mention certain moments (our first kiss, for example); anniversaries pass without celebration. No photographs exist to remind me of the time we traveled deep into the desert and slept beneath the stars. That day we climbed a glacier, then built a fire against the cold. Evidence must not be allowed to gather, you have taught me; in the end, it will always be used against us, however innocent it appears. So the presents I gave you at the beginning, before I learned this lesson, you buried in the yard, where they could rot safe from sight, crumble into only ash. And so we do not hold hands while walking together in the street; we offer no proof of ourselves as lovers to the world. Remember: once our very act of love was forbidden, illegal, punishable by imprisonment or worse.

From you I learned the value of silence, the purity of secrets. When you turn to me in darkness, without words, the gesture bears the weight of a thousand similarly unspoken movements, is heavy enough to prevent me from floating into the air. Once more our mute bodies move together. I receive private pleasure when you sigh or moan against your will. If I can make you cry out when you come, I count this as a triumph.

Later I waken in your arms. You are talking in your sleep, mumbling what you dream. I listen carefully, hope you will drop a clue. One word that contains a whole story. A name, some *Rosebud*. Of course I have studied the information concealed inside your wallet. I know the thin data that defines your name and age and place of birth—but little else. Family, former friends and lovers: who were they, what did they mean to you, where are they now? Upon the blank slate of your silence I am free to draw versions of the past that make you who you are today: my man has a thousand distinct histories, a whole horde of buried identities. As I must have for you. I study one alternative then another, according to my mood, my need. No, I do not pretend to know or understand you completely; but my loving imagination can create a dozen approximations of who you really are, and each is dear to me. For this reason, and despite our isolation, we are not lonely. Our multiple selves crowd these tidy rooms: all the boys we once were, all those gap-toothed, grinning ghosts.

These days and nights pass beneath the most ordinary cloak. We waken and go to separate jobs. In evening we share a meal, then stretch before the television, me in your arms or you in mine. We go to the gym and to the movies. Weekends are to clean the house and work in the yard. Domesticity. The telephone does not ring often; our doorbell insists upon silence. Outsiders pose danger, I have come to understand. They would bear witness in court, they would reveal what must stay hidden. As it is, our unknown neighbors will certainly speak to the television cameras upon discovery of your crimes; excited by brief, secondhand celebrity, they will offer mistaken impressions, skewed insights. ("They seemed such nice, quiet young men," those ignorant neighbors will puzzle.) Anyway, I have no wish to share you; we need no one besides each other, I try to tell myself. I can condone your bloody acts for the way each one drives you deeper into only me; we are entangled inextricably within your web of guilt. Where do you leave off, where do I begin? Sometimes, half-asleep, I touch your arm in bed and think it's mine. It is that difficult to discern the line of separation: what you do, what I do.

By now I know the pattern. Twelve or fifteen or twenty days after your last crime you grow restless, distracted, uninterested in making love. You complain of headache, and wear an inward expression as though inside your ears there were a buzzing you must silence any way you can. At our window you stand and search the dark, empty street. Out there is something you need that I can't give you: this is still difficult for me to accept. I wonder what it is I lack, how I could more completely fulfill your needs. (This is when I believe I am as guilty as you, a complete accomplice: I feel the shape and weight of your knife in my hand, see it slice and watch the red ribbons unfurl, share that satisfaction.) As it is I can only sense you build toward dangerous excitement; I become excited by suspense myself. Always I am prepared for the night when you say you wish to go for a drive. "Want company?" I ask—must ask—hoping you will answer yes, hoping we will only drive along the river and observe lights shudder in the water. I must offer you this chance to detour from your violent path, even as I know that altering your route would, in fact, mean leaving me behind.

But you do not want my company, you long to go into the dark night alone. Are you protecting me, preserving my innocence? Or do you selfishly refuse to share your pleasure? You put on your coat and kiss me coldly at the door; already your heart has turned toward the next unknown, unsuspecting victim that waits. I listen to the car's engine turn over at your touch, hear you drive away. Sometimes you are gone several hours, sometimes it is nearly dawn before you return. Then I will not notice the stain of blood on the hem of your jeans, the scratch on your arm hinting that this time there was a struggle. Afterwards you are tired and full of need. There is always heightened passion then; whatever lay between us, separating, has been eliminated. We move urgently toward our brief, false death, then lie together slick with sweat. The scent of crushed blossoms hangs heavy in the air.

Do you suspect I know? There are times, moving above me, when your open eyes confess. You seek my understanding. And when I hold you tighter, grasping the muscles that wielded the knife, this is absolution. My hands stroke forgiveness. *Be careful*, I nearly say the next time you go out alone. *Do it right*. Then while you sleep I check your clothes and shoes for splashes of blood, eradicate a clue you have overlooked. I retrieve the knife from the car's front seat to ensure that it is clean. Press its sharp blade against my throat as though I were both you and your victim at once.

Near the beginning you deliberately dropped a clue, I suspect. You wanted me to know. Through narrowed eyes you watched warily to see how I would react to certain news stories on television. How I would respond to understanding their connection to you. You knew me well enough to be sure I would not telephone the police: such acuteness of intuition has, in part, saved you from discovery until now. Watching those images—the body draped with a white sheet, the sobbing family, the perplexed police—I matched your silence and calmness. Instead of fleeing from you in fear, I stayed to love you with greater fervor. That was the moment we became linked by unbreakable chains. Complete acceptance: this is what we all seek, this is my definition of love.

Details don't interest me. I am not curious to know if it is men or women or children you kill, or why you need them silenced. What you do with the bodies, before and afterwards. If you like to hear them cry, beg, scream. How it feels. What it's like. I respect your secrets. After all, I have secrets of my own.

At first, it's true, I did feel jealous of your victims, of your special relationship with them. How their last earthly vision is of you. That interlocking of your eyes with theirs as they leave the world. How you carve out the shape of their unique destiny with your knife. Such shocking intimacy. But now I know you will always leave them to return to me. They hold your attention only briefly; our exchange lasts far longer than any death scream, any fading pulse.

Why I love you. After you are discovered (and the day draws nearer as surely as the next season) I will be the subject of curiosity, one more psychiatric specimen. They will hound me with questions, they will feed me drugs. Already I prepare for the silence I must maintain to preserve the holiness of our union. *Monster*, they will label you in an attempt to pollute our mutual devotion. Perhaps they will present me with a detailed description of your acts. How you gouge out a victim's eye with your teeth, roll that firm ball in your mouth, bite through its resisting outer layer to the satisfying squish of softness, chew up all the visions this eye has seen. *Inhuman*, they will say, anxious to place your deeds on a plane separate from their own existence, unwilling to admit that in all of us there is the capacity to perform every kind of act, and that these acts, however horrible they appear, may be an expression of the most human emotions such as desire, and hate, and love.

"He is my lover," I will only state. If they can't comprehend what this means, how the word wraps itself around everything you are, they will not be worthy of further information. If they had been just once inside your magic arms, they would not wonder at all. I will scorn them for accepting feeble, legal passion; I will mock their envy of our outsiders' ardor. It is simple to see how they will sensationalize and warp our story; but beneath their outrage will stir some glimpse of the true force of our love; really, this sight will disturb them more deeply than any of your actual crimes. It will drive them—the police, the courts, the media, the public—to hysteria. Without doubt they will work to prove that our love makes me an accessory to your crimes. They will not be able to leave me free.

The twisting of fate enthralls me. I see now that the inevitable end began long ago; the finale was written right there at the start. As a child my eyes hungrily swallowed dark-eyed boys who searched for trouble. Bad boys who did things I wished to do but could not do myself. There were never stains of dirt on my neatly pressed trousers; I did not dare cross the line that lies between what is and is not permitted. The misguided angels escaped from school, stole what they needed, drove with drunken recklessness through the night. At first their crimes seemed just an excess of boyish energy, a swagger of high spirits, such charming bravado; swiftly their needs turned darker, less innocent, and they flirted with Alcatraz, wooed severe sentences without parole. Danger burned inside them; I reached out for that heat, became branded a hundred times. There were handsome lovers and strong lovers, and lovers who carried me to all kinds of lawless lands and revealed to me any number of outlaw visions. Each of these dark desperadoes led directly to you. I followed their AWOL steps across the sand and found you there beside the sea, perched high upon the rocks, wind in your hair and salt sticking to your lips. Upon that shore we sealed an unbreakable pact, mixing our saliva and blood and semen.

We must take what we need. Every life you steal is a sacrifice offered only to me; our love is baptized upon an altar of blood. Certainly I do not pity your victims. I would stab them myself to keep you with me. Their lives are taken to preserve mine, I realize; if that seems a harsh equation, let me only say that all mathematics are cruelly precise. In fact, it is clear that your knife could easily press against my throat with the slightest shift of wind inside your heart. Anyone who doesn't know that even the strongest love must be this precarious is truly unaware.

Tonight the maple tree outside our window stirs and trembles. You look for car keys, you move toward the door. Suddenly my blood churns: their net may be drawn around you right now, this may be the night you don't return. The night you enter the magic door. When I do not visit you in prison, listen, you will understand: your spirit will escape its skin the moment you are captured; that body they guard with such care will be but an empty husk. Often I have caught your questioning glance: you wonder if I will be brave enough to slip from my skin also, and join you in the only place allowed for us to exist together. *You'll never take us alive!* we brag every outlaw's boast into the wind.

I don't know. I can feel impatient with abstractions that do not take into account the actual touch of your lips, the real pressure of your hands. Already I mourn your physical absence; knowledge of the brief time allotted for us here and now has made each glimpse of your tall form sweeter. Still, for a moment I am angry that you risk our earthly life together, court bodily separation enforced by iron bars. Is this what you finally want and need—to be apart from me in your lonely cell, your solitary confinement? Fleetingly I wonder what would happen if our roles were reversed: if I committed your crimes, would you be so understanding and accepting? While you pause in the doorway I doubt everything: you, me, us. I suspect your love just another con job, one more grifter's sleight of hand. Have I been set up as the fall guy who will take the rap, while you dance away at liberty to seduce a score of men unsuspecting as myself?

Don't go.

The words die on my lips, are swallowed by your goodbye kiss. No, finally I don't doubt, don't regret: I wouldn't change any of this even if I could. When you are gone into the demanding night I hear steel doors clang, strong bolts slam, heavy keys rattle a dirge. Someone cries for mercy. A knife stabs my heart, my opened veins afford release, we drown together in the red sea of love.

Sweet Jesus

They searched for a mother and they searched for a father, then Sister Mary said I belonged to sweet Jesus for eternity. She gave me a picture of a man with a long face and yellow hair floating in blue robes amid the clouds. Now they called me Matthew, but the name felt like my cracked shoes, too tight or too loose, always reminding me of another boy who'd once worn them new. The doctors peered down my throat for something hiding there, took pictures that showed what floated in my head. "If only you would speak," they sighed. "If only you would tell." They wondered again about the red coat that had been wrapped around me in a doorway on Union Avenue among the roaming cats and cars. A woman wore the coat, they said, a woman went away. "I was lost," quavered Sister Mary. "But now I'm found." At night the other children cried in rows of beds beneath the crosses and the smell of onions in the dark. I kept the picture of sweet Jesus under my pillow; he whispered when I moved my head, a sound I saved inside a secret box. Sometimes, when the thin nuns cleaned the corners and the bigger children played their bad game, I heard a voice from before St. Cecilia's and rainy Portland afternoons. During mass, sweet smoke curled behind my eyes, a bright red mouth was laughing through the cloud. Veils fluttered inside my skin, something shook me, Sister Mary placed the stick upon my tongue. After, they

stopped trying to teach me and the disappointed doctors went away. My broom swept mute years. I scratched
the floor and raised a cloud of dust and the priest with
spicy breath showed me inside his lavender robes. In a
circle the nuns clapped their hands at Christmas and
asked me for one more dance until I was too big, until I
had to go away. They gave me to the sour man near the
docks. I filled boxes in the back, waited for him to come
through the dark. His hot face moaned while big boats
moved slowly down the muddy river. The wafer melted
on my tongue. Disappeared. One day I lost sweet Jesus,
my secret box was empty, another boy belonged to him
for all eternity. My feet followed red coats in the street,
wondered where my prayers would take me. I'll never
tell, sweet Jesus, I'll never ask why.

Touching
Darkness

First things first:

You were not the prisoner; I was not the warden with the keys.

There was never a cage, never a cell. No bars of iron, no heavy chains.

Let's get that straight from the start.

Since appearances can be deceptive.

Once again, as originally, the room might at first glance look very neat rather than quite bare. Sparse furniture—a single bed, a night table, a wardrobe—is as unexceptional as its setting. A window, set fairly high in one wall, looks over our backyard; even when closed its venetian blind lets in light. The uncarpeted floor is laid with tiles, either much faded or never bold, of uninteresting design. The white walls are decorated with several generic prints of ships at sea. A large closet contains unmarked cardboard boxes whose obscure contents somehow do not intrigue: anything of value has surely been removed from them; nothing important enough to merit concealment likely remains in them.

Undisturbed dust dreams in silence.

Unbreathed air waits to be consumed by throats, caressed by lungs.

Certainly not a sinister or disturbing place. The room at the back of the house neither evokes nor deserves such description.

Perhaps only I, knowing it is there, am able to detect the slight stain on the tiles to the rear.

The subtle scent that lingers like a memory or dream of love.

For years we used it as a spare room, a guest room, a room to hold odds and ends that do not clearly belong in other rooms. Infrequently entered, except when something missing is searched for without particular hope within its walls, the room possesses an air of neglect born of indifference: neither of us feels sufficient interest to invest it with his attention, his energy, his taste. We do not really need the space; it is almost beside the point: we can bear no heirs. Often I forget the room entirely, as if nothing lies behind its door.

Kept closed, the door has no lock or key.

As your last wish, you will wordlessly beg for those interdependent mechanisms that deny entry.

Or prevent escape.

Yet finally this unremarkable space will be spoken of in the most lurid language.

Chamber of Horrors.

Dungeon of Death.

(Never mind that the room is situated on the ground floor and not in the basement. Upon the prosaic surface of the earth, not within its murky depths. Outrage often eschews accuracy.)

Prison of Pain, they will inevitably howl.

You would smile, I know.

If you could.

When you begin to sleep in the room at the back of the house, I am not unduly concerned. There have been a number of occasions during our long union when one or the other of us has felt the need to sleep separately for a time. A night, a week; at most, a month. Such nocturnal vacations from each other do not necessarily result from disharmony. There is no question of rejection, of withdrawal. Eventually the occurrence does not even require explanation, can pass without comment: for we are assured it will have a positive result. From our state of extreme intimacy, which to outside eyes may already appear suffocating, we move apart in order to come back even more closely together than before. We learn to miss and to want and to need each other fiercely again. To tremble anew at what was perhaps becoming an overly familiar touch. To receive fresh pleasure in the length of your body against mine, in the weight of my head upon your chest.

Simultaneous orgasms, syncopated sighs, osmotic dreams.

Our reconnection can possess the heightened excitement of the first encounter enriched by the wealth of erotic knowledge gained from ten thousand subsequent encounters.

But this time you do not return to our communal bed after a night, a week, a month.

I have no way of knowing that you will never share it with me again.

No understanding of what has ended, of what has begun.

At the time, as it happens, I am working and you are not. There is nothing unusual about this. Often we alternate holding employment; our life of love has always been more important than any amount of income. One leaves the other free to tackle long-postponed projects around the house, to assume the main burden of cooking and cleaning. Then more of our time together can be devoted purely to the act of love. (Though in more than just a sense every one of our shared activities—for example, putting up the storm windows in autumn—is a sexual exchange.)

It is a system that has worked well for us.

Because I sleep poorly without you beside me, I come home from work tired after my first solitary night. I do not have energy to wonder why you have not prepared supper. (This is precisely when you would be apt to fix my favorite meal as reassurance, however unnecessary, of your unfaltering love.) Why you remain in the spare room instead of sharing the meal I end up making. Why you don't feel like going to the cineplex, the café, the gym. You have already eaten, I think. You wish to spend a quiet evening at home, alone. During these phases when we do not join together physically, we often remain apart in other ways too. I shrug at the silence that leaks from the spare room. You are reading, you are resting, you are writing a letter. Once or twice during the evening, I find myself listening for hints of your nearby presence.

When I pass down the hallway, the spare-room door proves closed. Moving the sprinkler in the backyard, I glance toward the window of the room you inhabit, see that it is already dark at ten o'clock.

Mentally, I shrug again.

We have always respected each other's secrets.

The closer we have grown, the more important and necessary those secrets become.

The unknown is erotic. Darkness is aphrodisia.

The gap between what I don't know about your interior and all I know of your exterior can make me swoon.

Several days later I suspect you rarely leave the spare room while I am at work. The rest of the house lacks evidence of your presence. No crumbs litter the kitchen counter. No CD rests in the audio system. No damp towel drapes in the bathroom.

You continue to decline to share the meals I make, as you still do not wish to cook, to clean, to shop for groceries. While I am at home, you stay behind the closed door of the spare room, and are not overly responsive when I open it to say a few words at morning, after work, before bed.

Yes, you smile, when I ask if you're OK.

We have always told each other the truth.

Checking the odometer of your Jeep, I learn that the number does not change from one day to the next.

Of course you do not leave our house if you do not leave the spare room.

The other room, as I begin to think of it.

As it assumes greater importance, grows equal in significance to our room.

Or what was our room.

On the fifth day after we begin to sleep apart (or is it the sixth? I grow dreamy without the reality of your touch), I return from work to find the house filled with what feels like a new kind of silence. As if it has been empty for many hours during which all traces of human presence drained slowly from within its walls. Immediately my heart relaxes; just as suddenly I realize how tightly it has been clenched. I do not fear you have left me; the impossible is inconceivable. (Anyway, your Jeep rests in the driveway.) Instead, I hope that since morning you have been strolling beside the river or climbing the sweep of hill to where perfumed pines stir and moan in the breeze. You have looked increasingly pale (I know it is difficult for you too to sleep alone) and the weather is especially fine this June. (That last June, I will later think, as though June has never come again, as though all months, even current ones, are only memories now.) When I knock on the door of the other room, your voice does not answer. I open the door. You are sitting on the floor beside the bed; it is as neat as if it has not been slept in for more than just one night. Your face is turned toward me. I suspect your eyes have been watching for the appearance of mine since I left for work ten hours ago. All day you have done nothing but wait for me.

For my touch.

Our sexual life has always been intense. It is the reason we have remained together. (Only those few—in my experience, they are not many—who have fully explored the realm of all senses understand what a complete reason this can be.) Finely tuned bodies and sleek skin; swollen muscles and strong limbs; a pair of large penises: such is the medium of our communication, and to preserve this instrument of interchange we take considerable care regarding diet, spend several hours in the gym each day, forsake smoke and drink and other drugs. What I wish to tell you about who I am, how I feel, what you mean to me: all this is said through the language of touch. Now your and then my penis speaks slowly or quickly; the anus answers eagerly; lips elaborate the point. The few people to enter our daily life and observe us together invariably comment upon the extent of silence between us. Yet I doubt words could say more precisely or clearly what your hand conveys resting on the back of my neck as we drive into the mountains in search of the first or last snow of the ski season; what my multilingual lips say as they explore the various countries of your skin. In a unique, private sign language, your caressing fingers spell endearments upon my back. Intricate concepts, complex emotions: though silent, this idiom is not necessarily simple.

Before finding each other, we both experienced lovers who did not wholly understand the speech of sex, the tongue of touch.

That has allowed us to appreciate each other all the more.

Now my first touch in five or six days tells you I want you, I need you, I will never leave you.

More, you say soundlessly, unsmilingly.

(But that was long ago. Sometimes now, when the rooms around me are most silent, and the clock ticks its loudest, I can believe I inhabit this house alone. There is no sign of another presence, except for the scarcely distinguishable yet permeating scent of rot that travels from the room in the back. I can almost forget that in your ultimate, invisible form you are still there. Where you want to be. Need to be. Must be. Why? Love is the final puzzle of the world, the last secret of our galaxy, the true riddle of the Sphinx. I have had years to muse upon the question of what became of us. Like reaching out to grab darkness and ending up with empty hands, the answer still eludes me.)

The quality of your touch has changed since five or six days ago. It speaks with new force about hunger and need. After our initial, urgent dialogue is complete, you turn at once from me, curl into a ball on the hard floor where we have come together. You want me to leave when before our tactile conversation would continue long after the first explosion of semen.

Unlike myself, the single bed is undisturbed.

Leaving the room, I do not realize the full significance of the bed's unrumpled state.

Or of your silence before, during and after our act of love.

The next day I come home to find you have fastened heavy black cloth over the window of the other room in such a way that no light enters, not even a crack at the edge. The following day I discover you have removed the bulb from the light socket in the ceiling. Two days after that you rid the room of its furniture, the walls of their prints, the closet of cardboard boxes. You begin to use a bucket for your wastes. You no longer dress. When I enter the room, your naked body shrinks into the farthest corner from the light that falls in from the hall. Your eyes close until the door has shut and complete darkness returned. You have transformed the space into a void around you. Besides the bucket, there is nothing in the room except yourself; nothing to dilute that essence. No clothes interfere with my touch. No furniture stands between us. No light offers our eyes distracting, unnecessary images. Now we see only each other. See through touch, see through smell. To a slight degree (quickened breath, contrapuntal moans), through sound.

But you have ceased speaking in words.

And my voiced speech makes you cringe, as if it were fists.

The darkness is pure, your fingers spell upon my back.

The darkness is holy, they insist.

Would I have acted differently if at the time I had known that I would never hear your voice again?

That you would never leave the dark room to appear before me in light again?

Your touch soon informs me that it is not necessary to bring you carefully prepared and balanced meals twice a day. You will eat only a crust of bread, drink only a half cup of water. Nor is it important that I empty the bucket of waste regularly. All you want from me is my touch. As if this touch contains all light, all nourishment, all the comfort you desire.

What do I desire?

The same thing as always: your happiness.

I give you what you want, what I can, what I have.

More, your touch demands.

Harder, it urges.

Don't stop.

Driving home, I fear what latest development will await me there. I park next to your Jeep and from the outside contemplate the structure we share. It appears more or less the same as the other modest houses on this quiet street. Innocent, innocuous. The old woman next door, whose sidewalk we shovel in winter and lawn we mow in summer, waves until I lift my arm in response. (We have taken pains to ingratiate ourselves with our neighbors in order to forestall any unease they might otherwise feel from your presence, as in a foreign country one is careful to soothe potentially hostile natives.) A small boy pedals his tricycle furiously down the sidewalk, repeatedly rings its tinny bell. A sprinkler pirouettes with perfect grace upon green grass. Blue smoke from barbecues slants through the golden air of six o'clock. The scent of burning charcoal and cooking meat mixes with that of freshly cut lawns to produce the bouquet of suburbia.

The small boy's name is Billy. Often when you are working out in the yard, he will tag at your heels, tug at your sleeve, ask question after question. Changing the oil in your Jeep, you patiently explain each step, allow him to hand you tools. He stands beside you, scarcely reaching halfway up your long legs. His face tilts to find your eyes above. Your hand rests lightly upon his tawny head.

From what I understand, Billy has no father. My source of information, the old woman next door, shakes her head when speaking of him: plainly, she could say more.

I have seen the way you look at the son you will never have.

It makes the strings of my heart knot, tangle, twist.

From the driveway's perspective and distance, it is easy to summon such terms as "breakdown" and "psychosis" and "illness" to describe what is occurring in our house. It seems obvious that intervention and assistance are required for you, of me. In the end, they will ask why I didn't save you. Call that failure a crime, give it another name, turn it into something that demands punishment.

I will not try to explain.

That to drag you from the other room and to call an ambulance would have been failure to our eyes.

We have never lived for the world's eyes.

We have always lived for love alone.

Perhaps all lovers must believe they embark upon a unique adventure, undertake a brave new experiment, engage in unprecedented experience. You are daring me to follow you deep into the darkness. To search for the source of love, elusive as that of the Nile, which lies far beyond practical procreation and sanctified desire and convenient passion; only there at its origin, before becoming contaminated by time and space, is love pure. Long ago, I suspect, you planned this journey we are taking now, waited patiently until able to bring it about, always kept the larger picture in mind. An unremarkable house on a quiet street in a drowsy suburb far from the sleek center of the city: this particular setting is important to the success of your meticulously conceived design—as the room at the back of the house, the old woman next door and the small boy halfway down the block form further crucial pieces of the puzzle you hold whole in your head. And you selected me specifically because you believed I would not fail the challenges of your experiment, however difficult they might be. Half a dozen images of you closely considering me montage through my mind. You are wondering:

Am I strong enough, brave enough, man enough to love you?

The tricycle bell fades in the distance. I continue to feel you waiting within the house for me. For several days, I realize, I have come home hoping to find you gone. For one moment I am tempted to turn the ignition key and restart the still-warm engine, to drive away and not return.

This is my last chance to leave you.

From here there is no going back.

Slowly I approach then enter our house.

Gradually I stop thinking of the space you occupy as "the other room."

It is simply "the room."

The original room, the only room.

As if no other exists.

Sometimes your silence taunts me.

Sometimes it shrilly screams.

Seduces, begs, insinuates, cajoles.

Increasingly, what is left to me is interpretation.

Or rather: understanding that in love, always, interpretation is only what we have.

The adoring expression in his eyes, the tender tone of his voice: our own emotion, fatally subjective, elects the adjectives it requires to survive.

The air enclosed within the room becomes thick and heavy with the odor of your unbathed body, with the stench from the bucket of waste. It grows difficult for me to respond to your silent summons. I must remind myself that this aroma is produced by and is part of the being I love; therefore, I must love it also.

In love there can be no selective throwing out of chaff to keep the grain.

Take me as I am.

All or nothing.

In sickness and in health.

Till death do us part.

Threadbare clichés echo tinnily inside my head.

The darkness around you assumes the properties of solid matter. I stroke its skin, I squeeze its entrails. Rub it between my fingers, feel its texture. Touch it, learn it, know it.

Love it.

It requires increasing effort for me to touch you with the force you desire. I grow nostalgic for the days when the lightest pressure of my fingertips could make you quiver, cry out, come. In the darkness I read in braille a historical romance that features your clean hair's scent, the gaze of two green eyes, the precise pitch of a laugh. More and more, I feel I am making love with the past.

Or committing adultery with your ghost.

I wonder if our emphasis upon touch as profound communication was misguided all along. As your silence lasts, I am perversely compelled to speak to you in words, must fight to stifle that urge. When your birthday arrives, and then our anniversary, I feel helpless to convey the significance of these days. Especially since, exactly when its subtlety is most needed, my touch becomes reduced to blunt blows.

Still harder, you mutely beg.

Of course it is painful to realize that your body is losing weight, your muscles their firm tone. In the second that the door is open, as I enter or leave the room, a glimpse reveals how pale you have become. Gaudy sores and cuts and bruises decorate your skin like the haphazard work of some tattoo artist suffering a deficiency of sustained attention. With the nails of your toes and fingers, your matted hair grows long. But in the darkness your eyes shine more brightly than ever. Your touch tells me over and over that this is how you wish to live. Your previous experience was compromise.

Now you are completely satisfied.

Perfectly happy.

Summer passes slowly. I go to work each weekday. I visit you each evening. I mow the lawn and wave to neighbors and watch Billy pedal his blue tricycle back and forth in front of our house. He is hoping the sound of his bell will draw you to him. That you will play catch with him. Tell him about when you were a boy his age. Promise that one day he will grow to be as tall and strong as you. As loved as you.

When I return the emptied waste bucket to the room, you tend to shift it one or two feet from where I have placed it. After a moment, the metal's glint shows you have moved it halfway back to where it was. In my mind gleams a dozen occasions from the time before the room when you seemed to meditate upon the position of some unimportant object, consult a blueprint in your head, adjust the arrangement of the landscape to match it. The blueprint is of the past; what to me seems unprecedented is in fact repetition: this has happened before. I slowly understand how crucial it is that the room is at the back, not the front of the house. That the woman next door is old rather than young. That, for purposes of replication, Billy's hair is tawny instead of dark.

In my dream I sponge your body until it sings with cleanliness. I cut your hair and clip your nails and dress your sores. I feed you, cradle you, croon to you.

In our dreams we do what denied when awake.

Our telephone and doorbell have never rung often; we have always been enough—everything—for each other. Now when an acquaintance calls for you, I say you are at the gym, at the store, in the shower. When the old woman next door wonders once or twice why she hasn't seen you lately, I explain that you have gone away for the summer. By autumn I will say you have left me, I don't know where you have gone. I leave the keys in your unlocked Jeep until it is stolen. I scrawl *moved* on your mail, send it back. Calls for you cease; with one exception, questions about you stop.

You have gone.

You are not here.

Like any dream erased by dawn.

In what was our room, on what was our bed, I study photographs of you. Once I would have said, with complete conviction, that I would never have to do this. No matter how far you went away, no matter how long you stayed away. Light seeps from your snapshot skin, spills from your emerald eyes, escapes your Kodak smile. Women and other men turned in the street to catch that

light; they did not realize it was only a faint approximation of the dazzle to flood me when we were alone.
During our twelfth year we have wanted each other
more than during the first. In the supermarket your
broad shoulder brushes mine and I am nearly knocked
off balance by the force of electric charge. Spotting you
in the gym, my fingertips graze your wrists and blood
rushes to the lush surface of your skin. Always the taste
of your saliva blooms in my mouth. Always from us
wafts the spice of our mingled semen.

I do not possess a vial containing the precious essence
of your original scent.

No recording of the voice that throbbed my blood.

Before or after the last leaf falls from the maple behind
our house?

I do not realize precisely when I begin to think of you
in the past as well as the present tense. When the being
in the room, though still "you," assumes an identity separate from the one I originally loved. You have divided
into two—pre-darkness and post-light—like some
organism capable, with only the assistance of time, of
self-reproduction.

Which half received the indivisible heart?

Only Billy doesn't believe you have gone. He persists in
knocking on the front door and asking for you. As I
explain your absence again, he peers behind me for
sight of you. Dragging his heels, glancing over his shoulder, he leaves reluctantly. His unconvinced face is
pinched more sharply than ever with hunger.

At my least sound, you shake with such force I fear you will convulse. Now we do not even moan or grunt when we come together. There is only the dull thud of my fist against your face, the slap of my hand upon your skin. My kick, my push, my shove: all these gestures of love produce their particular sound, speak their specific language. It is unfamiliar to me; I can't understand it. Only you are fluent in this idiom.

I wonder where and when you learned it.

With whom.

We have always worn each other's clothes. We are the same size. Seeing you in my green shirt could make me feel we are interchangeable, identical, one. I would experience the same pleasurable confusion as of waking to wonder if the arm flung over my chest belongs to you or to me. Now I wear your clothes exclusively. At morning I look in our closet and imagine what you would wish to wear today. The faded yellow sweatshirt with a small hole in the left shoulder, an old favorite? I like to believe my dressing in your clothes allows you to share my experience within them.

To live in light as well as in darkness.

In our former room I make loud, guilty love with your photographed self. Sense you stiffen with outraged jealousy in the darkness across the wall. On my next visit, you retreat to the back of the closet and won't come out. Though I have long ceased receiving pleasure from our physical contact (except in the sense that your pleasure is always mine), on this evening I leave the room over-whelmed by unsatisfied desire.

Though the autumn proves surprisingly mild, I never feel warm in bed, wonder if your naked body suffers equal cold upon its bare tiles. Beneath heavy blankets I curl around my shivering self. The first time I waken to the sound of crying, I believe it comes through the wall. Then I understand this sound is produced by myself. Soon I am accustomed to being roused by weeping; it is no more extraordinary a nocturnal phenomenon than, say, darkness.

As you continue to deteriorate within the room, I grasp more tightly to life outside it. I do not miss a day of work. Attend the gym religiously, read the newspaper thoroughly, clean the house carefully. Leaves fallen from the backyard maple are raked, air freshener to combat the odor that leaks beneath the room's door is bought. My car is tuned, my teeth are examined. Respectful of the calendar, I have candy on hand for Hallowe'en. (This year Billy is a cowboy; last year he was an Indian.) At Thanksgiving I cook a turkey with all the trimmings, eat enough for both of us. When the first snow falls, I am acutely aware that you do not know the world has become white. As perhaps you are uncertain whether today is Tuesday or Friday, whether night has replaced day. (Or in your dark zone have you developed strate-gies, based on sounds from outside, to keep track of time as in the cemetery corpses methodically count off the weeks until their resurrection? Only the blunting of senses necessary for me to bear the room prevents me, surely, from hearing within it the song of birds and calls of children beyond.) At Christmas I am at a loss as to what gift I can give you. Then, on that silent, holy night, for the first time my hands draw your blood. At once I comprehend how much this excites and pleases you. You greedily lick the liquid that spills from your nose. I listen to the slurp, suck, slurp and recall the time I entered the room to see, in that second of illumination, you tilt the bucket of waste to your opened mouth. Then swallow, then lick lips, then burp.

Sometimes I wonder if my memory is confused. If it were I who unscrewed the bulb from the socket in the ceiling, removed the furniture, placed heavy black cloth over the window, took away your clothes. Sometimes it seems my body possesses physical memory of performing those actions. Then I shake my head: no. It has always been difficult to know where one of us begins and the other leaves off. Only that has caused my confusion.

At other times I ask myself if I could remain with you in the darkness. Share it with you as we have always shared everything important. Yet I know this is not possible.

I must remain in light so you can enjoy darkness.

I am the light, you are the darkness.

Complete love is the union of these opposite elements.

I repeat the formulae by rote, puzzle upon where I learned them, speculate that while I sleep someone stands beside the bed and whispers concepts and instructions that through the darkness sink into my subconscious to emerge as apparently my own thoughts upon waking.

There are moments, during daytime, when I can almost recall the sound of that voice.

Its familiar tone, its known timbre.

Anyway, if we did love lastingly in the darkness, our electricity would soon illuminate and destroy that element. Even now—still—sparks seem to shoot from our touch, swirl in haloes around our heads.

Repeatedly it strikes me how comfortable you are in the dark, bare room.

As if you have lived this way before.

You have realized in three dimensions the blueprint of the past that for years hovered only flatly in your head.

(Sometimes, entering the room, I feel I am stepping into the dark chamber of your mind.)

Or (to take the longer view) as if, over centuries of evolution, your species has adapted to these conditions until they have become a natural environment you can enjoy as well as endure.

Yet I can't permit myself to contemplate how you pass the hours while waiting for my next touch. What you remember of the past, what you experience in the present, what you hope for the future. I can't allow myself to calculate the number of dark hours you have survived so far. The thought causes a twinge of pain to shoot through my head.

Spring comes, spring goes. Suddenly it is a year since you entered the room. I mark the date by remembering:

The last words you spoke to me.

The last squint of your sun-drenched eyes at me.

The last cup of coffee you made for me.

If nostalgia is a second-rate emotion, surely sentimentality occupies a still lower plane.

In the backyard I catch Billy looking up at the window covered with heavy black cloth. He quickly runs away. The boy has always avoided me as much as, inversely, he has been drawn to you. He is aware that I know the truth about him. That I recognize the hunger in him. That I understand what he is prepared to do to save himself from starvation.

Need corrupts.

When you were not looking, his innocent gray eyes have leered at me.

His tongue has licked his pink, petalled lips enticingly.

If the woman he lives with—a relative of some kind, says my next-door neighbor—is in fact an alcoholic recluse, a mean and twisted spirit, that is really no excuse.

It could be much worse.

As I should know.

And you, I will learn, even more.

I abandon my habit of wearing your clothes. I do not want even to imagine your sharing the experiences and emotions I now have within them.

Certain stresses I must suffer and tensions I must bear because of the stupidity of the world.

Let's just say it has not been easy to sustain myself outside the room.

Arguably, you enjoy an easier existence within it.

Yet I do not resent the alignment of our roles.

Selfishly, unsuccessfully, I try to subvert your unspoken wishes, your undeniable happiness. At high volume I play certain music you have especially loved with the idea that it might draw you from the room. With similar hope I prepare the one dish whose tantalizing aroma you have never been able to resist. For one week I refrain from bringing you bread and water. Going away for a weekend, I deprive you of several visits.

None of these stratagems works.

I can almost sense you smirk at the naivety of my ploys.

Clearly you are the one in control here. The one to dictate the course of events.

I am merely your pawn.

Your prisoner.

Factor X in your investigation into the truth about love.

One evening during the second year you do not shrink away when I enter the room. For once the moment of light from the hallway does not seem to disturb you. Curious, I leave the door open and move silently toward your favorite spot to the rear of the room. When I wave my hands before your eyes, they do not blink. A clap near your ear fails to make you recoil.

You are blind, you are deaf.

Correspondingly, your touch becomes more urgent, more forceful, more demanding. *More, more, more.* Each time leaving you, I am exhausted from trying to fulfill your need, surprised by the sustained vigor of your response. I doubt I will possess the stamina to love you the way you need to be loved much longer.

Who is growing stronger?

Who weaker?

Yet I continue to close the door behind me upon entering or leaving the room. I cannot bear to witness with my eyes (it is difficult enough to accept what touch tells me) pus oozing from open sores, bones jutting sharply beneath skin coated with a second skin of dirt and blood, feces and urine. After each visit, I scrub myself mercilessly with powerful soap, but wonder if a trace of your decay clings to me still.

Unvanquished microbes.

Unbudged bacteria.

You have seeped into my skin, sunken deep inside my marrow, dripped into my DNA.

You are not deteriorating, I tell myself.

You are evolving.

I have failed still to rediscover how to sleep soundly alone. Perhaps this is a skill that once unlearned can never be acquired again? Where you occupied our bed yawns a bottomless pit beside which I huddle fearfully until dawn. (On the other side of the wall are you awake too?) And the voice that speaks to me in my sleep is waiting to pounce if I finally do drift off. Now it barks, growls, snarls obscene instructions. The morning mirror reveals a drawn, anxious face. My head throbs steadily. I fumble through the days as if half-blind, half-deaf. At work I continually make simple mistakes. My colleagues express concern. Those who have known about your presence in my life believe they witness evidence of suffering caused by your desertion.

It is not just a question of sleeping alone. I do not know if I am able to live alone. Millions do, I remind myself. Yes, but they have not known you. Often in the evening, battered by the pain in my head and the voice of my sleep, I sit on the hall floor, rest my back against your closed door, from your presence beyond seek to draw sufficient strength to carry on for one more day.

Billy's blue tricycle becomes a green bicycle. One Saturday I see him bent over its prone frame. One of the pedals is broken. No, he replies when I ask if I can help. He looks at me with a mixture of suspicion and dislike and fear. He believes I have taken you from him. Made you disappear.

Perhaps I am disappointed in the boy.

Perhaps I thought that, deprived of you, he would turn to me.

As if it were recently left there, or had been patiently awaiting discovery all along, a file concerning yourself, dated twenty-one years ago, appears at the bottom of the bag where you kept your hockey equipment. (I have been sorting through your things; it is time, snaps the voice of my sleep.) I glance quickly at the papers in the file. Medical reports, psychiatric records, police dossiers. Without assimilating their information, I stuff the papers back into the bag. If you had wanted me to know the contents of this file, you would have shared them with me. For reasons I can't articulate, it seems essential that I refrain from digging into your secrets now. The prospect makes the dull pain in my head sharpen.

We did not bring our pasts to our union. We were born anew with our first kiss. Yet I have vaguely gathered that no parents or siblings or close friends peopled your existence before myself; this kind of uncrowded history was one more attribute we shared. No one will look for you. Make inquiries. File a missing persons report. Even given the circumstances, it is astonishing that a human being might vanish without a murmur from the face of the earth. As if he were never here at all.

Melt away like snow that leaves no trace of itself behind.
Displaying what was there underneath all along.

After a certain point in the third year, there is no way to describe what passes between us in the room as sexual activity, however broad the scope encompassed by that term. Suddenly, swiftly, your touch grows weaker; you can no longer hold me, clutch me, grasp me. Eventually you do not have the strength to expel your wastes into the bucket, to swallow bread, to sip water. Your teeth have abandoned your gums. Your hair has deserted your head. Huge in your gaunt face, open wide, your blind eyes are covered with a film of white. Your limbs, appar-

ently broken some time ago in the course of our meet-
ings and never properly healed, dangle at odd angles
from your torso of bereft bone. You become an inert
mass upon the tiles. Now I am required simply to enter
the room and kick the shape of darkness. I must kick as
hard as I can for you to feel the touch. That kick is all
that keeps you alive.

It would be an act of violation, an explicit rape, to cradle
you in my arms, rock you gently, whisper into your
unhearing ears all the words of love that for three years
have been building up inside me, festering like the pus
that drips from your open sores.

Something snaps. With your last strength you sever the
unbreakable thread that has joined our physical selves
for so long.

You perform this superhuman act for the sake of my
survival—or, more exactly, since you are me, for our survival. I no longer need to crouch outside the room at
evening: what remains within its walls is dross; what is
essential, our love, lives on within my walls of flesh.
Though free from the contents of the room, from force
of habit I can't help continuing to visit it, to consider it,
to think of it as you.

Very carefully I sweep the house of all your belongings,
wipe your fingerprints from the walls, destroy every
piece of evidence that you were here. As a backyard fire
consumes photographs of your face and identification

from your wallet, as smoke from the liberating flames annoyingly tears my eyes, I remind myself that I require no sentimental souvenirs, no nostalgic knick-knacks. Long ago, I repeat, you were imprinted upon my cells, written into their code. Every expression of love between us was an act of genetic engineering.

I frown with irritation. The file of documents I left in your hockey bag lies open upon my bed. Yet I distinctly recall taking the canvas bag, in a load of your possessions, to the dump at the edge of town. I press my thumbs into the corners of my eyes; neither aspirin nor more potent medication relieves the pain of the headaches that have become a constant factor in my life. In addition, the dreaminess that I have suffered since your entry into the room has steadily grown stronger; my job performance has been affected to the point that last week my supervisor called me into his office for an interview that was highly unpleasant in its implications. (Once the golden glow that surrounded me—the radiance created by the light of our love—caused this man to blush whenever I looked at him, stammer whenever he spoke to me.) As a side effect of the headaches or of the dreaminess, or under their combined influence, I sometimes find myself now at a location without the least idea of how I got there.

It is a somewhat disorienting experience.

Almost disturbing.

The other night I woke up (perhaps, more correctly, came to consciousness) outside the house halfway up the block where Billy lives. I could not recall the series of steps that led to my crouching there upon the dirt, beside the chinaberry bush, beneath his window. My most recent memory was of opening and then quickly closing the door of the room. For the first time failing to transform my disgust of the stench and filth within into love for the substance that is its source. For the first time failing to enter the darkness and to satisfy the remains of its occupant. Beneath Billy's window, the spring dirt smelled amazingly rich: I would describe the scent as a clean darkness. Through the pores of its skin, the earth beneath me breathed in, breathed out. Pulsing at the edge of the yard, crickets kept time like a clock in the May night, reminded ascendant stars that they still had hours to glitter the dew. The touch of a breeze against my face reeled my head; the gleam of grass dilated my eyes; above, the hallucinogenic heavens swam, swirled, spun.

From the way this world overwhelmed my senses, I might have just emerged from three years within a dark, bare, fetid room.

From the nearest streetlamp, a path of light carried my vision inside Billy's window, exposed his perfect, unmarked face upon the pillow. Though slightly flushed with sleep, his face appeared pale under this illumination. I could see his chest rise and fall beneath a pyjama top patterned with what looked like superheroes; below, the covers tangled around his waist, left his concealed lower limbs to interpretation. The same breeze that touched my cheek lifted and let go the curtain of Billy's open window, with a delicate gesture offering then taking away my view, tantalizing, teasing.

Suddenly I felt quite angry.

How careless to leave the window open like that.

How irresponsible.

Inviting anyone to enter.

Even a sleepy suburb like this is not safe.

(Especially a sleepy suburb like this, I sometimes think.)

All at once the pain in my head became much more severe. I blacked out; that must be what happened. I next found myself standing in the shower, with powerful soap scrubbing and scouring my skin of its stink.

Your stink.

Apparently, at some point after leaving Billy I overcame my revulsion and visited you after all.

Perhaps my vision of Billy compelled the visit?

My vision, my experience.

I intuit an image is missing from my memory: its absence nags.

As the sound of Billy's bicycle bell reminds me of something I can't quite recall.

Something in the darkness I can't quite touch.

Something significant, I suspect.

Something known to the possessor of the voice that addresses me during sleep.

Trying to piece together what has happened during the blank spaces caused by the headaches in turn causes the headaches to grow worse.

I feel caught within a closed circuit.

The synapses in the circuit are produced by a struggle to escape it?

I reluctantly pick up the file on the bed. Quietly, as if across the wall you can hear, I examine its contents:

A physician's report concerning the physical condition of a boy who, it is estimated (see concurring psychiatric and police reports), spent seven years enclosed within a dark, bare room. Malnutrition: severe. Muscular coordination: poor. Sensory responses: poor. Inability to withstand light: temporary. Muteness: see psychiatric report. Recovery: *excellent* (underlined). Prognosis: no lasting physical damage.

A psychiatric diagnosis. Trauma: severe. Loss of speech: temporary. Loss of memory: severe; limited recovery anticipated. Loss of affect: severe; limited recovery probable. Perception of reality: poor. Sexual fixations: several. Prognosis: permanent psychological damage; eventual functioning at minimal levels. (For detailed analysis of case, see *International Journal of Psychiatry*, Vol. XXIV, No. 3, pp. 217–249.)

Social services report. Placement of subject into foster care. Follow-up visits: social (home and school) difficulties: noted. Sexual disturbances: see psychiatric records; acted out. Discipline difficulties: noted. Concern of foster parents: noted. Status: ongoing monitoring required.

Police file. Efforts to establish identity of Case No. _____: unsuccessful. Investigation into circumstances of criminal confinement: unsuccessful. Possible suspects in confinement: none. Possible motives: unknown. Final status of case: unsolved; closed.

Court document. John Doe No. _____ will henceforth bear the legal name _____.

At the bottom of these documents lie petitions, dated eleven years later, for their release to their subject.

I close the file.

In one sense, it has been closed for twenty-one years; in another, it is still open.

Those twenty-one years form a blank space for you?

A synapse in your closed system?

A period of limbo between one bare, dark room and the next?

Between one dream and another?

Across the wall, once more in darkness, you struggle to close the file.

Forever, for good.

If I did not know you better, this information might seriously disturb rather than briefly disappoint me. Initially, I must confess, I am somewhat surprised by your failure to destroy, long ago, documents that are essentially without meaning, that obviously bear no real relation to our love. I wonder at your decision to allow them to survive for my discovery. To risk our very special, very intimate experience being polluted this way by the uncomprehending world outside. Were my love for you less strong, it might now be soiled by the rough, clumsy touch of those systems that must always seek to control and to explain our existence.

Quickly correcting my mistaken sense of disappointment, I reject the documents as wholly as I reject the systems that produced them.

They mean nothing. They explain nothing.

They illuminate only the incomprehension of the unevolved world around us.

The stupidity.

Clearly, you left this information for me to destroy.

Call it a final invitation to partake in your experience.

A lover's last gift.

Once again, I am happy to comply with your wishes.

Another match scratches. More fire is fed.

Passing our house these days, Billy quickens his step, stares straight ahead. No longer looks lingeringly, hungrily toward where you once lived.

The smell of rot within the room is so intense I must hold my breath for the few moments I manage to withstand it. Though I continue to replace the bread and water that go untouched from one evening to the next, my visits are now perfunctory at best. More would be unnecessary. The entity upon the tiled floor bears as little relation to our love as did the documents I have destroyed. Frankly, I grow impatient with this mass of blood and skin and bone that you have left behind. I am almost resentful at your delegating me to deal with it. There is a danger that if your remains linger too long they will cloud the meaning of our love as much as the contents of the file threatened to do. The most important act of love I could perform at this moment might very well be to free us entirely of this mute, motionless mess.

This matter, this muck.

The periods of darkness—or blank spaces; or synapses—occur more frequently and last longer, as far as I can tell. Obviously, I am disinclined to seek relief from the medical profession for them or for the worsening, accompanying headaches. The quacks and charlatans have done enough damage as it is. Instead, I take the self-prescribed medication that, due to the stupidity of our legal system, I can obtain only with some difficulty. Unfortunately, it renders me unable to pursue certain activities that have long played a central, stabilizing role in my life; for example, I am unable to attend the gym. Also prevented from working, I take advantage of the considerable vacation time that has accumulated during these past three years.

The telephone rings unanswered.

Unopened mail accumulates.

Between the blank spaces I visit the cash machine, the supermarket, the supplier of my medication. At a building supply store I purchase a sack of lime, as the voice of my sleep has instructed. These excursions are necessarily as brief as possible: I must take care that the blank spaces occur within the house; to fall into them outside would be to expose myself to risk in several ways. Yet there is continuing evidence that I still wander during the dark episodes; that I do not come to consciousness in places I am without memory of traveling to is hardly a relief. It only means I do not know where I go or what I do during those times of blackness.

Guess, chuckles the voice of my sleep.

The unknown is dangerous, beats the pain in my head.

Interestingly, of late I have often "woken up" to find myself naked in the room. I am not equipped to describe the appalling loneliness of that experience. How the darkness tells me only that I would do anything, even leave life, to escape it. (I have never liked the dark.) More than once, I have discovered my hands to be stained red, as if with bright blood; a strange, bitter taste would haunt my mouth. For several days after my first encounter with these phenomena I was puzzled by the elusive nature of their source.

Abruptly, unexpectedly, the explanation slid to the front of my mind from its dark rear.

The house halfway down the block.

The chinaberry bush.

The obscure substance upon the tiles seems to produce a very weak, scarcely audible sound.

Mama.

Help.

Or so I think I hear.

The sound resembles the voice of a small boy who is frightened of the dark.

It is produced by my imagination, of course.

(The medication has more than several inconvenient side effects.)

The (imagined) voice does not speak again—at least, not while I am in the dark room.

I must have accidentally cut myself during a recent fall from consciousness. There is a deep gash in the flesh of my inner arm. The sharp sting appears to cause the pain inside my head to recede, if only temporarily. Perhaps one hurt erases the other. I work my tongue into the wound as my penis stiffens.

In the backyard I touch a match to a piece of cloth. As well as torn, it is soiled with what looks like the red juice of chinaberries. The pattern upon the cloth is made of men of comically exaggerated strength; they are patently capable of rescuing any situation no matter how desperate, of saving any being no matter how imperiled. Flames drop upon the site by the back fence where ash indicates other flames have fallen. A sound in the near distance lifts my head. The old woman next door is watching from her back steps. Realizing I notice her, she fades back into her house.

I wonder why I have not seen Billy lately. Since school is out for the summer, he should be playing on the block during these sunny days. Perhaps he has gone away to a camp situated among green, scented pines, beside a blue lake of crystalline water. With other boys like him, he swims and hikes and canoes; after dark, they gather around a fire to sing sweetly. Their voices lift high into the clear night, reach to touch glittering stars.

I can't help notice that lately I see better in the dark, as if my eyes have adapted to a prolonged lack of light. In the room I believe I notice the matter at its rear stir slightly. Bending closer, I realize this movement is in fact that of worms wriggling in and out of soft liquefying flesh. Matter is changing form, transmutating. I smile. This reminds me that our love has never been static; it has always evolved. Progress keeps it vibrantly alive.

I waken to hear Billy's voice cry through the darkness for help, mama, help. Something has happened to him at the summer camp beside the blue lake, amid the green pines. An accident. He has drowned in crystalline water or has plummeted from the cliff of a mountain trail. Long after its actual end, his voice continues to echo through the night. Though it travels from far away, the voice is distinct and clear as a voice within this house.

The proliferation of wounds I find on my skin suggests that when most heavily under the influence of medication I must be quite clumsy. I must allow myself to exist in too near proximity to sharp instruments. In the kitchen silver knives wink knowingly. The ax leers from the back porch; seductively, a razor shimmers in bathroom light. Where opened to the air, my stinging flesh sings so sweetly. My tongue tingles in anticipation.

Once such summer weather would have drawn me outdoors at every free moment; but each week I leave the house even less frequently than the one before. It is not that I fear falling into dangerous darkness beyond these safe walls; apparently, the synapses have ceased for the time being. There is no indication either that I persist in undertaking journeys and performing acts without conscious knowledge: it seems that phase has ended too. What needed to be done in darkness has been successfully accomplished, I assume.

(I can only speculate, at this point, upon those developments occurring within and around me; each new day I peek cautiously at whatever unexpected event unfolds. For you still control the execution of your secret master plan; and only the owner of the voice that speaks to me in sleep seems to share in advance that privileged information. Kept in the dark. This worn figure of speech now acquires fresh potency as its figurative and its literal meanings rub against each other, set off a vibration I feel in my teeth. In both senses of the phrase, as they pertain one to you and one to me, it is you who does the keeping in the dark.)

Still my head pounds, still that voice snarls during my sleep, still the curtains remain closed. Medicated, I stumble through shadowed, scented rooms. The one or two times I venture outside, I don't bother to greet my neighbors with a friendly wave, to interpret and to match their false expressions. The minor role played in my life by these unknowing people has been concluded; they don't matter anymore. (However, someone perhaps should warn the old crone next door about the direction in which she watches from her window, from her steps. Too late, she might come to regret the unwise habit.) Oddly, the street seems empty not only of Billy but of all children. It is the kind of absence that insists upon itself, like the silence that screams.

I am not surprised when you begin to speak from inside me. It is no secret that your essence entered mine some time ago; I have not mourned you because you did not leave. It is startling, however, to recognize that this is the same voice that has delivered instructions to my sleeping mind. Quickly I understand that the seeming harshness of its tone was due simply to the extra vocal force that is necessary to penetrate unconsciousness. For reasons not yet clear to me, your voice must now communicate during daylight as well as in darkness.

Of course it is overwhelming to hear again, after all that has happened during such a long time, the push of my lover's vowels, the catch of his consonants. At first I am so enchanted by your voice I disregard the words it forms. In some way, beyond the requirements of current circumstances, you sound different. I wonder if your voice itself has altered, if my memory of it is incorrect, or if my interpretation of its qualities has changed. Beneath the erotic throb that lifts the hair on my arms bites a cold, hard edge. Perhaps it was there all along. Carefully disguised, unperceived.

Hurry, it says.

The sack of lime, it insists.

Before it's too late, it commands.

The voice requires obedience. If its instructions are not carried out, I sense, the speaker will swiftly become enraged.

Summer heat has hastened the decomposition occurring within the room at the back of the house. The odor produced by this process is perceptible from the end of the driveway, from the farthest reaches of the backyard; slightly sweet, almost cloying, it mixes with the perfume of flowers grown by the old woman next door. Entering the room for the first time in several weeks, at your order, I notice at once that my approach raises numerous flies or gnats from the remains. They tremble above their source like visible ions of darkness. Then I see that the bones are nearly bare of flesh. They look quite small. I bend nearer.

This is the skeleton of a child, not of a man.

Someone has secretly substituted a boy's bones for yours?

What are you waiting for? hisses your voice.

I sprinkle lime over the bones.

It sifts through the darkness like a child's midnight dream of snow. In the morning we will toboggan down the big hill behind St. Cecilia's. You ride in front; behind, I wrap my arms around your waist, hold on tight, close my eyes as we speed faster and faster like the nuns' beads in the night. If we spill upon the snow, our arms will make angels until Sister Mary calls us in to feast on bread and water, all that is needed by orphans who have the rich, sweet nourishment of Jesus to enjoy.

Pay attention, snaps your voice. What are you doing?

I shiver as an angel's wing brushes my shoulder in the dark.

Start as a heavy lid slams in my mind, seals St. Cecilia's tight inside the coffin of the past.

Blink at my powdered fingers. Lick lime, taste chalk.

Rather than interfering with nature, I am aiding to quicken its process.

I remember how we would never ingest steroids to stimulate our muscular growth by artificial means.

For some reason the memory now strikes me as touching, tender.

It becomes necessary to turn more and more to my medication in order to silence the voice that otherwise speaks incessantly, steadily, scarcely pausing for breath. Yet you were never voluble; quite the opposite, in fact. Perhaps this stream of language is composed of all the words you did not speak to me during the twelve years before entering the room.

Late at night, exhausted, I am prevented from sleeping by the constant chatter.

It is malicious, cynical, inimical.

It delights in enlightening me on the subject of countless infidelities committed by yourself from the very beginning of our union. It gleefully paints in pornographic detail every illicit fuck and suck you experienced, and how your excitement in each encounter was heightened by my ignorance of its occurrence. Droolingly, it describes what really gave you pleasure, how your true desires were never satisfied in our bed, the way you only went through the motions with me, why you considered yourself a skilled actor for stifling yawns of boredom both beneath and above me.

Of course this voice is not yours.

The possessor of this voice has only imitated you in order to deceive me.

You would never do the things this voice describes.

Sickening acts. Disgusting deeds.

The motive here is laughably obvious. It was clear, right from the start, that the extraordinary combination we made would provoke inordinate jealousy and inspire all kinds of attempts to sever us. In each other's arms, we used to joke about the pathetic efforts made by those who panted to come between us. Their begging to join us upon the sheets. Their offering of large amounts of money to watch us. Instead of driving us apart, such machinations inspired us to dive more deeply inside each other.

The envious owner of this voice does not seem aware that even now, more than ever, efforts to divide us are doomed to failure.

But I can reason this out only with difficulty: for the venomous voice is screaming inside me. It shrieks out, over and over, one obscene scenario that above all others you enjoyed.

You don't believe me? shrills the impostor.

Ask the kid yourself. And why not give him a whirl while you're at it.

Afraid you might like it?

I am not offended by such an implication. I know what I have and have not done. Only that matters. It is interesting that, despite its purported omniscience, this voice isn't quite so all-knowing after all: Billy's accident, that unfortunate fatality, seemed to have eluded its notice. As to the real identity of the speaker, that is of negligible significance. Clearly, this voice is composed of all the frustrated longing, all the thwarted need, all the unsatisfied desire of all the cowards who populate the world around us. For the time being, for my own purposes, I am perfectly content to allow the voice to believe it maintains the upper hand.

Naturally my feelings were hurt by not being invited to Billy's funeral. It appears I will not even be informed belatedly of his death; the sad event will be kept secret from me, like the weddings and anniversaries and baptisms that constantly take place beyond the edge of my vision. Despite this slight, and the resulting tardiness, I consider bringing a tasteful wreath to the woman halfway down the block who was charged with Billy's care. My impulse is quickly killed by anger that such a being would be given a child to raise. I have seen this sorry excuse for a human from a distance; I can guess, quite accurately, almost as if they happened to myself, what sort of experiences Billy suffered at her hands. The kind of experiences that refuse to be buried despite the passing of twenty-one or more long years. Maybe the boy is lucky to be out of it after all. I glare accusingly at the street from behind my window. The nondescript block lined with modest houses appears hushed, holding its breath, in suspense or in fear or in horror.

When I next enter the room (I am not certain how much time has gone by; the medication interferes with my ability to calculate clearly the passing of days), the remains on the tiles to its rear resemble perhaps finely crushed bonemeal, perhaps the end product of the crematorium's furnace.

(Now my vision has grown poor, as if my eyes have strained for too long to see in darkness.)

I sniff an unfamiliar odor—something acrid, acidic, chemical. Something besides the sweet smell of decay, the smothering smell of lime. A further substance was added, by an anonymous assistant or by myself, to encourage the disintegration of bone?

I allow the puzzle to pass. There are more important matters to worry about.

I dig the mixture, whatever the full nature of its components, into the flowerbeds that edge our back lawn.

The lawn is brown from lack of watering, I notice dully.

The flowerbeds are choked with weeds.

The simple task is almost beyond my strength. My movements are clumsy, my coordination poor.

Weakling, sneers the voice.

Patsy, it snipes.

I have no idea if this concoction of bone and lime and other ingredients will act as fertilizer or as poison.

Finish what you started, orders the voice.

I dispose of the waste bucket at the dump.

Scrub the floor with disinfectant.

Remove the heavy black cloth from the window. Reinstall the single bed, the night table, the boxes.

Hang the prints of ships upon the walls. Screw a bulb into the ceiling socket.

Open the window to allow fresh air to enter.

Once again the room might appear very neat rather than quite bare.

Only a slight stain, perhaps invisible to unknowing eyes, remains on the tiles to the rear.

Despite the opened window, a subtle scent lingers like the memory of love.

For the first time in three years I am permitted to rest. Relieved of the painful pressure inside my head, apparently by the simple act of returning the room to its original state, I wander this shadowy house as if to reacquaint myself with it after an extended absence. I have been far away from here. During my long journey, the mirror informs, I have grown old. My face is pale and drawn and deeply lined. My hair is mostly gray; my eyes dull. My body is cadaverous as an anachronistic victim of the concentration camps. Beyond these physical effects, no souvenirs exist to speak of where my journey has taken me and what has happened to me there. There is no sign of what may have transpired within this house while I was away. What the world will call a crime. For which it will insist on finding a convenient scapegoat and on exacting harsh punishment.

I notice the outside of the house needs painting.

Inside, the clock ticks more loudly than I remember.

I move down the hall, past the door that, though without lock or key, remains closed.

Behind it undisturbed dust dreams in silence.

Unbreathed air waits to be consumed by throats, caressed by lungs.

The voice that once spoke within these walls is silent. It has received what it wanted. Surely satisfied, it is able to return to sleep behind the closed door. At least until the next time it is woken by desire.

Forgot something, teases the voice, with an approximation of a giggle, just when I am convinced of its dormancy.

I look around again. I am certain no evidence remains of the experience of love to have occurred during my absence.

The latest experience.

Of course I know, as I have always known, there have been other experiences in the past and there will be more in the future.

There are always more.

And I won't tell you what, chortles the voice.

A clue has been left behind by the owner of the voice. A piece of evidence has been deliberately dropped to tie me to its actions.

I am its victim, after all.

I will pay the price for its desire's fulfillment.

The pain in my head returns with vicious vengeance.

I reach for the medication, the instruments of injection.

Pale blood swirls the syringe.

The sting of the stab silences the voice.

I wait for the heavy fists to pound on the front door, the curious mob to gape from the sidewalk beyond, the television cameras to capture the easy images, the surface truth.

Darkness, pure and holy, creeps up behind me. Softly, quietly. Shadows gently stroke, obscurity caresses. I wait for the absolving hands of darkness, its tender touch of love.

Mama.

Help.

Understand.

Forgive.

The Cage

When I was a child it seemed the world was very wide
Oceans valleys plains and deserts all without divide
Then as I grew older, my wings began to stretch
My eyes grew slightly bolder and I could not stay at rest

So tell me why, now, is the cage so small?
Tell me why, Lord, am I here at all?
Within these walls of bone and these bars of flesh
In the lonely zoo there's not room for two
Within the cage
Within the cage

Sometimes the angels whisper that it's not so bad in
here
No one can cause you pain, my dear, no one can cause
you fear
And God can hear your prayers inside and we will sing
above
So don't lament for company and don't lament for love

Still tell me why, Lord, is the cage so small?
Please tell me why, Lord, am I here at all?
Within these walls of bone and these bars of flesh
In the lonely zoo there's not room for two
Within the cage
Within the cage

The Cage

One day the wise man will appear and speak outside my cell
Say son I think it's time you knew, I think it's time to tell you
The bars are in your mind, their keys are in your head
So step outside into the world and see what's here instead

Of crying: Why, Lord, is the cage so small?
Of crying: Why, Lord, am I here at all?
Within these walls of flesh and these bars of bone
Within this lonely zoo there's not room for two
Within the cage

Time to leave it, the cage
Say goodbye to the cage
Not going back to the cage
We'll never miss it the cage
Fly away from the cage

From the
Laboratory of Love

"Only the bird knows the wing," I remind myself at the completion of another investigation into the truth about love.

After the latest specimen to participate in my decades-long study leaves the laboratory.

This moment is always delicate, dangerous.

Involvement in the experiment has caused my pulse to quicken, heart rate to elevate, temperature to rise.

The specimen's scent clings to my skin, his secretions stick and smear, taste of him fills my mouth.

Electrical-biochemical reactions to our exertion continue in its aftermath. They so nearly resemble powerful, disturbing emotion, I am made vulnerable by what at the same time I realize are only simulations of loss and longing.

"It's all love," breathes the belly dancer, long before I find science, long before I leave the world, while we both stumble across deserts of desire, the same Saharas she searches still.

Immediately I embark upon the series of steps that, followed in exact sequence, with full deliberation, permit me to move from being the necessary participant in an experiment to being the equally necessary scientist who records what he has been observing all along.

Endow order and grace to what is otherwise a wrenching, confusing transition.

Follow standard procedures.

Change the sheets of the alcove mattress upon which the investigation occurred.

Snap off the music and blow out the candles that provide an appropriate atmosphere for its enactment.

Switch on bright light.

Swish potent mouthwash, spit in sink.

Beneath the shower allow a river to wash over me.

(A whole Nile, before it was poisoned, when all us dancers jangled silver and gold across the dark desert, fluttering flutes and veils, more swayed seduction upon the sand.)

As if, instead of scrupulous scientist, I were just another tired whore possessed by that profession's ancient mania to get clean.

One more killer with urgent need to dispose of the evidence that ties him to the bloody deed.

With antibacterial soap scrub it off, descend it through drain and pipe to the surface of the earth nine floors below; then farther down, underneath, away: adding to sewer or sea, evaporating into air tonight, falling in rain upon my face tomorrow.

Steam rises around me as proof that processes of transmutation occur continuously, occur now.

Liquid flays like something solid; lashes hot, hotter, hottest; lasts longer than any civilian shower.

Afterward, veils of vapor float around the bathroom.

Mist prowling the earth on its very first day.

From which any original, unknown form of life might emerge.

Or me.

My physical self, lent again in the service of science, returned.

Hello, you've survived, you've come back.
   Did you miss me? Do you still need me?

I dress in a clean uniform of simply cut loose-fitting clothes.

Unlock the metal filing cabinet in the corner, remove the notebook pertaining to current experiments.

At the round white table prepare to record data and observations.

Trace graphs, draw charts, solve equations.

My heart rate has slowed, my temperature has lowered.

I become calmer, cooler.

Like the scientist who was here all along.

Although this post-experiment procedure has been created according to highly sophisticated mathematical principles, like any sequence of precisely ordered, perfectly executed acts, it contains the power of ritual.

Moves me beyond science.

Allows illusion that fresh fingerprints do not smudge my scalded skin despite efforts of ablution.

Encourages denial that they do not add permanently to a million older, equally obdurate traces of oil and sweat, saliva and semen, glandular and chemical secretions; fragments of genetic material and broken chains of DNA, fractions of molecules and atomic particles of all the specimens who have moaned beneath my touch during twenty years of investigative effort.

Do not contribute to the tattoo of a million caresses, imperceptible to the unaided eye, as if drawn with invisible ink, that decorates my flesh as extensively as a second skin, one I will never slip from, a species of shroud.

Likewise, the scent of the most recent specimen and of all those to precede him, an overpowering accumulation and combination and concentration of myriad odors, is ordinarily by ritual rendered inaccessible to unassisted human sense, detectable only by the most sophisticated mechanisms of olfactory registration.

Tonight my attempt to exceed science, surpass the senses, fails.

As I open my notebook, the scent of all the flesh known by mine steams from its pages, distilled into a substance nearly solid, almost available to touch, clearly invasive, certainly toxic.

Signals of warning smoke through my mind: danger is coming, danger is near.

The fumes still sicken as they dissolve beyond vision.

My belly clenches, my laboratory spins.

Settle down, instructs the scientist inside me.

My sight shifts back into focus. My fingers grip the table's edge.

I remind myself that investigations are always challenging.

Methodology requires that I participate in procedures while simultaneously studying them objectively.

Control for precise ends that which by its very nature embraces chaos.

Manipulate activity that seeks to disrupt itinerary.

Work what is wild to determined purpose.

Near the beginning, I experimented with method by employing two "outside" specimens to make up the pair required for research. Removed from the equation, empowered by that perspective, I hoped to be able to enhance the scientist's observations with my own.

Quickly I found this tactic unsatisfactory.

Incorporating a second subject into an experiment means lessening control over an already unruly act.

Increased rewards of observation do not compensate for loss of critical data obtainable solely through experience.

I realized I had to overcome the challenges presented by my necessary involvement in research.

I still need to trust that emotional makeup, physical constitution and early experience have uniquely prepared me for success where most would fail.

I must reassure myself that I was chosen for this work.

Selected for sound, supportable reasons.

Not by accident, from whimsy, for fancy.

Say that twenty years ago I awake one unwitting morning in whichever city has received my most recent flight from the boys I once was. Persistently eluding my escape, continually clutching at my sleeve with hungry fingers, they have driven me back and forth across the globe, jealously chased away every lover to try to claim me. They have drained my resources, they have exhausted my youth. How the weary light becomes clearer and truer on each of those afternoons in Tangier or Paris or Jakarta, always revealing more than yesterday, as if I were moving from blindness to sight, from confusion to faith, from death to life. Yet for a while I am unable to understand what my eyes newly see; I lack the knowledge to interpret what is revealed. The purpose of an existence never before glimpsed remains obscure even as its contours are created with clarity, without hesitation, in accordance with instructions murmured perhaps in sleep, directions offered by nightingales in the dark, apparently the echo of every lost lover's voice. An extensive number of complex factors work together at this moment, when they would at no other, permit me to receive the muffled voice that grows increasingly audible during day as well as night, while the illumination it casts becomes more dazzling. My eyes aren't accustomed to such pure light, it takes them time to adjust. Time to understand the purpose for the special landscape I have been constructing. Time to comprehend the aim of systems I have established for operating within that matrix. It is not until the first laboratory has been created in exact obedience to his instructions that the source of the voice materializes in brilliant light: I summon the scientist by creating the correct air for him to breathe, I invoke him by establishing the appropriate setting to receive his words, his vocabulary, his language of love. Even as he carefully explains the goal of our experiments, the parameters within which we will conduct them, the rules of operation that will permit them; even as the scientist explains every shining law of my new life, I swoon inside his original seduction, the first syllables he slid into my ear: Leave the world behind, come beyond with me. I will show you the dungeon, deep beneath your skin, whose hundred cells can hold a hundred boys in solitary confinement. I have the power to keep them down in that dark chamber below memory. As long as you remain loyal to the laboratory, they will never escape to haunt you again. Quid pro quo.

"This is only one more night," I try to convince the cold light of science that surrounds me.

My skin prickles, as when frozen flesh is invaded by blood, as upon the painful process of thawing.

Listen for mirror to glassily agree that, yes, this is just another night on the way to where we're going.

From the outset I understood that my investigation into love must be conducted through the medium of flesh: what I seek lies beneath the skin, below bone, under organs, deeper than blood, beyond scalpel's reach.

I accepted, too, that this path would not travel through lush surfaces, shapely limbs.

(Pure science must always practice discrimination for which no apology is required; embracing one theory means coldly denying others.)

Beings encased within less aesthetically fortunate shells have always provided the richest raw materials for research.

My thesis is built upon a single fundamental principle.

When desire denied too long is finally fulfilled, when withheld beauty is belatedly possessed, when longing for wing and flight is at last unshackled: such ecstatic experience unleashes extraordinary reactions, which originate from the deeply buried molten core of love.

My physical self, this form shaped and honed for satisfaction, provides the catalyst.

Bend your bones into a boomerang that will always return you to my arms.

Long before tonight I learn to suppress distaste for the more physically unattractive subjects that participate in my project.

To stifle instinctual responses to rancid flesh and sagging skin and ominous rashes during intimate contact.

To disregard odors, to quell rising nausea, to bear dry heaves in the bathroom afterwards.

("Aren't we the sensitive soul," sneers the scientist.)

To prize what appears repellent as especially valuable to my work.

To honor unpleasant surfaces that challenge me to dig deeper, to dig harder, to unearth from my own subterranean center responses to what was once repugnant.

Slowly I grow to welcome the appearance at my laboratory door of a decomposing carcass.

Clasp carrion tightly within my arms.

Graze my lips in prayer over every inch of rotting flesh.

Bless each wrinkle, wart, imperfection.

On the evening, several years into my work, when I close my door against a subject brimming with youth and beauty and every other attraction, an embarrassment of physical riches, any doubt that I can successfully complete my experiment vanishes.

I leave longing behind, move beyond loss, enter the sacred zone.

Envision involving specimens according to an equation of ever-decreasing beauty, whose enactment can trace a straight line on a graph, until I embrace only beings with missing limbs, running sores, cancers.

I will learn to kiss the abscessed eye, caress the shriveled limb, enter the infected anus.

My study's final participant will be scarcely recognizable as human, resembling more an appalling multitude of genetic mistakes: a tongue for an ear, a seven-toed foot stemming from a shrunken head; of indefinable sex and age and race; more dead than alive; untouched by another hand, never blessed by a kiss.

This will provide the ultimate data for my investigation. Illuminate the holy heart of love.

After seven years in darkness, I couldn't see by light, I could only negotiate the brush and fields when they were black as the sky above, except for stars that spell a story about a dancing blonde, with her striptease sidekick and her son she orbits between stages, sometimes sings about a sailor, that was the real truth of before, not seven years inside a cage. Now in the night was what followed the glitter, yes, this sea of sightless stumps came after the rouge.

There is no reason why this evening's encounter should threaten my controlled cocoon.

The specimen was unexceptional.

The experiment proceeded without incident to a satisfactory conclusion.

If anything, it was disappointingly mundane, unlikely to offer up startling insights or important revelations.

Unlike, for example, a session with a specimen who hates what he needs.

Who reacts violently upon receiving what he wants, upon satisfying what he despises.

Fists against my face, hands around my throat.

Boot in my back, blood in my mouth.

The scientist becomes excited by these instances. They permit him access to especially interesting expressions of love, provide opportunity to collect rare, precious data.

"Excellent," he enthuses as I spit a tooth.

Whether I find such intense experience pleasant or unpleasant is irrelevant.

Whether I am able to successfully defend myself from it, with the knife concealed beneath the alcove mattress, is incidental.

I never asked who, I never asked why.

Still, every encounter, including the latest one, holds value.

My investigative skills are by this point so highly evolved I am able to uncover in the least promising material any number of minor points of interest that might, factored into earlier data, be of use.

My post-experiment disturbance tonight may, upon analysis, provide more important data than the activity in the alcove to precede it.

Even after twenty years of investigation, I remind myself, occasional unsettling responses to an encounter are only to be expected. These have always occurred. They have always proven to be isolated incidents, little more than freakish phenomena; nothing to worry seriously about, only a test of my strength.

"Love is our only religion," intones the dancer in Damascus dusk, interrupting her eternal prayer for his appearance. "We invoke

his love with faith, we resurrect his ardor with our adoration, he saves our soul with his sex."

Instead of beginning to record, I warily study my laboratory.

It resembles any of the studio apartments housed in any of the buildings that seek ascension above this city on the Pacific coast of North America.

(This city is merely the latest in a long series to provide setting for my research; except as a location for another laboratory, it holds no meaning.)

Although I have been operating in this apartment for three years, it resembles one newly occupied, before the placement of furniture and hanging of prints and other evidence of a life.

One wall, facing south, is entirely windows; the others are bare white.

Between them, upon clean hardwood floors, are visible the few articles necessary for research.

My apparatus:

A free-standing mirror, positioned at the end of the alcove, reflects visual data pertaining to what occurs upon the mattress.

In the main room, besides the round white table of metal and single matching chair, besides the filing cabinet and boom box, only a telephone through which potential subjects make contact.

There is little to snare the eye, claim attention, provide comfort.

No plants or rugs, no television or sofa.

Compact kitchen, spartan bathroom, shut closets.

Curtains and windows kept closed.

Antiseptic sharpens the air; formaldehyde hones its edge.

The telephone is usually silent; the boom box is not played unless an experiment is in session. It was necessary to cease listening to music for pleasure upon embarking on my project. The thinnest melody still evoked in me the most ridiculous response, altered the chemistry of my emotions to countereffect, loosened and softened and encouraged to dream what must remain clear, hard, precise. Now music is merely a mathematical pattern of sound for my manipulation.

Nothing to offer distraction from the essential procedures occurring between these walls.

Sometimes, upon entering my laboratory, a subject appears unsettled by the space. Realizing his disturbance could impact on our activity, I provide false assurance, say I live somewhere else, keep this apartment merely to meet men like him.

In a sense, this is true.

My laboratory is settling only for controlled experiment, for pure science.

For love.

"Are you going to mope and moon all night?" interrupts the scientist.

Turn to a fresh page of my notebook.

Number and date tonight's experiment.

Identify time, temperature, weather.

Pinpoint phase of moon and tide, position of influential planets.

Target specimen's height, weight, age.

Ethnicity, race.

Every word uttered by both specimen and myself, with deconstruction of syntax and vocabulary and grammar.

Every moan made, every sigh produced, with interpretation of timbre and tone.

From extensive experience, by means of highly evolved senses, I am able to make finely calibrated estimations with conviction.

The exact temperature of his touch.

The precise key in which he groaned.

Alterations in barometric pressure at orgasm.

It was always foggy outside the blue room in Sidi Ifni where you found me. We couldn't see the ocean through its thickness, we could only hear the boom below, what went echoing against the hills behind, interrupting the meditation of camels in the desert beyond. Even the balcony was tiled blue, it floated in the fogged breath of all the boys who had drowned for love, hovered us in silver ascended from the depths, until I slipped away to Goulamine where you lost me to the dancer's dunes.

However powerfully developed, my senses remain subject to limitations. Once I considered the value of supplementing their capabilities with sophisticated technology.

To exploit audio, video, digital options.

To explore possibilities of playback, frozen image, slowed motion, amplified sound, computer enhancement.

Our investigation is observed best through unaided senses, documented best through the written word, the scientist insists.

Commitment to process is key to every important endeavor, he stresses.

(Perhaps such insistence actually indicates something else, I do not permit myself to wonder.

(Fixed philosophy, hardened ideology, limited vision.)

The eyes of the boy in the snow were frozen open, but he couldn't see.

Of course I record in code—precisely, in constantly changing code.

It is necessary to remain vigilant concerning security.

While a fairly simple computer program could probably break my cryptography, precautionary measures must still be taken.

Work in progress, particularly that of late—of increasing danger and of elevated intensity—needs to unfold and flower in secrecy.

When a cycle of completed experiments is ready to be offered to the world through publication, I painstakingly transcribe code into ordinary language.

Erase its complicated keys from my memory.

Destroy the original notebooks, dispose of their remains.

Bury them like atomic waste deep in earth above which ground burns, becomes barren.

We sleep in the thistles and weeds, dream of sailors navigating boats through the stars, steering toward a port of peace, it will resemble Eureka, California.

What they don't know won't hurt them, the scientist explained amusedly when, early on, I wondered if the unwitting involvement of participants raised a moral question.

They should feel honored to be involved on any basis, he snapped the second time I expressed such qualms.

They should understand that pure science operates in a sphere beyond muddy morality; in a space devoid of legal niceties, social conventions, polite parameters.

They should know that every act of love is an investigation, whether documented or not.

Upon my parchment skin you drew a treasure map to what you found beneath. It would become creased and soiled by ten thousand clumsy fingers, memorized by as many gold-fevered, glittering eyes.

Now a clear physical sensation runs down my right arm as I record.

What transpired on the alcove mattress travels through my hand and onto the page.

Safely there, encased in code, it is removed from my memory, erased from my experience.

Dissociated from me.

I will be able to access this experiment only by reviewing the notebook that contains it.

From the start I understood that it would be impossible to complete my long, difficult search for answers without the release that documentation provides.

Impossible for any being to bear, prowling through his blood, the memory of all the eyes to widen before his at the moment of truth.

He lay staring in the snow, a jagged grin gashed into his throat, a second mouth that couldn't tell who or why.

After recording an experiment, I typically study the notes from previous ones for purposes of contrast and correlation.

Tonight I fail to find release from the act of documenting, the encounter continues to perplex me, I close my notebook unsoothed.

Each action has its reaction.

The air I cause to move stirs the dollars left on the table by the departed specimen.

This donation will be slipped between the pages of one of the five volumes, secreted at the back of the alcove closet, which contain the published records of early investigations.

Which function as my bank.

For the moment, the money is disregarded, unimportant, beside the point.

It is never enough to sustain my work even on the most basic level: electricity and telephone always verge on disconnection; cupboards loom too frequently bare; a single thin dime to make it through the night.

All money is magic, chanted the belly dancer before swallowing another silver coin inside the incense.

I rise from the white metal chair, move to the window.

As if responding to a muffled call from the world beyond the laboratory.

The call of my lost name, my real name, my secret name.

His summons threads through the imam's wail from the mosque in El Jadida and as a Paseo de los Santos penitent he prays eternally for my return and in airport terminals and train stations and bus depots he crackles distorted directions back to his untrue eyes.

The curtains scratch open; the window uncloses with a resisting scrape.

Behind me, the scientist clears his throat in disapproval.

He doesn't have to tell me that I am disobeying standard procedures.

That science must almost always be conducted in secrecy.

A multitude of untitled research projects are currently under way at myriad unmarked locations upon the planet. Like mine, they deal with flammable material, tread hazardous ground. They are politically sensitive, morally risky, subject to sabotage. In the wrong hands, their findings could prove destructive on a catastrophic, global scale. They may be officially forbidden by governments that covertly fund them.

Denied by multinational corporations that instigate them.

Clandestine labs operating behind fronts in unmarked buildings at the edge of strip malls or inside industrial parks. Within gated compounds far off public roads, high up in mountains, deep in jungle or desert.

My current laboratory functions in similar anonymity.

In this undistinguished cement apartment building on this unexceptional street.

The intercom at the street door that is linked to the laboratory is labelled Occupant.

The laboratory door itself has triple locks.

The telephone number is unlisted.

In fact, there are two numbers, each with its distinct ring.

One through which candidates for experiments make contact with the scientist.

(A newspaper advertisement, infiltrated among those offering straightforward sexual services, provides the number.)

The other allows access to the front behind which the scientist can safely operate.

To an assumed identity, an approximation of a civilian self, a construct.

A manipulation of tone of voice, facial expression, body language, behavior.

A facade of fashion meticulously adopted from magazine layouts and advertisements.

It is essential, when outside the laboratory, that I blend in, escape attention.

Let's say I'm as much skilled thespian as scientist.

Say it suits my purpose that you judge me to be a prostitute or addict.

Damaged being, lost soul.

Zombie.

Whatever.

Sometimes he assumes another form in hope that it will be the one to dissolve my blinders, erode my shield, attract my eye. In a Teutuan derb he impersonates a beggar, from rags reaches out a broken hand, whines for dirhams. On a plazita bench in Madrid, behind the church that is always locked, he clutches a cane as an ancient man. At the mall in Santa Monica a skinny teen stunts a skateboard, rolls another blunt. He is the overly solicitous flight attendant during an Air India non-stop between Bombay and Algiers. He is the officer who conducts the strip search at Canadian customs. The cabbie who drives me into the ghetto of my mind.

Over the years, as I become more deeply immersed in investigative activity, as the scope of my existence narrows to encompass only this sphere, there occurs less communication unrelated to science.

Each relocation of base of operations, and corresponding changes of telephone number and address, moves me further from reach of an earlier life.

(When I was lost, until I was found, before I was set free.)

Because my research is funded in cash by its participants, I am able to avoid bank accounts, safety deposit boxes, credit cards. I pay no taxes; I have no employment record. No health insurance. No driver's license. I have a criminal record only in several countries, which are easily avoided; there are no outstanding warrants. There are six passports, each issued to a different name, each issued by a different government. The name I use at any given period is likewise fictitious.

Except to telephone and electric companies, my address is unknown.

Except for bills from these two utilities, only advertisements appear through the slot in my door.

As much as possible, almost completely, I cease to exist in official as well as private terms.

Slip through the cracks, off the face of the earth, from my original skin.

Did you miss me?

  Do you still need me?

The open window confronts me with a hundred apartment towers rising through the night.

Confuses me with the lights of their ten thousand rooms.

The same overwhelming number shine across the inlet, on the far side of the bridge.

The light in which I stand is one of many, one more.

"Painted scenery," mocks the scientist at my elbow, *"paper view."*

Against the black velvet backdrop, purely silent and hallucinogenically near, an ascending aircraft illuminates a sloping line that replicates the graph of desire I have just traced in my notebook.

The rising light hooks my eye, lifts it toward the spangle of stars above, the black ocean beyond.

We row across the moonlit lake, toward Christmas Bay, each at an oar, bending backs in time while the train whistles midnight down the valley, pools its echo in the hollow of my bones until your tongue licks my eyes, our abandoned oars sway a waterdance, we drift and cluster, let cold dark current pull.

My skin ripples, as if in response to a subterranean disturbance.

The scene before me shivers from stasis, emerges from muteness.

Video screens flicker across darkness and distance; shapes shift in their strobe.

The city breathes and traffic streams below; stars pulsate above.

"Moons and Junes and Ferris wheels," mutters the scientist.

Like an alarm, the telephone emits the three short rings that indicate another possible candidate for experiment is calling.

I ignore the signal, though once I was always greedy to gather more research, keen to conduct a dozen experiments a day.

Lately, only one encounter an evening is usually possible; even the avid scientist does not advise attempting more.

"Stay away from the window," he suggests now, *a sharper edge to his voice.*

As the world outside surges into sound, roars like surf inside a shell, amplifies the echo of the distant ocean.

As the swelling air sharpens with salt, stings my skin.

A moment after falling silent, while its aftertone still intrudes upon the air's liquid hiss and foam, the telephone rings again.

This time it emits only single sounds.

Summoning not the scientist but the civilian.

The first such summons since establishing this current laboratory, I realize.

The first, therefore, in three years.

This realization vibrates like a plucked string inside my mind.

Quivers questions to life, triggers mental motion.

How many political systems have failed since I stepped out of time?

Have wars been won and lost? Journeys made to stars?
Who? I didn't wonder. And why? I didn't ask.

As the ringing stops, I turn to the white table to record its occurrence.

Instead, my attention is drawn back to the rooms that illuminate the air outside.

Now I am able to detect that, like me, their occupants poise before open windows.

They wave like flags in greeting or in warning, call a thousand impersonations of his voice into the city's clamor.
You've survived, you've come back.

We lean into saline air, slant toward its suggestion of spring.

In interior canyons, snow melts, uncovers, exposes.

In the alley directly below my window stirs a shape darker than the darkness it fills.

He magnetizes himself into a substance always attracted by my atoms.

My shoulders twitch; their muscles burn.

The scientist purses his lips.

Impossible that he has found me.

"Watch it," warns the scientist, his voice now pitched a single note away from the one that preludes punishment.

The one that sounds as overture to finding myself slumped against the wall, its white surface stained from another night of cutting, the word *Help!* smeared with blood beside my head, the knife still in my hand and my sliced skin still singing, the scientist explaining once

more that it hurts him more than it hurts me; if I followed standard procedures, this would be unnecessary.

Back away from the window, retreat from its clutch.
　　Breathe the laboratory's familiar air; accept its acrid taste.
　　The world's din fades, then mutes.
　　It must have been a mistaken call.
　　One random voice thrown through the night.
　　One incorrectly pressed digit among six others.
　　No one knows where I am, who I am, that I am.

*I will never keep you from flying, he whispered like a thousand
oceans in my ear.*

Varicolored pills spill brilliantly upon the white table.
　　My fingers hover above possibilities, linger over choice.
　　Pluck blue.
　　Float its essence on my tongue, loll in its luxury,
swallow with satisfaction.
　　"Another," seduces the scientist.
　　"Again," he purrs.

*At the edge of my vision, where light meets darkness, where what is
known melts into the unknown, his hand hovers in invitation. He
wants me to join him on the balcony off the bedroom, beyond the
French doors. Once more we will lean together against the iron rail
above the narrow Macarena street during the hour when afternoon
meets evening and the twang of a plucked guitar ascends from the
music store below. Garlic from the corner café sautés geranium air,
the slot machine in the bar halfway down our cobbled block pings*

tunes of chance. His arm across my shoulder holds me inside this winged moment at the same time as we soar above the azoteos and the spires, the river and its bridges, all the way to Matalascañas.

Daylight.

I am curled on the hardwood floor, in the corner of the laboratory farthest from the alcove mattress.

Without blanket, pillow, clothes.

As usual.

Again.

(As a child, after what happens in the beginning, I form a dislike of beds. I am afraid of sinking and smothering in asphyxiating softness, seek the safe surface of hard floor, prefer most of all the cube of partly contained darkness beneath a boxspring. The people who say they are my parents worry. This is something else for them to whisper about in the next room; their clawed voices scratch through the wall. They consider returning me to the clinic, adding this latest unsettling behavior to records of others the doctors can't diagnose, can't cure. Instead, for my birthday they buy me vibrant sheets patterned by bold superheroes against whose image any boy would like to sleep. They buy a firmer mattress for the bed. They tie me to its posts, fasten me in the harness, force more pills down my throat. Finally they give up, acknowledge one more defeat, accept something else they can't change. Something else from the cage I have to keep, something else too late to forsake.)

Gulls wheel through my line of sight, shriek that last night I neglected to close the windows, draw the curtains.

Failed to return the notebook to the locked cabinet, to secrete donated dollars inside a book.

My sleep has lasted longer than usual, the clock informs me; the setting of its alarm was shirked.

These minor lapses in discipline annoy my need for rigorous order.

The itinerary leading up to an experiment requires execution as exact as that which follows.

Stiffness of the muscles in my upper back, just below my shoulders, suggests that last night's encounter in the alcove was unusually demanding.

Elements of wrestling were incorporated into the activity?

Or of a more unusual sport of love?

What happened last night?

Something went wrong.

Something isn't right.

A wing of memory wheels across my mind as I shut the window.

Trace of a dream swoops past the corner of my eye as I close the curtains.

I rub the sockets of sleep, grind away its physical consequences, rid my vision of unscientific conceits.

Sleep is only the necessary process required for physical and mental restoration.

Dreams are not permitted to invade my subconscious, to infiltrate my waking.

Traces of geranium are not allowed to linger in my sterilized air.

"Careful," murmurs the scientist, announcing that he too is awake.

Move cautiously through morning, as though I have wakened upon a landscape mined with the bones of all the ones who died for love.

As though their rigged, unmarked graves lurk to explode me into the sky.

Make allowances for aftereffects of last night's pre-sleep medication.

The dosage of which I realize, at the very beginning, functions as a tool in the pursuit of my investigation.

Like the recording of experiments, a valuable device for release from them.

Obviously, I cannot afford to ingest substances that might negatively affect the mental clarity required to organize and cross-reference and analyze masses of detailed data, intricate formulae, sophisticated calculations.

No crude narcotics to damage the prime physique required for my research.

No tobacco, no alcohol.

No crank, crack, crystal.

Shoot up only the heroin of love.

Employ only substances refined with purity, designed with delicacy for precise effects, in laboratories as clinical as mine.

After extensive trial and error, I discover those compatible with my most productive performance as scientist.

Certain nights require a pink pill.

Record my intake precisely; monitor milligrams strictly.

Other nights need silver powder.

Remain on guard against the tendency toward an annihilating dosage, which the challenges of investigation can prompt.

A blue pill is saved for extreme circumstances.

Upon discovery after an experiment of tearstains on the sheets, feces on my fist.

Last night there were two blue pills.

The scientist doubled my dose in order to accomplish one of his special experiments?

The kind that, much to his displeasure, I still cannot bring myself either to participate in or witness?

Please, no.

Not again.

Or the blood in the morning isn't mine, there's still too much of it, a sickening surprise, my stomach heaves at the mess as the scientist shrieks: "Clean it up, it's the least you can do, excusing yourself from essential work with silly scruples, dreaming of valentines while I'm left to dispose of the remains."

I should feel relieved that the laboratory is not splattered with serum of brain or shreds of skull this morning.

Grateful to be spared the scientist's endless lecture concerning the long tradition that allows that sometimes lives must be sacrificed to experiment in order to make important discoveries that outweigh such loss.

His rant that I am completely hopeless, quite unsatisfactory, he will find another associate if I don't shape up at once, there are a dozen boys bursting with promise on every block, he can pick and choose, who needs a weakling, a parasite, a nonentity like me.

His silence after a night that went wrong is suspicious.

Quite likely, strategic.

After twenty years of intimate coexistence, we harbor few fantasies about each other, the scientist and I. I continue to be grateful that he saved me, that he set me free. But my blind devotion to his beliefs, when I worshiped at his feet and admired each of his ideas, has long passed. And it is many years since the scientist has been equally enamored of me. At the beginning, he was ecstatic to have found the apparently perfect colleague for an unusual undertaking after half a century of unsuccessful searching, after decades of disappointment. He was thrilled to have uncovered what was surely the ideal disciple. That was when I basked in his belief in me, delighted showing him my fervor for his religion, burned with desire to embrace it as my own. I loved to exceed his wildest expectations. I adored to drop his jaw by drawing the richest data from specimens, by offering his eyes the most powerful articulations of love. Until with astounding banality, as a surprising cliché, the honeymoon ended and the bubble of illusion burst. Gradually I learned I can never satisfy the scientist. I discovered that he will ruthlessly use any weapon available to ensure the success of his experiment. He will employ a whole arsenal of unscrupulous effects to get what he wants. By turns he flatters or criticizes, encourages or exhorts, congratulates or condemns: always according to a concept that does not take into account my well-

being except as it furthers itself. Yes, he is as tempera-
mental and moody and selfish as any artist. Yes, I am
intermittently resentful and restless as any prisoner.
Ours is a complex union, subject to the stresses of
extreme circumstances, intensified by uninterrupted
intimacy. We bicker and nag. We humor each other, we
ignore each other. I know that secretly the scientist
despises me precisely because he needs me. I also know
that despite his protestations he would abandon me in
an instant, without a thought, if a more suitable assistant
appeared. And while it has always been clear that my
existence will end with the final experiment, as a necessary given, it seems the scientist will survive our endeav-
or undamaged. Once or twice he has let slip of a future
experiment in which I will not be involved or needed. I
do not deceive myself that he will miss me or mourn me
in the usual sense. He has never pretended that the usual
sense applies in our zone. We have left the usual sense
behind. Beyond the usual sense, I have considered
leaving him only once. If I did leave, he would unlock
the dark dungeon inside me, release the boys who after
twenty years of solitary confinement would kill for love.

Frown over last night's record, seek in its pages what has
gone wrong.

I am unable to decipher my own code; its key is missing from my mind.

"It doesn't matter," the scientist assures me.

Sometimes he censors an experiment he decides isn't
significant for our research or that otherwise fails to
meet his exacting standards.

"I know you'll make it up to me tonight."

An expression of forgiveness. A vote of confidence. A note of warning.

I ingest the first in a series of meals composed with dietary precision and accompanied by an exact assortment of supplements for maximum effect.

Material to be chewed thoroughly and swallowed untasted at calculated intervals.

Merely a combination of proteins and minerals, fibers and starches, carbohydrates and fats.

Solely the necessary means for maintaining the physical beauty that is my investigation's essential raw material.

"We have secrets," revealed the dancer. "Let me show you what we learn in the huzzelas behind the bazaar, beyond the myrrh. How to magic into the magnet for his eye, how to incarnate into each image he needs to touch, how to create the illusion he loves to believe in. Let me show you tinctures and essences, powders and proteins. Roots and leaves, fire and ice, earth and sand and mud. We have secrets."

Wait for effects of nourishment to register.

Study the free-standing mirror, consider the body in it coldly.

As always, it appears an alien entity, detached from myself; like its contents, donated to science.

Despite inevitable processes of aging, despite damage presumably inflicted in my life before the laboratory as well as more recent injuries, still serviceable.

I trace the maze of scars, wonder where they lead.

"Don't start," advises the scientist.

Refocus on smooth taut flesh flushed by veins visibly swollen with blood.

Curves and ripples, ridges and mounds of muscle.

Large penis ready to engorge and lift.

My instrument, my equipment.

There is no physical evidence to suggest I may not be able to continue my investigation indefinitely, whatever twists or turns it unexpectedly takes.

See it through to the end.

I don't have to look at the face I cradle with my roughened hands at last, it has already been revealed to me by a thousand and one nights of sculpting your features from only air.

Telephone silenced, laboratory sealed.

Make minute adjustments to apparatus, ensure its immaculate condition.

Employ disinfectants and antibacterials, chemical solutions and compounds.

(Though insisting I perform them flawlessly, the scientist disdains such menial tasks, refuses to cook or clean at all. We all have our own talents, he mutters, pondering hypotheses while I scrub the toilet. Privately, I wonder if he knows how to boil an egg, how he survived before meeting me.)

Put myself on autopilot. Pretend that nothing is wrong.

Whatever has happened, I have lost only a single night of work.

That's all, nothing more.

There is no significance to the fact that each week it takes me longer to summon the strength to begin work.

There is no indication that the correct execution of the proper series of steps will fail to prepare me for optimum participation in an experiment tonight.

"Your name is Billy," I baptized him too late.

Ominously, I don't feel stronger and clearer as morning reaches noon.

Perhaps this is one of those days when I find myself off balance without explanation, for reasons beyond cause and effect, inaccessible to logic. One of those difficult days when I wonder if my mood coincides with, say, the arrival of my forgotten date of birth, the erased anniversary of our first kiss, the unremembered time I last saw your eyes: information harbored within my cells, imprinted upon them like a genetic code whose key I have lost.

A closed curtain twitches.

A locked door strains to open.

I struggle to accept that I am always affected by invisible forces with the power to infiltrate the zone of sanctity around me.

They must be acknowledged, recognized, understood, factored in.

Nullify threat by naming it.

"Is Billy you?" they wondered in their white coats, waiting for my answer.

Such problematic days occurred most frequently during the second spring after I embraced science, when my first dedication to its holy commandments had abated, when I was still near enough to the world to hear the calls of boys young as myself outside the window, close enough to see their long-legged stride down the street. Those eager eyes, such frank faces, that absent arm an ache across my shoulder. In the midst of an experiment, I had to blink away an image of pink cheeks above the petalled O of promise, focus instead upon the specimen writhing below me like a snake desperate to shed its skin. In the hours between experiments, I had to dissolve the clean line of a neck from the April air, turn from the temptation of teenagers in trees. For a period of several months it was uncertain whether I possessed the capacity of complete dedication demanded by my calling after all. The scientist made it clear he had second thoughts about my suitability; I was on probation now, he let me understand. Certainly his supreme act of political cunning was to pretend ignorance of the two instances during that dangerous season when I sought selfish satisfaction, pursued private pleasure, sinned against science.

On both occasions I was conscious of the threat to which I was exposing the laboratory.

On both occasions such awareness conquered the power of the beauty in my arms, defeated my illicit enterprise.

When a third occasion presented itself, upon the appearance at the laboratory in Sydney of a corporeal composition of surf and sand and salt, I closed the door before he could surge inside, foam into my arms.

On that day I knew I was capable of saving every sigh of breath and ounce of semen for science.

Saving, not wasting.

The tattoo artist pricks patterns of Pisces upon my skin, colors constellations to orbit you into my arms.

As if a rainstorm were passing through me, I suddenly gush self-pity, stream torrents of tears upon the hardwood floor, wallow in the puddle.

I am getting old. Soon my hair will gray, my flesh sag, my skin cave. I will grow sick, weak, crippled; brittle bones will break. It will become increasingly challenging to maintain an illusion of the physical beauty required to catalyze experiments; eventually even the compassion of candlelight will not suffice. Specimens will leave ever smaller donations behind, then nothing at all. I will find it difficult and finally impossible to pay prosaic bills. The strongest dose of medication will fail to produce effect, the most forceful touch will not be felt, the final breath will pass unnoticed.

I am a victim of science, I am a puppet of delusion, I am a page of pathology.

An aging, addicted prostitute, an abortion of the world, a mistake of God.

Imminently, a body in a dumpster, a decapitation beside a dam.

A final tear forms in the corner of my eye.

A harsh giggle emerges from my mouth.
Who else but me to offer pity for myself?
Since I've fucked God to death.

The scientist finds this episode deplorable. He is aghast by such exhibitions; in the corner he whistles tunelessly over his theorems until my self-indulgence has run its sorry course.

(They say the scars are the result of an accident. They say they were inflicted in an instant. They say they weren't produced systematically, slowly, deliberately during seven years behind locked bars.)

"You must leave life to know love," I mumble on this latest difficult morning, repeating by rote one of the old mantras that once cast clear, sharp light. As if making sound realizes its meaning, actualizes into the air, allows it to be seen and heard and held on to.

Cling to the knowledge of all the other beings working secretly across the world to uncover, illuminate, discover.

Draw strength from their unwitnessed activity, their heroic sacrifices, however different from mine.

In Oslo my attention is drawn to drapes closed across an apartment window in afternoon, registers the palpable presence behind them, catches the subtlest tell of the curtain's twitch.

At the end of a dirt road in Macedonia a dog barks on a chain before a cabin that is boarded up, though smoke rises from its chimney.

In an Akron, Ohio, mall a blonde woman in a tennis dress ascends an escalator while across the synthetic space, in perfect symmetry, I descend.

I am not alone.

There are many of us who have chosen to endure harsh circumstances to discover what the world has not yet dreamed of. Though we cannot meet, though we cannot even acknowledge each other, I take comfort in their existence. I know they read the published records of my research with understanding, absorb its information, augment it with their own insights.

You must lose love to find it, I chant to chase away my doubtful morning.

"Greeting-card clichés," the scientist critiques.

"Dimestore platitudes," he pans.

"Hop to it," he instructs.

I visit the gym, several blocks away, in emptiest early afternoon.

As usual, as though nothing were wrong.

Few forms move with mine among the weights and pulleys and chains.

Among machines that resemble crudely constructed instruments of torture whose pain must be endured for the sake of love.

The scientist is always mute in this setting. While he recognizes the vital importance of exercise, its repetitive nature bores him; he prefers to spend this time in more intellectually stimulating activities. *They wouldn't interest you*, he remarks loftily when I wonder. I shrug acceptingly, suspect the scientist's silence in any location outside the laboratory stems secretly from fear. Removed from his controlled environment, he huddles inside me like a frightened child inside a dark cage. I feel grateful for respite from his demanding, critical attention.

During two and one-half hours move between the mirrored walls.

Earlier inspection of my physical form, in the laboratory, has informed me which aspect of it must be developed today to create lines provocative of greatest desire tomorrow.

I squint enough to see muscles are manipulated with perfect form, for optimum result.

Not enough to notice my eyes.

Not enough to notice the forms that shift around me.

Upon my first appearance in a gym, several of these shapes will attempt to engage my attention.

My lack of response usually aborts such efforts.

Their immaculately developed surfaces, primed and pumped for love, render them useless for my purposes.

They do not sufficiently require my touch, they find satisfaction easily.

When displays of interfering interest continue despite my dampening, I switch gyms.

Standard procedure.

He grins from the shower's steam, tongues of vapor lick smooth skin I once licked, that tattooed butterfly above the hip, wing on bone, it made me soar. The body whose weight and length my arms measured precisely during a thousand and one nights has been extended by several inches, augmented by five or ten pounds. Eyes have been

recolored, hair dyed, foreskin cut. His false flesh drips deceit, he
towels it dry, opens his mouth in invitation. Offers himself as the
one who gives birth to love. Not the one who double-crosses desire.

Strain to lift unease.

To handle it, control it, use it.

Each dull clank of iron drives away the name called
in the night.

Each drop of sweat defeats the power of geranium dreams.

Each heave of weight moves me surely toward ability
to conduct the next experiment.

Heart rate increases, body temperature rises, pulse
elevates, sweat forms.

Dress rehearsal for physiological phenomena that
will occur during tonight's investigation.

Push past painful production of lactic acid.

Force released endorphins to shoot through brain.

Expel from lungs exhausted oxygen to cloud the
mirror, to conceal a pair of wakened, hungry eyes that
look like mine, to blur the glass long after I have left the
reflected space.

Cross the short distance between gym and laboratory
unsteadily, as if exercise has weakened rather than
strengthened me.

Train eyes upon the sidewalk, see only enough to prevent stumbling into traffic, into some stranger's arms.

Protect myself from becoming daunted by the multitude of possible specimens for experiment, more than
I will ever be able to use, too many to undertake.

Blind myself from faces that turn in my direction,
deafen my ears to following footsteps.

*He has pursued me from our El Pozo balcony, back and forth
across the globe, in and out of time. In a doorway across the street
from the Lisbon apartment he stamps his feet and shivers until I
emerge at last into the iced evening. At the harbor of Naxos he
surveys the ageless Aegean in anticipation of my disembarkation
from the afternoon boat from the mainland. He suffers the heat of
Havana until I appear as a darker shadow at the end of the shadowed arcade.*

A murky shape at the end of the block emerges from
bright daylight.

A pair of entwined lovers slaps my sight.

Once I would have been enraged to witness such ersatz
ecstasy; once I harshly condemned all polite passion,
civilized lust, legal longing. Filled with the fervor of any
convert to a new religion, one more zealot, I took the
pursuit of pale pleasure as a personal affront to my
search for truth. A frivolous force against which my
discoveries must strain for assertion. I had to learn to
remind myself that against a background of unevolved
exchanges my message can only stand out more boldly,
more brilliantly, more necessarily.

The two bodies press together, press against my eyes,
insist upon recognition.

Are they familiar from before the laboratory or from
inside it?

They separate into two slivers that waver away, vacate
the wincing light.

At the bottom of my belly fists pound, feet kick.

Moving mannequins, I try to convince myself.

Cardboard city, tissue-paper trees.

From the little church on the opposite corner, across twenty or thirty feet of grass, a solo tenor ascends a hymn. The praise of God twists pitch, assumes every song of faith psalmed by the encaged, swivels my head. I perceive only darkness waiting beyond the ajar door.

Although its triple locks appear untampered with, my laboratory has been infiltrated during my absence at the gym.

Even before studying the space for evidence of intrusion, I know it.

My scalp tingles in alarm, stiffened hair registers danger.

Dusted surfaces would reveal fresh fingerprints not my own.

Infrared equipment would register heat retained in the prints, betray they were left only minutes ago.

Yet at first glance the laboratory appears undisturbed.

The lock of the filing cabinet is, like the laboratory's door, intact.

Last night's donation still rests on the round white table.

These signs that simple robbery did not motivate the invasion raise alarm.

That the notebook for current investigations has been moved from the table elevates it further.

An inch of the notebook protrudes from beneath the alcove mattress.

An incomplete attempt to bury, to hide.

There is no way of knowing whether its code has been broken. If what I failed to understand has been understood by other eyes.

A miniature heart, drawn with red ink and steady hand, decorates the point where my record leaves off.

A single flower stains the exact center of the alcove mattress scarlet.

Geranium.

An imprint of unrouged lips smudges one corner of the mirror.

Whose?

Only the kite knows the wind.

Close the notebook, clean the mirror.

Float a flower out the window. Sigh it down into the empty alley.

Only the sail knows the breeze.

I will have to leave this laboratory.

I will have to relocate to a safe setting.

Usually, I make geographic adjustments at my own will, in my own time.

Or upon the advice of the scientist, his insistence.

Sometimes from intuition that Asia instead of Africa, for example, might contribute most usefully to my work.

Each shift requires a certain amount of adaptation.

Research conducted in a new language, maintained by another currency, enacted in altered air.

Close analysis reveals that the results of experiments themselves are largely unaffected by modulations in language, culture and political system.

The truth lies beyond primarily superficial differences.

The truth smelts such differences into substances as pure and essential as semen.

Once I am forced to move because of overly curious neighbors.

Once due to unwelcome attention from police.

On several instances because a subject persists in pursuing me after participation in an experiment, refuses to understand that only a single encounter is required of him, won't accept that his desire is of no use to me now.

Or I am driven over borders and across oceans for reasons less obvious, less tangible.

When the forbidden view outside a laboratory attaches itself to my sight like a lover's face that can never be studied long enough.

When the slope of a hill becomes his broad back I must lean into.

When the face of a child who plays in the park at the end of the block appears below me as I rock above a specimen.

When the child's voice emerges from the mature mouth at his moment of climax.

Piercing the zone of purity necessary for my equilibrium, my dedicated existence.

"Why don't you call the airport?" the scientist will suggest, *trying to mask panic beneath a calming croon. "A change would do us both good."*

I have relocated before, I remind myself.

There is no reason why I might not do so again.

And again.

And again.

Shaken like a leaf on its stem, stirred by the force of his breath,
the kiss blown strong enough to break me from this branch.

Don't panic. Don't run.

Place last night's notebook in the filing cabinet.

Place last night's donation inside one of the five books
at the back of the alcove closet.

Whatever happens, they will tell who and why.

Publishing early research has presented the only serious
threat to my underground existence.

Has created a subtle tension between exposure and
concealment.

It was simple to present my manuscripts, transcribed
from private code to public language, as work of a fictitious author with a fictitious biography.

Simple to provide, for this author's photograph, a
clipping from an obscure European magazine.

A smiling young man advertising the beauty and joy
of gin.

Less simply, publishers are made nervous by my
reluctance to meet, to offer an address.

By my unwillingness to sign documents but, instead,
verbalizing contractual agreement through an unlisted
telephone number that changes after I hang up.

I am not interested in receiving reviews of these books.

However much I need it, I am not interested in
money offered in advance or generated by their sale.

Insist, rather, that all earnings anonymously fund
clinics.

Specifically, clinics that provide abortion on demand, without cost.

It won't stop crying however hard she shakes it, however loud she plays the music to drown it out, however long she shuts it in the storage shed outside. A mechanism that won't turn off, won't break. It's still crying on the floor when she returns from the bar the next morning. Ruth said I told you so, hung up after she asked if she could come back with it to Brale when it was two months old. The Jupiter Circuit had let her go in January, Diamond Lil had left for Vegas, the hotel was going to lock her out. Snow piles the tail end of dirty winter around the trailer the bouncer lets her have if he can come by now and then. He didn't mention bringing his buddies. Didn't warn her of the spike on the table where she tries to change the baby, something is wrong with it, it won't stop crying. Another headache pounds the answer to make it end. You cross the highway, go through those fields that end in brush, follow the sound of the river. Walk away from the silence in the snow, you hear only the river, they won't find it until spring.

Because hesitation over unusual conditions imposed upon publication is overcome, because it is deemed worthwhile to make exceptions to standard business policies for its sake, I am encouraged, during moments of doubt in the real value of my research, to believe in it anew.

Until I realize that once again fact has been published as fiction.

Science presented as art.

Perhaps I don't find out for several springs.

Except to pore over my encoded logbooks, I cease to read at the inception of my investigation: like music, words inspire fantasy and longing, which play no useful role in my essential occupation but damage it instead.

I avoid bookstores and libraries.

But accidents still happen.

Perhaps, after carefully avoiding the terminal's paperback kiosks, my sight stumbles upon a woman who sits facing me in the departure lounge at Schiphol for the next direct flight to LAX. She is reading the Dutch translation of the third volume of my research. The book is held in front of her to prevent the observation of her expression as she reads. She sits alone, posture erect, although the seats in this lounge are especially comfortable and invite ease. On the unoccupied seat beside her, carefully folded, lies her coat. Beside her feet rests a briefcase. I look up from it and meet, on the back of the book, the smile of the intoxicating young man who advertises gin.

The woman looks at me, looks away.

I will steal the book before our flight is over.

Add it to the first two volumes, also abducted.

But rarely read.

I cannot afford the threat to my morale that even a quick glance at these published volumes incurs.

I am invariably disappointed by the crudeness of my early efforts.

The significance of experiments seems diminished by translation from code to ordinary language.

Though only scientist, I need the clarity of a seer and the power of an artist to communicate my results.

I am plagued by the doubt of publishing initial conclusions, which may be interpreted as final, though it is clear that my research is cumulative, always leading up to and preparing ground for stunning revelations reached at the end.

I am conscious that I may not survive to express such conclusions.

Balance these two conflicting concerns, realize the importance of disseminating preliminary research, however imperfectly, without delay.

Even misinterpreted, it still holds power, has use.

Serves the world better than untranscribed notebooks left behind to appear to unevolved eyes as nothing more than gibberish, just desperate scratches into the surface of the cell, only hieroglyphs smeared with excrement upon the asylum wall.

They say that, technically, you were not locked inside a cage for seven years.

Since the key was always in your hand, the bars only in your brain.

The scars a product of your own knife.

Hesitantly, I open the first volume.

The text appears as untranscribed code.

Like last night's record, one whose key I have forgotten.

Worse, one whose key I have never known.

The other four published volumes are similarly indecipherable.

For an inability to find poetic effects that soar my meaning, I have consoled myself with achieving the straightforward and clear and exact.

If I fail to communicate the results of research on this basic level, my experiment is worthless.

"My?" interrupts the scientist with ironic emphasis.

"Not yours. Not even ours. Only mine."

The scientist seems as unperturbed by my loss of literacy as by the invasion of the laboratory. I sense with sudden force what I have often felt in flickers during our long association: I am involved in a scheme whose ultimate aim is kept secret from me; all along the scientist has provided me with false or incomplete information in order to manipulate my involvement in an experiment that, in fact, has nothing to do with love, and everything to do with deception.

I am as ignorant as the unwitting specimens who visit the laboratory, only another specimen myself, we squirm together beneath the microscope, fry in its focal light.

Everything that is happening now has been arranged as perfectly as a poem to elicit from me reactions to an experiment now inaccessible to my comprehension?

They want me to draw pictures, they want to talk about the pictures. Why the boy lies naked in the snow. Why he doesn't wear clothes, why he wears only one shoe. Why he doesn't move, why he doesn't breathe. Why a second mouth grins open on his throat, it looks like lipstick, Diamond Lil drew red hearts on the speckled mirrors, laughing.

Reaching farther back into the closet, I remove the valise that, despite the scientist's disapproval, I have carried with me since he found me.

Some of its contents, I suspect, pertain to my forgotten life before the laboratory:

A plastic whistle, a Cracker Jack ring, a purple feather from a boa.

A shell that holds the echo of a sea, an envelope filled with grains of desert sand.

A postcard of Eureka, California, its message *Miss you like crazy* signed with a lipstick kiss.

Some of the valise's contents were, I believe, left behind by specimens upon departing the laboratory. Dazed by their experience within my arms, scarcely able to remember their own name, they drop pieces of themselves as they stumble away.

Maybe I find a comb fallen beneath the table.

Sunglasses left beside the bathroom sink.

Or articles whose abandonment is puzzling, implausible.

A wedding band, a driver's license, car keys, one shoe.

A wallet-sized snapshot of a family in front of a Christmas tree.

I turn all these objects over in my hands, feel which ones radiate the heat of meaning for me.

It is difficult to judge which mementos pertain to my forgotten history and which hold value only for a stranger. I sift through uncertainty, wonder if in fact everything in the valise belongs to me, as talismans of experience I have had but which the scientist has kept secret from me.

I have piloted an airplane, worked in an office, fished with friends.

I have danced at my own wedding, balanced my son on my shoulders.

Try on the wedding band, try on the single shoe.

See if they fit, if they claim me.

Imagine constructing a being who belongs to this assortment of disparate objects.

Who would he be? What would he look like? How would he love?

The scientist peers over my shoulder, snorts in disgust.

"*Do you really want to remember? Do you really want to know?*"

I snap the valise shut, shove it back to the rear of the closet.

Knuckles knock the closed chambers of my heart.

Let me in, let me out.

I weave to the bathroom, claw at a vial.

No.

Medication at this hour would incapacitate tonight's experiment.

The correct response to this situation has been drilled into me:

With a brief period of rest, place what are only minor challenges into perspective, transform what are only inconsequential irritations into actual insignificance, restore what is still a perfect instrument for science.

Rest for which the hardwood floor appears inappropriate for once.

My alternative, the mattress in the alcove, is almost acceptably hard.

But it is disarming, deceptive, dangerous.

Even unoccupied, apparently innocuous within a skin a sterilized sheets, it throbs with the unmet longing of all the specimens who have squirmed upon its surface, vibrates tensely with undissolved energy of their unreleased desire, seethes with the toxins of their tears.

Even when I give them everything, it is never enough.

After, the dancer declaims, we are only the mirage of their oasis.

Even after they have sucked every drop of fluid from my spine, they slather thirst.

Even after they have masticated each muscle of my heart, they drool hunger.

It swamps the alcove mattress, it would sponge into my porous body.

Soak through bone, seep through cells, infiltrate blood, osmose into dreams.

Confuse me with belief that I am the specimens I study.

As though the brief rest of a single blossom upon a surface has the power to permanently banish all fever beneath it.

The power of a poppy opening its opium arms.

Offering perfumed invitation into the alcove, push into the drift and descent of dream.

Tap your cane blindly across the Algeciras square toward me and at Tarifa boom your voice beneath the surf beyond the green wall and drum your reach through beaten Morogoro night. Or it's only a branch knocking against the cabin that turns the world in my arms, breathes you into my back. Only some pine outside, unsettled by a wind risen from the lake, swept down the valley. Only the Morse code of the indivisible dream.

The knocking isn't random.
  It is a determined sequence of sounds.
  A prearranged code to gain entrance.
  Persistent, insistent.
  The percussive pattern raps my memory.
  Let me in, let me out.

You knock on the stone wall that separates our cells for several dark years before I understand your coded language of love.

It takes too long to pour myself back into my sieved skin, the signal stops before my scattered bones gather themselves into a body, my cane of hand gropes darkness too slowly.
  Open the laboratory door upon empty hallway as the elevator sighs shut, begins its hummed descent to the surface of the darkening world.

He was here again, he has gone again.

The echoed pattern of knocking unravels its code in my mind.
  Informs me that I have been forced to alter my landscape with exponential frequency over the last ten years, each time toward an always narrower escape, away from always more dangerous circumstances.
  Informs me that in fact I have not inhabited this laboratory for three years.
  Informs me that in fact it has been only a matter of months since the last close call.
  Since the last time I was found.

Or since the last body was found.

"If I conceal information from you," hisses the scientist, "it's for the greater good.

"If it weren't for your incompetence, relocation would never be necessary.

"So grease your lips and get ready for the salt mines, sissy."

Time lost to temptation, day lost to night.

Neglected procedures have left me hungry, dirty, disoriented.

My shoulders' morning ache has turned into a throb, as if I have been heaving heavy burdens instead of resting.

Quick:

Flick switch, elicit light.

Shower, shave. Fix hair, fix face. Slope into uniform of seduction.

Make mirror hot with what they want to see, have to reach for, need to touch.

Ready for tonight's specimen, ready to receive his call.

It occurs within five minutes.

I answer it correctly, on the second ring.

As the correct identity.

With words and voice that reel a participant in.

With modulated vowels and assumed accent he attempts to pass himself off as a suitor for science initiating telephone contact. A catch in his tenor, a crack in its pitch, causes me to break the line in Toronto and Jakarta, in Ankara and Toulouse.

Shake my head, toss away its tricks.

Not his voice. Not my voice.

A suitable candidate for experiment. Yes. Perhaps even an especially interesting one.

Provide him address, intercom code, floor and door number.

I am not overly excited, not inappropriately pitched, not unfavorably flustered.

I am calm and blank as I need to be.

"You've done this ten thousand times before," soothes the scientist.

"Do it one last time until you need to do it again."

Dim lights, close windows, draw curtains, light candles, begin music.

The scientist coils on the metal chair, prepares to witness, watch, observe.

Should I remove from the alcove closet one of the props stored on its shelf?

Did I intuit on the telephone that tonight's specimen might usefully respond to one of these implements?

Whips and chains, restraints and gags; vari-sized and -shaped objects of insertion.

Probes to delve deep into the truth.

Less obvious experimental aids:

Carefully chosen symbols with power and purity to evoke heightened responses.

Responses beyond rational proportion to their banal source.

Something simple as the most ordinary article of clothing.

Any uniform of innocent youth, any carefree costume of athletic endeavor.

Pristine, perfect.

A skateboard aslant the hardwood floor.

A dumbbell at rest before the window.

A baseball glove to take him back, to release twenty-five years of longing, to expose the truth about love.

Like the one he wore playing catch with the boy across the street on summer evenings when the quality of air, its pressured composition, alters the pitch of their voices as they toss their secret back and forth, tunes what they call to one another into a newly discovered language, sharpening its note to one they have never before heard in their own voice or in the voice they receive across twenty or thirty feet of dampening grass, enough twilight distance now to blur faces, warm and cool at once, a medium for moths and the squeak of the Carpenters' screen door, such soft thuds of old leather.

I glance from the closet toward the scientist.

He shakes his head as knuckles tattoo the laboratory door.

"Not tonight."

"Get ready," he repeats in the special tone, electric with excitement, *that he adopts whenever he feels my dedication to our cause might be wavering, whenever he wishes to falsely inspire me for one more unshared reason, whenever he wants to trick me into believing that the next experiment will be the final experiment, the one we have been working toward all these years, the one I was born to die for.*

I'm not ready after all.

Not ready to investigate his familiar eyes, not ready to admit what they ask.

Not ready to watch him undress, expose his humble flesh, its erected need.

Its quarter-century of longing, its known lines.

The seam of scar across his throat.

The butterfly faded upon his left hip, frozen until I kiss breath into its wings, make them flutter with my tongue.

"You don't have to watch, I'm the one who watches, it works best that way, you learned that long ago."

Once certain images would rustle the darkness after each experiment, interfere with required rest despite recording, *a drop of water falling from an oar, a curtain breathing before the balcony, his face against the snow,* touch me where I didn't want to be touched, fondle what I didn't want felt, insist on squirming beneath the chemical blanket slid across my mind.

Until I trained my eyes to stay half-closed behind curtaining lashes while rendering required kisses, while fulfilling fantasies of flesh.

Until I learned that what isn't seen won't be remembered.

Until I mastered standard procedure.

I have never stretched my bones around this shape, never curved its contours with my wrists, never sutured its wounds with my stapling lips, never heard my secret name breathed by this scarred throat across twenty or thirty feet of dampening grass as geranium explodes sharp as amyl nitrate through my wires, floods my circuits, overloads their sockets. This body pressed into my body shifts form again and again, transmutes into every form I have inflamed, evolves into every one not sparked. Their knowing fingers find the mound of muscle on each of my shoulders, press both springed locks to allow what has lain beneath to unfold, expand, rustle.

Go away.

The words emerge from my mouth as a moan, inspire the shape beneath me to become further excited by this suggestion of passion, cause it to groan itself into my vision, below me appears the face of a stranger, of any stranger, of every stranger, I squeeze it away with a squint.

Come back.

I stand above a body that lies naked upon the snow of sheets.

Why doesn't it move? Why doesn't it breathe?

Look closer.

Find him beside the creek, beyond the wooden bridge, where moss upholsters stones and roots, sponged green clings winter water. Exposing spring has melted snow that covered him, melted flesh that draped him; his faith in me has faded with his breath, his bones have already bleached with broken trust, they don't believe in my approach across rusted needles fallen from the towering pines. The creek insists upon the exuberant season, throws itself upon your slate skull, splashes through your silence. Billy, it's me, remember. In the cage my knuckles delivered an oath upon the wall between us: even if our escapes are individual, even if survival separates us, even if we alter into unrecognizable forms, I will always find you.

I nudge the body on the mattress with a fearful foot, apply cautious pressure with my heel.

Billy, it's me, remember.

The scientist's voice emerges harshly from my mouth. As at certain times of stress, when judging me unequal to the moment, he has decided to intervene.

He spits: "Get up, get dressed, get out."

Snaps: "No use crying over spilt milk, splattered semen."

The body doesn't move.

The scientist's voice rises in pitch, assumes a shriek of fury, a scream beyond any language I understand, a howled code my mind can't break.

A sound like the one swelling from the snow, a sound I must stop.

I reach for the precautionary knife concealed beneath the mattress.

Sieve my skin, unlock its pores, free its contents from their dark dungeon.

Dig harder, dig deeper.

Release the scent of plasma, sweet and rich and cloying.

Fetuses wriggle in the red pool, like ameba in a petri dish.

They fight a losing battle for life.

The scientist's scream wanes into a whine, weakens into a whimper.

Then a hum, then silence.

Goodbye, so long, miss you like crazy.

I am standing in a candlelit space that the illumination of leaving exposes to be a sparsely furnished apartment, small and shabby, with illegible graffiti scratched into its walls.

There is a man on the mattress before me; a butterfly pulses his hip.

In the morning he will awaken to wonder who and where he is, what happened to him while he slept.

With a mop he will eradicate bloody evidence of an unknown, aborted past.

He will remove the valise from the closet, hold its contents in his hands, puzzle over which belong to him and which to a stranger.

Turn the pages of five books, look for clues within them.

Until the light around him becomes stronger and clearer, until a voice emerges from that light to illuminate the meaning of his surroundings, their purpose.

How they will serve science, defeat memory, lead from life to love.

Before employing the power of my plumes, I wish to leave a message for this new associate of the scientist. Words for him to hold on to during what will be a long, difficult experience within the laboratory. A single sentence that will abbreviate and ease such an experience. I unlock the filing cabinet in the corner. On the round white table, beside the candle burning there, open the notebook to where my efforts to record the truth left off last night. Stare at the red heart beating on the page, then bend to write in the blank space beneath it.

Flame leaps from the candle, my new wings blaze.

Smoke enfolds me like mist at the very beginning of the world from which any original form of life might emerge.

"Love lifts," promised the belly dancer's final postcard from the
pyramids, her last telegram from Tangier.

Throw open the window, invite air to stream inside the
magic door.

It feeds and fans my feathers of flame, enlarges and
strengthens their span.

Encourages them to try the sky, to take a leap of faith,
to trust in the end.

Ash falls into the alley, sparks ascend.

Sail me and my helium heart above the ocean of sky
toward the upper port of peace.

Only the bird knows the wing, only the wing
knows flight.

Marie

During the day he had his buddy, Old Jack D, while Marie got by on the hard food he puts down for the cats. He didn't know if she fell or what. Comes in from the other room, finds her licking the floor on hands and knees. She seemed to like it down there, Marie. At dark they attempt to chew from foil plates while first frost creeps past the county line. Not many souls out this way: another trailer across the field, smoke in the sky above the stumps. He made her feed herself supper, she could do it if she tried. Her noise starts, her left arm floating stiff in the air. You had to knock it down. The spoon hits the floor, scares the cats out into the cold. They stayed inside, Marie and him, the TV on. Voices ricochet between the pasteboard walls, echoes carry him way back. Marie by the grill, behind the smoke; him at the blurred counter. That's how it began. Ammonia ascending from bent spoons, eggs twitching in café grease. Praise the Lord and praise the holy hunchback. His heart jumped, she flipped it over, squinted at the edges curling crisp and black. Seeing what was there, if it was any good. You never know what will happen. Just ask Old Jack D, maybe he holds all the answers, deciphers static scratching from radios as years slouch by. Taking the truck to town alone, you finally have to tie her to the trailer door. Have to avert eyes from the rearview mirror. How she looks there, behind, in clothes she fights him not to change, gray eyes still fierce sometimes. It's for her own good, sure. A knot left over from fishing trips up in the Saquomish, loons crying to the lake. Once he rattled back to a tilted porch, hollow bottles, no Marie. She'd left him before, when she could. Tried more than once to stay away across the hills. Another awkward woman off balance awhile in another small town. Now, at the same time, she was here and she was gone. Marie, he called. Where are you? It steamed the air, smoked inside his heart. For forty years he'd liked to call her name even when there was no need. Marie, my own Marie. Something stirs the brush past the next clearing. He sees her barefoot in the stems and weeds, the rope trailing from one wrist. Time to cut her hair. To put plastic on the windows. Find a winter coat for the stoic scarecrow. He could do it if he tried. Marie, he keeps calling while she snaps November twigs brittle as old bones. This time her face would turn and know him. Next time, another time. Some magic time. Come on, Marie. She starts that noise, loons at lakes. The ammonia circle swelled. Back home, it's time Old Jack D grinned him to sleep. Marie curls on the kitchen floor, a purring corner.